THE LAST HAPPY SUMMER
THE DAYS OF WAR SERIES
BOOK ONE

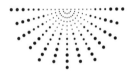

JONATHAN CULLEN

LIQUID MIND PUBLISHING

All rights reserved. No part of this book may be reproduced, distributed, or transmitted in any form or by any means, including photocopying, recording, or other electronic or mechanical methods, without the prior written permission of the author, except in the case of brief quotations embodied in critical reviews and certain other noncommercial uses permitted by copyright law.

Copyright © 2022 by Jonathan Cullen

www.jonathancullen.com

Liquid Mind Publishing

This is a work of fiction. Any resemblance to actual persons, living or dead, or actual events is purely coincidental.

ALSO BY JONATHAN CULLEN

The Days of War Series

The Last Happy Summer

Midnight Passes, Morning Comes

Shadows of Our Time Collection

The Storm Beyond the Tides

Sunsets Never Wait

Bermuda Blue

The Jody Brae Mystery Series

Whiskey Point

City of Small Kingdoms

The Polish Triangle

Sign up for Jonathan's newsletter for updates on deals and new releases!

https://liquidmind.media/j-cullen-newsletter-sign-up-1/

CHAPTER ONE

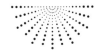

 une 1941

No matter what her age, no matter what joys or hardships life would bring, Abigail Nolan knew this: the morning she woke up each summer to go to their cottage on Point Shirley, she would always feel like a little girl.

Like most years, she was so anxious that she had packed the night before. She took mainly skirts and light blouses, knowing it would be a long, hot summer. Downstairs, she could hear her mother and brothers getting ready, their frantic footsteps and movement of luggage. Their father had already gone to work, rising before dawn to take the streetcar down to the shipyard. He had been a crane operator at East Boston Works for over twenty years and never missed a day, even when his children were born.

Abby dragged her trunk out of the bedroom. Her older brother George was coming up the stairs as she stopped on the landing to catch her breath.

"Can you help me?" she asked.

Looking at the trunk, he just snickered.

"Looks like you can handle it."

She frowned and pulled it down the stairs, lifting it over each step so it wouldn't scratch the wood. When she got to the bottom, her twin brother Thomas helped her take it out to the sidewalk.

"Abigail, help your brother," Mrs. Nolan said.

Abby looked over and her mother was holding the door open for George, who had two suitcases in his hands.

"Why should I? He didn't help me."

"Stop your bickering!"

Abby went up and took the door from her. George brought the luggage down the steps and put it on the sidewalk.

"Ma, have you seen my coat?" Thomas asked.

"Why on earth would you need a coat?"

"In case it gets chilly."

"Then put on a sweater, you pansy," George said.

Thomas ignored him and went back inside. Abby loved George, but he was mean, and she was surprised he even had any friends. As the oldest, he had a lot of expectations put on him, and their parents were disappointed when he dropped out of East Boston High during his sophomore year.

"Abby!" she heard, but it sounded more like *uh-buh*.

She looked over to the next house, and Chickie Ciarlone was on the porch.

"Hi, Chickie," Abby said.

The little girl just stared, her arms wrapped around the railing. The Ciarlones had moved in five years earlier, the first Italians on the street. Mrs. Ciarlone was a widow whose husband had died in a WPA project during the Depression. Aside from Chickie, she had an older son Salvatore who everyone called Sal. He was the friendliest in the family, but no one ever saw him because he worked nights.

"Play! Play!"

"I can't play," Abby said with a sad smile. "We're leaving."

Chickie dropped her head with a pout. She was a strange child, and Mrs. Nolan called her *funny*. Abby didn't know if it was mental retardation or if she had had an accident as an infant. Either way, she never left the house, always staying on the front porch or in the yard, never playing with the other girls on the street.

Abby wondered if she even went to school. But she didn't know much about the Ciarlones because their families didn't talk. When Abby's mother was growing up, the area was all Irish with a smattering of Jews and other ethnic groups. The Italians had started moving to East Boston just before the Great War, settling in the slums around Maverick Square. Over the years they slowly migrated north, horrifying older residents with their strange customs like growing tomatoes on their roofs and raising rabbits to eat. There were so many of them now they made up half of the congregation at St. Mary's church.

"I don't know why you bother with that mongoloid."

Abby spun around. George was sitting on a suitcase, a cigarette between his teeth.

"It takes one to know one."

"*Takes one to know one*," he said in a mocking voice.

"And she's not a mongoloid."

"Sure looks like one."

"Go to hell!"

Abby stormed back up the steps, almost colliding with her mother at the door.

"Where're you going?" Mrs. Nolan asked, sweaty and agitated. "The cab will be here any minute."

"Your son's a bastard."

Her mother gave her a sharp look. Abby used to get scolded for foul language, but now she was an adult, having just graduated from East Boston High with Thomas.

"Did you bring the tablecloths?" Mrs. Nolan asked.

"You didn't ask."

"I'll get them, Ma," Thomas said.

"Teacher's pet," George said.

Thomas stopped and looked over, and Abby could tell he had had enough of George's taunts.

"How 'bout I smack that smirk off your face?"

George flicked his cigarette and looked away. As boys, they always clashed. It wasn't the normal back and forth of sibling rivalry because George was a bully. His years of picking on his younger brother ended in their early teens when, after a sarcastic remark, Thomas knocked him over the kitchen table while their mother was making dinner. At the time, Thomas had been on the high school boxing team, rising to the top of his weight class. Mr. Nolan walked in from work as it happened but seemed in no rush to intervene. Abby suspected he wanted Thomas to keep going, if only to teach George a lesson.

"Oh, for heaven's sake," Mrs. Nolan cried.

They all looked, and a taxi was coming up the street, red and white with the word *Boston* written across the doors.

"What's wrong?" George asked.

"I asked for a DeSoto."

"And you got a Model A."

It pulled up, and a short man with a mustache and flat cap got out.

"Sir, this won't fit everything."

"Would without the trunk," George said under his breath.

Abby crossed her arms and gave him a dirty look.

The driver smiled and walked over to inspect the luggage. There were three suitcases, Abby's trunk, some smaller bags, pillows, linens, and dry goods from the kitchen. In Mrs. Nolan's hand was a cardboard box with the cake she had made for her husband's birthday.

"Trunk in the trunk," the man said, speaking in a heavy accent.

"Go on," Mrs. Nolan said, looking at her sons.

George and Thomas walked over and lifted it in, and the only time they ever cooperated was when their mother asked them to do something. Next, they loaded two of the suitcases but couldn't fit the third, so they put it in the back seat. When Mrs. Nolan told Thomas to take the front instead of her, Abby knew it was to keep the boys apart. The rest of them piled into the back and shut the doors.

"Where to?" the man asked.

"Point Shirley."

As they pulled away, Chickie was waving with both hands. Abby was about to wave back when, suddenly, Mrs. Ciarlone came out, grabbed her by the arm, and took her inside.

"Gonna miss her," Abby muttered.

"You're the only one."

"Mind your tone," their mother said, seated between George and Abby like a referee. "But I do wonder what's got that woman."

"She's a widow," Abby said. "Maybe she's just lonely."

"Then she should learn English. You can't expect to make friends when you can't talk to people."

"Amen," George said.

Mrs. Nolan frowned, but it was one of the few things they agreed on. The Ciarlones had lived next door for years and still felt like strangers.

The car made a U-turn, the luggage creaking in the back. As they rolled down the hill, Abby stuck her head out, getting one last look at the house. She had warm memories of leaving for Point Shirley each summer, the excitement as much as the sadness, and she could measure the course of her life by the days they departed. Before her uncle died, he used to drive them in his Velie Royal Sedan, the finest car in their neighborhood at the time. Once when she was little, they even went by oxcart. Life was simpler back then, with fewer automobiles and fewer people. She missed those times when the hours felt like days, the days like months, and the months sometimes like an eternity.

Somehow Abby knew this year would be different, a great dividing point in her life. She had been accepted to college, the first one in her family to go, and Thomas had applied to be on the police force. After George left high school, he'd always had odd jobs, and now he had steady work driving a newspaper truck, delivering to shops and newsstands. Abby was happy they were continuing the family tradition, but she knew it wouldn't last—nothing ever did. And it wasn't just because they were all adults now. With the war in Europe, she had a sense that the world was changing fast. More than anything, she feared it would be the last summer they were all together.

CHAPTER TWO

*A*s they drove across the strand, Abby could see the white house across the bay. Everyone called it a cottage, but it was more like a shack with a roof and a porch. Any value it had was more sentimental than real because it had been in the family for generations. It was built by her mother's Irish grandfather, who had come to America when much of East Boston was still farmland. He had started as a printer's apprentice before getting a job at the shipyard where he made turret sheets for ironclads during the Civil War. With the money from the plots he sold off from his land, he bought a small parcel on Point Shirley, a narrow peninsula in the neighboring town of Winthrop. At the turn of the century, East Boston was experiencing a construction boom, and he built the cottage in his free time using the discarded wood and rusted nails he found on job sites. It was plain but sturdy, having withstood over forty years of storms, including the Hurricane of '38.

Even from a distance, something about the home looked off, like a wall painting that wasn't quite level. With its faded clapboard shingles and crumbling chimney, it wasn't much to look at, but they were lucky to have it. No one they knew had a summer house; most people in their neighborhood struggled just to pay the mortgage or rent.

When they came around the bend, her father was sitting out front in a chair. They hadn't expected him until dinner, so her mother got suddenly anxious because she now had to hide the cake. Dressed in his shirtsleeves and shorts, he sipped a cold drink through a straw. It looked like an aperitif, but Abby knew it was cream soda. Her father hadn't touched liquor since she was seven, giving it up after decades of heavy drinking only after their mother threatened to leave him for good.

Even though she was young, Abby could never forget those terrible years, their parents arguing and shouting while she and her two brothers watched from the top of the stairs. Once he knocked over an entire cupboard, shattering the glasses and china plates, heirlooms from her mother's grandparents. Abby never resented him for it because the moment he quit, he became a completely different man. And for her, the actions of the present always meant more than the mistakes of the past.

As they got out of the cab, George stretched his legs and mumbled some complaint they all ignored. Abby felt a similar relief, and although the ride from East Boston to Winthrop was only five miles, it had been uncomfortable with all the luggage.

"Did you quit your job?" Mrs. Nolan asked.

Their father smiled, his head back and eyes shut.

"No, but wouldn't I love to," he said.

The driver opened the trunk and Abby's brothers took everything out. While Mr. Nolan sat basking in the sun, his wife grabbed the cake and rushed to bring it inside. Just as she passed him, he raised one eye.

"Is it a cake you brought me?" he asked.

Abby grinned. As his daughter, she couldn't detect his Irish accent as other people could, but the way he phrased things was funny.

"Stop being so nosey," his wife said, swatting at him.

"Me birthday's not 'til Sunday," he said, but she was already in the house.

As George and Thomas carried the luggage up the path, Abby tried to help, but they wouldn't let her. She was about to go inside when she noticed someone waving in the distance. She walked across the street to the grassy headland that descended to a pebbly beach. Unlike the outer side of Point Shirley, which had miles of soft sand, the harbor was rocky. Stepping carefully, she made her way down to the shoreline where she saw two girls on a towel and a large umbrella stuck in the sand. One of them stood up, a short brunette with a large bosom. Abby got excited when she realized who it was.

"Sarah?!" she exclaimed.

"It must be summer."

"It is now," she said, and they hugged.

"Remember Noel?" Sarah asked. "She's on Foam Street."

Abby looked over and waved.

"Right around the corner," she said.

Abby had known Sarah since they were kids, those long summers spent walking the beach, wandering the sandy streets after dark. At one time, there were hundreds, maybe thousands of kids on Point Shirley. But during the depression, a lot of families lost their cottages or had to sell them. For those who didn't, many of the children were now grown up, living their lives somewhere else.

"How was senior year?" Sarah asked.

Abby bit her lip. She had gotten the acceptance letter in May and was still as excited as the morning she opened it.

"Going to BU," she said.

Sarah's jaw dropped in surprise. Even Noel was interested enough to look over.

"Boston University?"

"A full scholarship."

"Oh, Abby. We gotta celebrate—"

"Abby?!"

She looked back, and Thomas was standing at the top of the bluff, his sleeves rolled up, hair blowing in the wind.

"Ma needs help," he yelled.

"My, my," Sarah said, clearing her throat. "Hasn't he grown up?"

Abby made a sour smile.

"Haven't we all."

"Not like that," Noel chimed in, leaning up on her elbows.

As hard as it was to judge her own brother, Abby knew Thomas was handsome. And she was sure it was one of the reasons why he and George didn't get along. While Thomas got the good looks and personality, George seemed to have inherited all the worst qualities of each parent: their mother's awkward nose and their father's large forehead.

"Who's here?" Sarah asked.

"All of us. You?"

"My brother Frank joined the Army. He's in Georgia."

"And your sister…?" Abby asked, hesitantly.

She couldn't remember her name, one of the consequences of going a year between seeing people.

"Sissie got married."

"Married?"

Abby was surprised because she was only a year older than them.

"She moved to Hartford. Her husband is in the insurance business."

Abby smiled, but the news was bittersweet. There was a time when all the families she knew returned each summer intact. Over the past couple of years, however, that had started to change, with older siblings getting married or moving away. Some even went to college, although most of the people who came out to Point Shirley were working class and couldn't afford it. Abby was one of the few girls she knew attending university that fall, a fact that made her feel proud or pretentious, depending on the company.

"Are you still living in…?"

"Quincy," Sarah said. "Yes."

It seemed like a silly question because no one Abby knew ever moved.

"And you?" she asked Noel. "Are you from nearby?"

Before she could answer, there was a sudden roar in the distance. It grew by the second, so loud that Noel got up and came over. The ground started to shake and then, moments later, a half-dozen Army planes flew over so close the water rippled. They crossed Winthrop Harbor and veered west, all in perfect formation.

"Holy moly," Sarah said.

"That was low."

Abby stood spellbound, watching the planes until they disappeared over the horizon.

"Why didn't they land?" she wondered, looking over to the airport.

"It's just an exercise. Probably headed to Fort Devens," Noel said.

Sarah turned to her.

"How do you know so much about the Army?"

"My uncle works there. He said they've been getting all sorts of things: planes, tanks, guns. In case of war."

The word *war* left everyone at a loss for words. On the summer shore, at the beginning of their vacation, it was the last thing anyone wanted to think about.

"I've gotta head back," Abby said.

"See you at the beach tomorrow?"

"Sounds good."

"Bring your brother," Noel said.

Abby smirked, but she couldn't help but feel flattered.

"Bye," she said, and she walked up the bluff.

CHAPTER THREE

By the time Thomas finished putting all his clothes away, he was covered in sweat. The small bedroom on the second floor faced the sun and got hotter as the day went on. In August, it was unbearable, and he remembered many nights as a child when he and George would drag their sheets and pillows downstairs to sleep out on the front porch. In most cases, they didn't cooperate or get along, but when it came to comfort they were allies.

George walked in with his shirt untucked, pulling his suitcase behind him.

"Why do you get the good bed?" he asked.

With the angle of the roof, the bed by the window was cramped but had better ventilation and a nice view, while the one by the wall had more headroom.

"Shoulda got here sooner," Thomas said, sliding his empty suitcase into the tiny closet.

"We swap next month?"

Thomas frowned but didn't say no. A month was too far into the future to negotiate anything.

"Agreed?" George said.

Thomas turned, and they locked eyes. Whenever he looked at his brother, he got a strange mix of pity and disgust. As a boy, he was terrified of him, a fear that had long since faded. Thomas wasn't cruel, but he got some dark thrill in knowing that, at any time and any moment, he could have knocked him out cold.

"I don't agree to anything," he said, then he stormed out.

As he came down the stairs, Abby was walking in. He had told her twenty minutes earlier that her mother needed help.

"Where were you?" he asked.

"We just saw fighter planes."

"Get used to it. Who was that you were with?"

"You know Sarah Lerner."

"Is her brother Frank here?"

Abby shook her head.

"He's in the Army," she said.

Thomas nodded and walked out, feeling a slight jealousy, or maybe even guilt. Not a week went by that he didn't hear about some friend or acquaintance who had joined the military. He had considered enlisting, and the only reason he didn't was that his father said cops were just as important as soldiers when it came to protecting the nation.

Out front, Mr. Nolan's chair was still on the lawn, but he wasn't in it. Thomas heard voices, and when he walked around the side of the house, the picnic table was set with a flowered tablecloth and dishes. His parents were sitting together, talking in the shade of the tree. Abby came out the back door carrying a casserole, and Thomas walked over and took a seat, careful not to shake the table.

"A fine view," his father said, sipping his cream soda.

"A lovely view."

Thomas smiled and looked behind, where the sun was setting over the city in a haze of yellow and orange. In the foreground, a plane was taking off from the airport, the loud hum of the twin turbines rumbling overhead.

"Off to Bermuda, I'd say," Mr. Nolan said.

"There's no way of knowing that, Daddy," Abby said, taking the covers off the serving dishes.

"I'd like to think so," he said, and he smiled at his wife.

"Where's your brother?" Mrs. Nolan asked.

"Coming!" George shouted from the second floor.

For all the trouble with his eyesight, he had the hearing of a wolf. He walked out the back door in his bare feet, his hair wet and slicked back. He was holding a drink, but with its cloudy yellow color, Thomas couldn't tell if it was lemonade or liquor.

George sat down, and as he reached for the plate of ham, Mrs. Nolan stopped him.

"I propose we say grace first," she said.

Everyone moaned except for Mr. Nolan, who never disagreed with his wife. They clasped their hands and bowed their heads.

"Dear Lord," Mrs. Nolan started. "We thank you for this bounty we are about to share, and we humbly ask that…"

Once she finished, George grabbed the ham and took more than his share. Abby picked up tongs and passed around ears of corn, still steaming from the pot.

"A bit early for corn, no?" Mr. Nolan said.

"It's from all the rain we had in April," Abby said.

"So, you're a meteorologist now?" George snickered.

Thomas could tell the remark stung by the twitch in Abby's eye and the way she turned away. He knew if he let George start teasing her now, it was going to be a long summer.

"Beats hawking newspapers," he said.

George didn't slam the bowl of potato salad, but he put it down hard enough that everyone noticed.

"Who hawks newspapers? I drive a delivery truck."

"And what are those trucks full of?"

"At least I have a job."

Thomas chuckled, something that always antagonized his brother.

"I work at the theater. Remember I got you tickets to *The Fighting 69th* two weeks ago?—"

"Now, boys," their father said, his firm voice always enough to stop their bickering. "Speaking of jobs. They're looking for security men down the dockyard."

With his fork to his mouth, Thomas looked up.

"I'd be interested," he said.

"Pays fifty cents an hour."

"Then I'd really be interested."

"Beats taking tickets," George said.

Thomas didn't respond, knowing his brother's sarcasm was more out of regret than for amusement. In his teenage years, George had been arrested twice, once for stealing a horse from the Bennington Street stables and another time for breaking the windows of a synagogue. As someone with a criminal record, he could never work in security, which was why their father hadn't asked him as well.

"And it might look good for your résumé," Mr. Nolan added. "For when you get a letter from the Boston Police."

"*If* he gets a letter from the police," George said.

Thomas smirked, but his brother was right. The war in Europe had stirred up the patriotic passions of young men everywhere. Those who hadn't already enlisted in the service were lining up to join police departments across the country, making the job more competitive than ever.

"Could you put me in touch with someone?"

"I'll march you into the hiring office meself," his father said.

While they talked, the women had quietly gotten up and gone inside, and Thomas knew what they were up to. Minutes later, Mrs. Nolan came down the steps holding a chocolate cake, Abby beside her in case she stumbled. On top were several dozen candles, their flames flickering in the soft evening breeze. There weren't nearly enough, but it didn't matter because Mr. Nolan didn't know how old he was. After his parents died of typhus, he and his eight siblings were separated, sent to institutional workhouses across Ireland. Somewhere in all the confusion, his birth certificate had been lost or misplaced. He estimated his age from the memory that he made his First Communion the same year the Boer War began.

Mrs. Nolan walked over with a wide smile and put the cake down in front of him. While they sang "Happy Birthday," he stared at the candles, a look of mild embarrassment on his face. Once they were finished, he paused to think, everyone waiting in suspense.

"To many more happy summers on Point Shirley!"

Thomas clapped, and everyone joined in, a moment of poignant celebration. Even George, who had a scowl in the best of moods, found the decency to smile.

"You're not supposed to tell your wish out loud," his wife said.

He peered up at her with a mischievous grin.

"That wasn't me wish."

She rolled her eyes and frowned like she was dealing with a fresh child. Abby gave her a knife, and she cut the cake, handing out pieces on the brittle plates that had been in the kitchen since her grandfather's time.

In the dusky light, they sat and ate under a contented silence. Thomas looked across the bay, the light shimmering off the water, a couple of trawlers returning to port. It was a scene no different than years past, and he hoped it would continue. But now that he was an adult, he felt a deep restlessness, and it wasn't just about getting older. The threat of war was in the air, and even if America wasn't involved, everyone worried it soon would be. Beyond the death and suffering, it represented some great shift, and no one believed the world would ever be the same again. For anybody young and eager about life, it seemed an awful time to be starting out.

CHAPTER FOUR

Abby awoke to the smell of bacon and French toast. She had slept without a blanket, but even with the window screen, gnats and mosquitos had gotten in, her arms and chin now covered in little welts.

She got up and changed into a dress, crouching low so she wouldn't bump her head. The tiny back room had once been a closet, the pitch of the roof taking up half of the space. As a young girl, she had slept with her brothers, the three of them crammed into the bedroom. With all the giggling and farting, she couldn't stand it; a girl had no place being around two rowdy boys. After several years of pleading for her own room, her father finally gave in, relocating the vent stack and putting in a window.

She walked down the stairs and went into the kitchen, where her mother was standing over the stove.

"Where's Daddy?" she asked.

"At work."

"But it's Saturday."

"He was called in. Hungry?"

"Yes," Abby said as she sat at the table.

Mrs. Nolan made up a plate and put it down in front of her. Abby had been right about the bacon, but instead of French toast, it was fried potatoes.

"Your friends stopped by," her mother said.

"Sarah?"

"And another girl."

"Probably Noel."

"They said they'd be at the beach. The good beach."

Abby smiled because she knew what she meant. Winthrop Harbor didn't really have a beach, more like a rocky shore interrupted by patches of coarse sand. On the other side of the peninsula, however, was Point Shirley Beach, facing the sun and always busy.

She finished her breakfast and went into the bathroom, a small space behind the kitchen with a metal sink and tub. For much of her life, the cottage hadn't had running water, and they would bathe in the ocean. Their father dug a well and installed plumbing in the early '30s, a time when so many men were out of work from the Depression that help was cheap and easy to find.

She splashed water on her face and brushed her teeth with a tube of President toothpaste from the summer before, now flat and curled up. Before she left, her mother handed her an orange and said, "Don't get sunburned!"

"I won't."

Abby left and went down Bay View Avenue. The air was warm but comfortable, birds darting between the trees, the smell of lilacs in the air. The streets had once been lined with chestnut trees, but they had all died from a fungus epidemic years before.

At the end, the road turned to sand, the homes along the coast worn and weather-beaten. She walked along the path between the seawall and came out on the beach.

"Abby!"

Ahead, Sarah, Noel, and another girl were lying on a blanket. As Abby approached, Sarah got up, her skin shining with baby oil.

"Abby, this is Angela," Sarah said.

The girl sat up, her dark hair pouring over her shoulders.

"Nice to meet you," Abby said.

"The same."

"Maybe you know each other," Sarah said, and Abby was confused. "She's from East Boston."

"Maybe. It's a big place."

She could tell Angela was foreign and most likely Italian, something about her hair or the shape of her face. If Abby hadn't inherited her mother's prejudices, she had at least become more aware of such qualities, which was sometimes the same thing.

"Where's your brother?"

"I have two," Abby said, tilting her head with an ironic smile.

George never got much attention from girls, or at least the respectable ones, and with his constant puss and bad manners, it was no wonder. The only people he related to were his hoodlum friends from Bennington Street, who he went back to visit most weekends.

"How about a dip?" Noel asked, standing up and dusting off her legs.

When Sarah looked over, Abby gave her a reluctant nod. She loved the ocean, but she didn't like swimming in it, the saltwater being sticky and harsh on her skin. The sand was rocky too, and once as a little girl, she cut her foot so badly that her father had to carry her back to the cottage.

Nevertheless, she got up and fixed her bathing suit, which was tighter than last summer.

"Look what the cat dragged out," someone said.

She looked over and saw George walking towards them, his pants rolled up and barefoot. With him were two other guys, hands in their pockets and cigarettes between their teeth.

"Aren't you working?" she asked.

"That's Dad. I don't work Saturdays."

"Since when?"

He ignored the question and looked at her friends.

"This is Paul. This is Jimmy," he said, making introductions.

Abby always got anxious around him, worried he would say or do something embarrassing. But the girls were interested enough that they came over.

"You're Dave's sister?" George asked Noel.

"You know him?"

"I wouldn't have asked," he said, trying to be clever. "Hey, we're having a shindig here tonight. Some beers, a bonfire."

Abby gave her friends a sharp look, hoping they would take the hint and say no.

"I'll go," Angela said, raising her hand like it was a request for volunteers.

"Terrific. Nine o'clock."

"I'll guess I'll go too," Noel said.

"You guess?"

"No. I'll go. Why not?"

Abby kept a straight face, but inside she was outraged. When she was younger, he never would have interfered with her friends. Now that she was eighteen and out of high school, she was no longer entitled to the privileges and protections of youth, something she had never considered about getting older.

"Catch you girls later then," George said.

He nodded to his buddies, and Abby watched them as they swaggered off.

"Abby!"

Startled, she turned, and Sarah, Noel, and Angela were halfway to the water.

......

ABBY SAT on the front steps with her mother. While she had lemonade, Mrs. Nolan drank something stronger. It was late afternoon, the sun hovering over the skyline, the smell of dinner in the air. Hearing voices, she looked over and her father was coming around the bend with Thomas. Even after a long day, he would always be smiling, which she attributed to his upbringing. People who had tough lives never took happiness for granted.

But today her father looked tired, and she knew driving a crane was hard work, loading freight in the heat, rain, and cold. Whatever his exact age, he was getting older, his shoulders starting to slump. He once claimed he had wanted to be an accountant like his cousin in London. As a man without an education, he had no chance at a profession, remarking that "America was generous, but it wasn't foolish."

"Aren't you two a pair," Mrs. Nolan said.

"A pair of what is the question," her husband joked.

He took off his cap and wiped his forehead, which was red and glistening. His commute was longer in the summer when he had to take a bus to East Boston first before getting the streetcar to the shipyard.

"Celebration is in order," he said, leaning on one knee.

Mrs. Nolan smiled and looked at her son.

"Do we have a new employee at East Boston Works?"

"I got the job," Thomas said, somewhat bashfully.

"Well, that didn't take long."

"We need to hire twenty men," Mr. Nolan said. "Just got a big contract with the government."

"With the Department of Defense," Thomas explained. "To expand operations."

"Two more berths. Adding capacity to send more supplies over to England. Like they deserve it."

Mrs. Nolan rolled her eyes and sipped her drink.

"Don't be such a sourpuss. They're our allies."

Like any Irishman of his generation, he hated the British, but it was more out of principle than from experience. As a ward of the state, he had lived mostly in rural institutions and probably hadn't met an English person until he came to America.

"Let's hope they live up to the task," he said.

Abby smiled and moved over to let them pass. But inside she had a nervous feeling, somewhere between anticipation and dread. Europe had been at war for almost two years, the stories of death and destruction all over the news. She had a friend from school whose grandparents lived in Germany and another whose aunt had died in London during the Blitz.

Aside from a few personal stories, most people seemed too busy to worry about what was happening three thousand miles away. Still, there was tension in the air, growing every day like a dark storm on the horizon. It seemed cruel to come of age now, Abby thought, but her parents' youth hadn't been any easier. Her mother lost a sister to the Spanish flu, and two of her father's friends had died in the Great War. They had raised their three young children in a depression, Mrs. Nolan planting a vegetable garden and her husband painting houses on weekends to make up for the lost work.

"Abigail?"

She came out of the daydream and realized everyone was inside. With her mother holding open the door, she quickly got up and went to join them.

CHAPTER FIVE

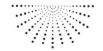

Thomas sat out front under the elm tree, planted almost fifty years before when his great-grandfather bought the land. The sun was down, and it was dark. In the distance, he could hear the laughter of children as they ran through the yards, playing tag and hide-and-seek. He remembered those magical years of childhood when summers felt like one long and lazy afternoon. He would meet so many new friends and do so many fun things, he sometimes forgot they had another life in East Boston.

It was on Point Shirley where he had almost all his significant firsts: his first crush, his first kiss, his first drink. At fourteen years old, he fell in love with a girl from Hawaii, rubbing her breast in the shadow of the seawall beneath a full moon. He never saw her again, but he wasn't heartbroken because nothing back then seemed real or meant to last, something he was reminded of every September when they returned to the crowded streets of the city. Still, he longed for those times, or was it his youth he missed? For four years, he couldn't wait to graduate high school and become an adult, but now he would go back in an instant.

"Where's your brother?

He jumped in the chair.

"Jesus, Ma!" he exclaimed, looking back.

She walked over in her bare feet, a glass in her hand.

"Where's your brother?" she repeated.

"In hell."

"Mind your manners," she said, her tone changing.

He offered her the chair, but she said no. Instead, she sat on the grass beside him, crisscrossing her legs and smoothing out her dress. In the low light, her skin looked as smooth and vibrant as it was when she was younger. She was beautiful and had always been beautiful, those tender eyes and high cheekbones that Abby had been fortunate enough to get. Thomas felt sad thinking that she, like everyone else, was getting older.

"Your brother…" she said, stopping mid-sentence. "I don't worry about you. I don't worry about your sister."

"You shouldn't, Ma."

Pursing her lips, she gazed out at something in the distance.

"I worry about George though. I always have."

"He's an odd sort."

She chuckled.

"That's one way to put it," she said, stirring her drink with her finger.

After a short pause, she turned to him.

"Don't hate him, Thomas. Please."

"Ma, I don't—"

"No. I mean it. Tell me you won't hate him. Ever."

Their eyes met in the dusky light.

"I won't hate him," he said.

She nodded and looked away, and he got the feeling she didn't believe him. He never thought he could despise his own brother, but considering that hate was the absence of love, he wasn't so sure.

"We're all getting older. When your father and I are gone, I don't want him to be alone."

She put her hand on the chair for balance, and he patted it.

"I know, Ma. I know."

The front door swung open, and they both turned. Abby walked out in a long, flowered dress, her hair in rolls with a bow at the top.

"Are you sneaking off to elope?" their mother asked.

"Where's Daddy?"

"Probably asleep in the hammock."

"The mosquitoes are out strong."

"Your father has been bitten before."

Abby approached, tiptoeing over the bumpy grass. Thomas had been helping his father pull rocks from the yard for years, and it still wasn't any smoother.

"I'm going down to the wall," she said to him. "Wanna come?"

"The wall?"

"That's what I said."

He looked over at his mother, who raised her eyes. On summer nights, the seawall had always been a gathering spot, the place where all the youth of Point Shirley met to mingle. For Thomas, as well as for Abby and George, it was the source of many fond memories. But it was mostly kids, and he felt foolish going at his age.

"Nah, I'm too old."

Abby frowned.

"Then that makes me too old," she said.

"Then there you have it."

"George might be there."

"He's ancient."

Their mother giggled, putting her hand to her mouth, and Thomas could tell she was tipsy.

"Go for a bit, dear," she said. "Keep an eye on all those ruffians. Maybe you'll make your first arrest."

"I'm a security guard, Ma. Not a cop."

"Not yet anyway."

He sighed and got up.

"Sure. Let's go down to the wall."

IN THE DISTANCE, Thomas could hear voices and laughter. He tried to keep up, but Abby was walking too fast, either out of eagerness or impatience. They reached the end of the street, and he saw a couple of dozen teenagers sitting on the seawall, more down at a campfire. As they walked through the crowd, he nodded to people he recognized, mostly younger siblings of guys he knew, but it was smaller than in years past.

He kept his hands in his pockets, feeling out of place and not just because he felt old. Socializing at the beach wasn't as exciting as it used to be, and he only came to watch out for his sister.

"Abby?"

Sarah walked over holding a beer, Noel trailing behind her. Thomas could tell they had been in the sun all day, their cheeks red and hair wispy.

"Hello, Thomas," Sarah said, and Noel waved. "Nice to see you again."

Thomas gave a reluctant smile.

"You as well."

Even if they were just average, they were pretty enough that he didn't mind the attention. Each year, girls who hadn't been approachable the summer before would blossom into young women, something he always looked forward to.

"Where's Angela?" Abby asked.

"Over at the fire."

Thomas looked towards the water where he saw sparks and heard the crackle of burning wood. Any gathering with booze and fire was a risk, but the Winthrop police never bothered anyone unless a resident called to complain.

"Who's there?"

"Lots of people."

"Your brother," Noel said.

Thomas got tense—being around his brother always made him uneasy. But he wasn't surprised he was there. When George wasn't with his friends in East Boston, he was usually at the beach. At one time, they even had the same summer friends, but as they got older, George drifted to a rougher crowd.

"I guess I should go see what he's up to," Abby said, then she looked at her friends, fluttered her fingers. "Toodle loo!"

Thomas followed her down to the beach where the tide was out, leaving a long stretch of flat sand. Several figures stood huddled around the fire, their hoots and hollers echoing down the shore.

When they walked up, George was at the front, his shirt open to reveal his sunburned chest. He had a beer can in his hand and his arm around a brunette girl.

"Abigail!"

"Abigail?" one of his friends asked.

"Our parents named us after the first three presidents."

"I don't remember no Abigail."

"George Washington. Thomas Jefferson. John Adams was in the middle. When they had Abby, they couldn't name her John Adams. So they named her Abigail after his wife."

Thomas chuckled because it was probably the most he knew about history. George had done poorly in high school, finally dropping out after he realized he would have to repeat the tenth grade. Thomas always thought it was sad because, for all his brother's faults, he was actually pretty smart.

"Want a beer?" George asked, looking across to them. "Over in the bag."

"No—"

"Sure," Abby said.

When she walked over to get one, she saw some girls she knew and started talking. Standing alone, Thomas listened to the conversation, which was mostly drunken rambling. He hated booze and hardly ever touched it. The last time he got drunk was junior year when he and his friends got some wine and drank it behind the pool hall. As a boy, he would see the bums on Bennington Street begging for nickels to buy jugs of cheap gin. Most of all, he remembered what alcohol did to his father, turning a gentle man into a slobbering lunatic.

"What if Germany attacks us?"

Thomas looked up. He didn't know who said it, but it was the first interesting thing he heard.

"Hitler won't attack America. It's too far."

"They could with their U-boats."

"They'd need ten thousand."

"You gonna join up?" someone asked George.

The guy looked like a hoodlum with his pug nose and gold chain. Thomas had seen him before, although he wasn't sure if it was there or back home.

"When the time comes," his brother said, smiling at the girl beside him.

Thomas wondered who she was, whether George knew her from previous summers or if they had only just met. In some ways, he felt bad for her, and maybe for them both, knowing how flings on Point Shirley never lasted.

"Howz about you?"

The young man went around the circle, asking everyone like he was testing their patriotism. Some were just teenagers, too young for the military, and it seemed like a cheap shot. Thomas hated the bravado, wondering why it was always the smallest guys who were the most obnoxious.

"And you?" the guy asked, looking at Thomas.

"Naw. I'm going into the seminary."

When everyone laughed, the guy looked confused, like he didn't know whether it was a joke or not. And George wasn't there to tell him because he had stepped away to piss.

"A priest?"

"That's right," Thomas said, keeping a straight face.

"Maybe you can pray I get a piece of tail tonight."

"That would take a miracle."

Again there was laughter, this time more subdued. A quiet tension filled the air.

"How about you scram?"

"How 'bout I shove that beer can up your ass?" Thomas said.

Suddenly, everyone stopped talking. Thomas stared across, and the man glared back. He wasn't afraid because he was a foot taller and thirty pounds heavier. He was sober too, the best advantage of all, and he knew he could have taken down two or three of them if he had to.

The standoff ended when George returned, and Thomas was relieved. He had been dealing with bullies all his life, and on the streets of East Boston, there was no shortage of them. He had learned long before that if you backed down to one, you backed down to them all. And once you showed fear, there was no coming back.

He stepped away and walked over to Abby, who was standing with some girls by the water. They all wore summer dresses, the colors muted in the darkness.

"I'm going back to the cottage," he said, and Abby turned around.

"Now?"

"Now."

"On such a lovely night?" he heard.

He looked up and forced a smile, unsure who said it.

"George is over there," he said, nodding towards the fire, "in case—"

"In case what?"

Their eyes locked, but there was nothing to dispute. They weren't kids anymore, and Abby could take care of herself.

"Just don't drink too much," he said.

She tilted her head with a mischievous grin.

"And what if I do?"

"You'll have a wicked hangover!" someone said.

Thomas glanced over, and one of the girls smiled.

"Just be careful," he said to Abby.

"Aren't I always?"

As he walked off, he headed away from the fire, wanting to avoid his brother more than the guy he had argued with. George was annoying when he was drunk, and his friends were just as bad.

Thomas was almost at the road when someone called his name. Turning, he saw a girl come out from the shadows.

"Noel?" he asked.

She approached with a timid smile, walking on her tiptoes. The top of her dress was loose enough that he could see her cleavage.

"Where're you going?" she asked.

"Home."

"So early?"

"I'm tired."

When she came closer, he could tell she was drunk. Her eyes were sagging, and she spoke in quick, scattered bursts.

"There's a meteor shower," she said.

"I didn't know."

"Wanna watch for shooting stars?"

He thought for a moment.

"I don't—"

"Please?"

She looked up, her lashes fluttering, and he couldn't say no.

"Sure. Just for a bit."

She grabbed his hand, and they walked, the sounds of the party fading behind them. They reached a quiet part of the beach and sat on the seawall, and Thomas emptied the sand from his shoes.

"It's so beautiful out here," she said.

The sky was clear, a stretch of infinite stars, and on the other side of the sound, the lights of Nahant sparkled.

"Haven't you been here before?"

"We came to Point Shirley when I was little. My great-uncle had a house on Yirrell Beach."

"Not anymore?"

"He died a long time ago. The house is gone. Destroyed in the hurricane."

Thomas nodded. The Hurricane of '38 was something everyone remembered. In East Boston, they lived on a hill, so they didn't have to worry about flooding. But they lost power for over a week, and when they finally came out after the storm, the streets were covered in debris.

"*Noel?* Is that for Christmas?"

"Noella. My family is Portuguese," she said, then pointed towards the sky. "Did you see it?"

"I think so," he said, looking up.

"I saw you put Anthony in his place tonight."

"Anthony?"

He knew who she meant but wanted to downplay it.

"The guy at the fire. He's a creep."

"He's just a bigmouth."

She laughed and turned to him.

"That's what my friends say. That I'm a bigmouth."

She stared at him with a curious wonder, and he knew that look. Without another word, she leaned forward, and they kissed. Her lips were soft, but he could taste the beer and didn't like it. Finally, she pulled away, breathing heavily, her face glowing.

He was just about to say something to break the awkward silence when she giggled and shifted on the wall. In a single motion, she pulled down her dress and lifted her bra to reveal her breasts. Thomas gasped, his eyes fixated on them. There was something shocking about seeing a girl suddenly topless.

"Noel," he said, hesitantly.

"Go ahead, touch them."

"I really—"

"Please."

She took his hand and brought it to her chest. When he felt the soft warmth, he reached for the other, squeezing them both. He had the urge to maul her but didn't, and it wasn't out of decency. If things got hotter, he didn't have a rubber, and the last thing he wanted was to get a girl pregnant at eighteen. All his life he had watched people act on instinct, and sometimes he thought the one thing he had going for him was his discipline.

"What's wrong?" she asked.

"It's just that—"

"You don't like me?"

"Of course I do," he said, but it wasn't completely true.

She was pretty but also naïve, and he never liked anyone or anything that came too easily. Besides, they had only just arrived at Point Shirley, and it was too early to get hitched. If he slept with her now, he knew it would be a long summer, especially if things went sour.

"What do we have here?"

She pulled up her dress, and they both stood up. Coming down the beach was George and the girl he was with at the fire.

"Where's Abby?" Thomas asked.

"Beats me, brother. You know I can't see nothing at night."

"Hi, Noel," the girl said.

Noel got up, fixing her dress, looking embarrassed.

"Hi, Angela," she said.

"What're you two up to?" George blurted, so drunk he swayed. "Don't tell me. Watching shooting stars?"

Thomas grinned at the comment, both its accuracy and its tact; he had expected something far more sarcastic. They all stood facing each other, the girls smiling and George trying to stay upright.

Finally, he looked at Angela.

"C'mon, doll," he said, hiccupping. "Let's leave my baby brother to his girl."

Thomas cringed at *his girl*, but he appreciated the sentiment. Angela waved goodbye to Noel, and they walked away, Thomas watching until they disappeared in the darkness. When he turned back to Noel, she was stooped over, her arms crossed.

"What's wrong?" he asked, and he could tell she was crying.

"I feel like such a heel."

"Don't."

"I do."

She looked up like a frightened child. Her eyes were glassy, mascara smudged. He was overcome by a warm sympathy that made him smile. Women were always more attractive when they were vulnerable.

He held out his hand.

"C'mon. Let me walk you home."

"You sure you don't mind?" she asked, her voice strained and emotional.

"I insist."

CHAPTER SIX

When Abby woke up Monday morning, everyone was at work except for her mother. She crawled out of bed, her head still sore from Saturday. She hadn't drunk that much since graduation the month before, a night she would never forget. She and her classmates had started at the Lenox Hotel in the afternoon and ended up at the Cocoanut Grove until midnight. The drinking age had been twenty-one since Prohibition ended, but someone knew a doorman who let them in. One of her friends broke her shoe dancing; another girl almost left with a sailor. Although they would have stayed until closing, they were making so much noise the bar manager finally asked them to leave.

Abby crept downstairs in her slippers, the steps bending under her feet. She could sense the fragility of the old cottage, its thin frame and drafty walls, something she never noticed when other people were around. It was strange to be alone, the first summer that both of her brothers were working. Thomas had always had a job at the theater, but he usually only worked weekends. George's employment history had been sporadic since high school, seasonal work and low-wage jobs. Delivering newspapers was the steadiest thing he ever had, but it was hardly a career.

She walked into the kitchen and saw bread on the table, a pat of butter and some jam. But she wasn't hungry and could never eat right when she got up. Hearing someone whistling, she walked out to the back porch, and her mother was on her knees in the garden, trimming the daffodils.

"Good morning," she said.

"My, my," her mother said, looking back over her shoulder. "Look who has arisen."

"What time is it?"

"Close to ten anyway. Make some toast. There's bread on the table."

"Thanks."

"Abby, dear," she said, straining to stand up. "Your father tore his good pants. He'll need them for church. Can you take them to the tailor?"

"Sure."

"They're on the counter beside the icebox. There should be a few dimes for the bus on the sill."

Abby laughed to herself, remembering hearing her father groan when he split his pants playing horseshoes the evening before. He loved to socialize with their neighbor Mr. Loughran, a former police captain who lived next door with his wife. Their three sons were all grown up and living out of state. Like most families on Point Shirley, he bought the house cheap before the Great War and used it as a summer place. Once he retired, he made it into a year-round residence, one of the first cottages to be winterized. As a ham radio enthusiast, he had a large antenna in his yard, and many nights Abby would listen to the static and chatter of his conversations with people far away.

After washing up, she got her father's pants and put them in a knapsack. She reached for her purse and was just about to go when her mother rushed out from the kitchen, her cheeks red and a wisp of hair on her face.

"Can you fetch a couple cans of peaches from the house? I'd like to make a cobbler tonight."

"Yes, Ma."

Abby walked out, the screen door snapping shut behind her. It was a beautiful summer day, the sun strong and the winds low. She went to the end of Bay View Avenue and waited on the corner for the bus. Already, the beach was busy with cars parked along both sides of the street, and people walking by with parasols, blankets, and coolers. When five boys in a convertible drove by gawking, she turned away with a frown.

She often resented the visitors, invading their quiet corner of paradise, and her family had always been protective of Point Shirley. Her mother said she could spot people from the city because the wives smoked, and the kids would spit in public. Mrs. Nolan talked about their neighborhood like she was from somewhere else, a snobbery Abby sometimes had too.

When she finally got off the streetcar in East Boston, the noise and traffic were overwhelming. She never felt like she lived in the city until she returned to it. Crossing Bennington Street, she approached Gittell's Tailor, where some boys were shooting marbles on the sidewalk. With their dark hair and ragged clothes, she knew they were Italians like most young kids were now. They stood up as she went by, eyeing her with a mix of suspicion and curiosity.

"Afternoon, Miss," one of them said, tipping his hat.

Another whistled at her, and two men in front of the pool hall laughed. Feeling self-conscious, she rushed over to the door and went inside.

As she waited by the counter, someone looked out from the back room. She assumed it was Mr. Gittell, but she really didn't know. They never used a tailor, her mother doing most of their alterations at home. But Mrs. Nolan struggled with the needle lately because her hands were so jittery. While she claimed her nerves were wracked from age and housework, Abby knew her drinking didn't help.

"Madam," the man said, walking out.

He was about her father's age, with thinning dark hair and glasses. When he smiled, he had kind eyes, which put her at ease. Like any woman, she hated to be leered at or catcalled, and the incident out front had shaken her up.

"Yes," she said, taking out her father's pants. "These need to be repaired."

The man laid them flat on the counter, examining the seam with the precision of a surgeon. Then he reached for a ticket, wrote something on it, and handed it to her.

"Ready by end of week," he said with a thick accent.

"Thank you."

"My pleasure."

She walked out and the gang was gone, replaced by a group of young men who stood smoking around a parked car. They all wore leather jackets and pleated slacks, the standard outfit of street hoods. When she glanced over, they stared back, and she quickly looked away.

It felt strange to be alone because she hardly ever was. In high school, she was always with a lot of girls, whether they went to the theater or shopping downtown. There was safety in numbers, something she had learned when a friend of Thomas' was murdered in Maverick Square one night after missing the trolley. East Boston was a tough place and *getting tougher*, as her mother said. Considering women were always the most at risk, she was lucky to have brothers.

She started up the hill to her house, a white colonial with black shutters and brick stairs. It was hard to believe it was once the only home on the street, built during the Civil War by her great-grandfather. He once owned all the land down to Chelsea Creek, and her mother remembered playing along its banks before the highway was built. But that was a long time ago, and now the neighborhood was dense, houses crammed together, buildings on every corner.

As she walked up the steps, someone called, and she turned to see Chickie.

"Hello, dear."

"House," Chickie said, pointing.

"Yes. I'm going in the house.

"Play?"

"I can't play now."

Chickie whimpered and looked down. Abby always tried to be kind to her, braiding her hair and teaching her pat-a-cake while Mrs. Ciarlone peered out through the curtains. But she couldn't raise the girl, and it was sad to see her spend so much time alone.

"I have to go inside," she said.

"Tomorrow. Play?"

"Not tomorrow. Maybe next week?"

"Next week. Play."

Abby smiled and went over to the door, reaching for the key and unlocking it. Inside, the air was warm and musty. They used to leave some windows open, but her mother insisted they stay closed. There had been a lot of break-ins recently, and burglars were always on the lookout for families that were away.

She walked into the pantry and found the canned peaches, putting them in the knapsack. She took some corn and green beans too, not wanting to make the trip back if they ran out. There was a small shop on Point Shirley, but with money tight, she knew her mother would send her home rather than buy something.

Smelling smoke, she went over to the back door. When she looked out, she was surprised to see George with two guys on the porch. She didn't recognize them, but then she didn't know a lot of his friends. On the table were some beer bottles, an ashtray, and a jar of Planters peanuts.

"Am I interrupting a party?" she joked.

"You're interrupting. But it ain't a party."

"Aren't you working?"

"What're you doing here?" he asked, ignoring her question.

"Ma wanted me to get some things."

She glanced over and saw a newspaper with *Social Justice* across the top. The name was odd, especially since George had never been involved in politics or things that concerned the welfare of others.

As she stood in the doorway, the two men sat quietly, one with his hands clasped, the other having a cigarette. She could sense an underlying tension and didn't like feeling unwelcome in her own house.

"You coming back to the cottage?" she asked.

"When I'm ready."

She gave him an icy stare but was too polite to retaliate. So she went back inside, walking through the rooms to check on them. The only thing unusual was that the clocks had all stopped, but there was no reason to wind them because it would only happen again.

She threw her bag over her shoulder and left, locking the front door even though George had a key. As she turned around, a black taxi pulled in front of the Ciarlones' house, and a young woman got out. She was tall and pretty, with a red dress and a headscarf. She paid the driver, and he got a suitcase from the trunk.

The car pulled away, and the woman stood on the sidewalk alone, looking confused or maybe just tired. Moments later, Mrs. Ciarlone burst out the front door, exclaiming something in Italian before rushing down the stairs. They embraced, kissing each other's cheeks, a show of affection that would have shocked some of the more traditional neighbors. All the while, Chickie watched from the porch, peeking over the railing with shy curiosity.

Abby didn't know if the lady was a friend or a relative, but she spoke in Italian and had the exotic look of a foreigner. Either way, the reunion was sweet, and as unfriendly as the Ciarlones were, Abby never felt any personal scorn towards them. Mrs. Nolan was quietly offended, if only because she had lived there all her life. George was more open in his hostility, once calling them *dumb guineas*, a strange remark considering many of his friends were Italian.

The woman took her baggage, struggling with her slender arms. Mrs. Ciarlone tried to help, but with all her extra weight, she could barely get herself up the stairs. They made it to the door, and Abby was surprised when the lady looked over and smiled. As she started to smile back, Mrs. Ciarlone yelled for Chickie and rushed them all inside.

CHAPTER SEVEN

Thomas stood on the tarmac with fifteen other men, his back arched and arms at his side. They had all been given uniforms without the time to put them on, his blue pants and shirt folded on the ground beside him. The first day was for training, touring the facility and getting familiarized with the procedures. With a ten-foot-high barbed wire fence, East Boston Works was well-protected, but the shipyard was expanding fast, and there were rumors it would eventually be operating 24/7.

Just three months before, President Roosevelt had passed the Lend-Lease policy, which provided food and supplies to England and other allied countries. Along the docks, there were already hundreds of barrels of oil and pallets of rice and potatoes. Once the ships were loaded, they would go north to Portland, Maine, where they would join a convoy to make the journey across the Atlantic, escorted by warships. Thomas and the other new recruits were advised not to talk about what they saw so civilians wouldn't get alarmed. But as lowly guards, they weren't bound by oath or law, and gossip was a hard thing to stop.

"I wanna know if you hear a rat fart!"

The supervisor walked up and down the line like a drill instructor, his cap set straight on his bald head, a clipboard in hand. The hiring agent had called him *sergeant*, but Thomas doubted they had official ranks for security staff, and everyone else called him Mr. Barrett.

"Presently, we're loading a thousand tons a day. We expect that to double by the end of summer…"

He had a thick Scottish accent, rolling his r's in a way that reminded Thomas of his father.

"That level of cargo is bound to attract thieves."

As he approached Thomas, he stopped and turned to him.

"Watchman, what's your name?"

"Thomas Nolan, sir," he said.

"Do you go by Thomas or Tom?"

"My friends call me Thomas."

"Then I'll call you Tom."

Thomas remained still, a grin on his face.

"Tell me, Tom. What do you do when you see a suspicious character on the lot?"

"Ask for his ID card."

"What if he doesn't show it?"

Thomas thought for a moment. In the training room, they had explained the order of procedure, and he didn't want to get it wrong.

"Tell him he needs to come to the office," he said.

"And what if he kicks you in the balls and runs off?"

"I blow the whistle."

Barrett held up the whistle around his neck and looked everyone in the eye.

"This is our single most effective tool as watchmen," he said. "Not only does it signal there's been a breach, but it allows us to come to your aid and quick. Crooks will stab you in no time to get away. Especially all these dagoes around here."

There was some uncomfortable laughter. Thomas couldn't tell if he was joking, but there were several Italians in the group.

"Now," the man continued. "Your field training has concluded. You're welcome to join me in surveilling a couple pints at Sonny's in Maverick Square."

Everyone fell out of line and collected their things. At his interview, Thomas was told they would receive batons as well as pocket watches to time their rounds. He never mentioned he had applied for the Boston Police, worried they would think he was a hothead or worse, that he was only using the job as a steppingstone, which he was.

Barrett headed across the lot, and most of the men followed. Thomas would have gone, but the day shift was almost over, and he had planned to go home with his father. So he walked towards the pier and through a narrow gate where, in the distance, he saw a tugboat pushing a barge in the harbor. Along the dock were two ships, their thick lines tied to the bollards. With the gangways down, he could see inside, crates of supplies stacked against the wall, some marked U.S. Army.

"Hey, you!"

Spinning around, he saw a man in coveralls and boots, his face soiled and sweaty.

"What're you doing?"

"Looking for my father," Thomas said.

Noticing the uniform in his arms, the man's attitude changed, but it didn't quite soften.

"This area is restricted. You on duty?"

"I just finished training."

He stepped closer, took Thomas around the shoulder, and pointed. "Between the buildings," he said. "Locker rooms are on the right."

Thomas thanked him with a friendly nod and walked away.

The shipyard was so large it took him five minutes to find the door, and when he did his father was coming out carrying his bag and thermos.

"Thomas? You made it through your first day, did ye?"

"We spent all morning studying maps."

Mr. Nolan turned his head, gave him a sideways look.

"It helps to know what you're looking after."

"Of course, Dad."

"Now how's it feel to finally be a man?"

Thomas smiled. His father's praise was never excessive, but it was clear.

......

THE TRIP from the docks back to the cottage took almost an hour, and the streetcar was packed. Mr. Nolan had once considered buying a car, but he couldn't drive. Like most of the family, he spent his life on trains and buses, and one of the advantages of living in the city was you could get around easily. Despite his bad eyesight, George was the only one who had a license, which was ironic because he almost never left East Boston.

At Orient Heights, they boarded the bus to Point Shirley. As they rolled across the strand, Thomas looked over at his father, who lay slumped on the bench, hat in his hands and staring out at the sea. Even in the dusky light, he looked old, and Thomas wondered how much longer he would continue working. Thomas liked these small moments, traveling quietly beside his father, especially because they were never alone. Out of everyone in the family, they were the least alike, and yet they got along the best. While Thomas' mother always said he was too serious, his father had a more relaxed, philosophical view of life.

By the time they got home, Thomas was exhausted, and it was only his first day. The month since graduation had been a long and lazy slog, and he hadn't had to get up so early in weeks. He was still working two or three nights at the theater, but it was only for spending money, and on Point Shirley, there wasn't much to buy. Now he had to tell his old boss he was leaving, a sentimental departure because he had had the job all through high school.

He put his new uniform under the bed, changed, and washed up. When he got downstairs, his mother had set the table outside. It was still early enough in the season that the bugs weren't bad, but once the greenheads arrived, they would have no choice but to eat inside.

"How was your first day?" his mother asked as he walked out. She had on a blue flowered dress, her hair in a bun.

"Good. Can I help?"

"Get the potato salad, would you? It's in the icebox."

As he turned to go back inside, his father was coming out, a cold glass of cream soda in his hand. Thomas hadn't seen him drink in years and sometimes forgot all the chaos from when he did. His mother was a different story, however, and although she went days, sometimes weeks without any alcohol, once she started, she didn't stop. She could be silly, sad, or sentimental, depending on her mood and the company.

When Thomas and his siblings were young, the country was still under Prohibition, but she had a friend at the pharmacy who got her a prescription for *medicinal liquor*. Like any good drinker, she kept it together, staying sober when she had to and letting loose when she could.

Thomas walked back out, and Abby was in the yard. With her wrinkled dress and bare feet, he knew she had been at the beach or wandering around town. Only a week before, he had dreaded coming out to Point Shirley, and now that he had a full-time job, he realized he was going to miss those carefree days.

"Your nose is burnt," he said.

She stuck out her tongue, and he laughed. He put the potato salad down beside a tray of cold, sliced ham and a dish of relish. With everything ready, they all sat down.

"Where's George?" their mother asked.

"He was at the house today with some men," Abby said.

"Friends?"

"I don't know."

"What's that boy up to?" Mr. Nolan muttered, reaching for the ham.

After they ate, Mrs. Nolan went into the house and came back with a dish of peach cobbler. She scooped it onto their dirty plates, but no one cared; they didn't have small bowls anyway.

"What a delight," their father said, sipping the last of his drink and gazing out at the water.

The sun was going down, casting a soft haze over the city. In the distance, a Navy frigate was passing behind the airport, headed into the harbor. All the dockyards were now doing work for the U.S. military, something Thomas learned from his supervisor, and the number of warships entering the port was growing each day.

All the activity was good, especially after the previous winter when commercial shipping along the Atlantic seaboard had come to a halt. Mr. Nolan's hours were reduced by a third, and his union had warned of layoffs. The fighting in Europe was disrupting international trade routes everywhere. And although German U-boats had been ravaging British merchant ships, they hadn't been bold enough to attack an American one.

President Roosevelt's Lend-Lease program had changed all that. By giving aid to Britain and Russia, it was putting men back to work, and industries were booming. Thomas was proud to be part of the effort, but he was also nervous. No one in the family talked about the war, and aside from a couple of food drives at their church, it seemed like a distant worry. But signs it was getting closer were everywhere, and a month before, the government had seized five foreign vessels in Boston harbor: Italian, Danish, and German.

"Tell me about the job," his mother said, finally sitting down.

In her hand was a cold drink, either vodka or gin.

"We work in shifts," Thomas said.

"Nights?"

"Maybe. We won't get our schedules until next week."

She smiled and took a sip, sweaty from taking in the dishes.

"I like the uniform. But aren't wool pants too heavy for summer?"

"There's shade."

"Shoulda asked for silk," his father joked.

"Mrs. Flynn says there are some big ships."

"What's inside them is bigger..." Thomas said, stopping when his father gave him a sharp look.

Abby walked out, and it was enough of a distraction that he didn't have to explain. She had on a clean dress, and her hair was brushed out.

"Where are you off to, miss?" Mrs. Nolan said.

"The beach."

"In your satin shoes?"

"I'll be careful."

As she got closer, Thomas saw she had covered up her sunburned nose.

"Wanna come?" she asked him.

"No thanks."

"Noel will be there," she said with a hint of sarcasm.

When his parents looked over, Thomas squirmed in the chair. They were always curious about his love life, especially his father, who once warned *woe to him who does not have the counsel of a good wife*.

"Go on, son," Mr. Nolan said. "Wanna be a bachelor all your life?"

Thomas scoffed, but he appreciated their encouragement. He wasn't interested in Noel, something he realized the night she flirted with him. But that didn't mean he couldn't socialize, and even if the crowd at the seawall was mostly younger kids now, he knew he would someday miss it.

"Sure," he said to Abby, and her face beamed. "Let's go down to the beach."

CHAPTER EIGHT

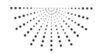

*A*bby staggered up the front steps, sweaty and hot. She had gone with Sarah and Noel to Deer Island, a rural stretch of inlets, paths, and bluffs at the end of the peninsula. Besides a lighthouse, it hosted the House of Correction, an eerie stone structure surrounded by a barbed-wire fence, with guard towers on each corner.

She always got a thrill in knowing seven hundred criminals were just down the road. Years ago, six men had escaped, and all of Point Shirley went on the lookout, men scouring the streets with shotguns and baseball bats. Only five or six years old at the time, she remembered it not for the escape, but because it was one of the few times she had ever heard her father curse.

When Abby walked into the kitchen, her mother was bent over the slop sink, washing the clothes.

"Did you have lunch?" she asked.

"I'm not hungry. Can I help?"

Mrs. Nolan stopped and looked over panting.

"If you want something to do, go pick up your father's pants."

Abby had forgotten and probably would have left them at the tailor all summer.

"I'll go now," she said.

"There's change on the windowsill."

After drinking some water, she reached into the jar and got two dimes for the ride and seventy-five cents for the repair. She had her own money, but it was all bills, everything she had saved working at Betty Ann Bakery on weekends in high school. Her mother never wanted her to have the job, more concerned with her image than her daughter's development. Her family had been in America for four generations, and she was determined to finally have someone go to college. Mr. Nolan won out in the end as he did with most things his wife was stubborn about, insisting it was never too early to learn the value of work.

Abby caught the bus at the end of the road, sitting next to some girls who were heading home to Saugus after a morning at the beach. She loved listening to them, their gossip and silly chatter, because it reminded her what it was like to be thirteen. They seemed so carefree, but life never was, and everyone had problems, only kids dwelled on them less. When she was their age, the country was in the middle of the Depression, and she remembered coal relief trucks driving through their neighborhood, and the C.W.A. workers building the playground at the end of their street.

She got off at Bennington Street and crossed over to the shops. Seeing some men in front of the pool hall, she looked for George, knowing he often hung out there. He hadn't come home the night before, which wasn't unusual. When he was younger, he used to stay at Point Shirley for the entire summer like the rest of them. But after he quit high school, he got restless and was always going between their house and the cottage. While Thomas said he couldn't wait to get out of East Boston, George couldn't seem to leave it.

She walked into Gittell's and saw a young man behind the counter. He was tall and well-dressed, his hair parted to the side.

"Hello," he said, looking up.

When he smiled, she felt a slight chill.

"I'm…I'm here to get my father's pants," she said.

"Do you have your ticket?"

She cringed, looking in her purse even though she knew she had forgotten it. All year, she had been as disciplined as a librarian, keeping notes of chores and tasks, a timetable of her homework. But when school ended everything fell apart, and some days she had trouble remembering to brush her teeth.

"I don't, I'm afraid," she said.

"Not a problem. When were they dropped off?"

Again, she was stumped. She counted back the days, but in the endless monotony of summer, there wasn't much to distinguish them.

"Last Monday," she blurted, hoping it was right.

"Was it for a cleaning?"

"The seam had to be mended."

Again, he smiled, and this time, it put her at ease.

He went into the back room, and she heard him moving hangers around. As she waited, she looked around the small shop, the walls decorated with pictures of the latest styles, men in double-breasted suits and women in A-line dresses. In a Sears Roebuck poster, a couple stood arm in arm in some tropical paradise, Bermuda or St. Thomas; places she had dreamt about but not been. She had never given much thought to love or romance, having spent her adolescence focused on her studies. Her mother once said that nothing could sideline a young girl's ambitions like a man. Abby took the advice, although she was never sure if it was sincere or from bitterness about her own dashed hopes.

"Miss?"

Startled, she turned, and the young man was at the counter.

"Pardon," she said, embarrassed.

"Are these the pants?"

"I believe so."

He handed them to her and then rang it in.

"Do you live locally?" he asked.

"No…I mean, yes."

He looked up, narrowing his eyes with a hint of flirtation.

"We stay in Winthrop in the summer," she explained. "But we live just up the road."

She was about to ask him too when the register dinged, and the cash drawer opened.

"Seventy-five cents, please."

Handing him the change, she noticed his watch, gold with a leather band. He was more refined than the men she knew, and she even detected a faint cologne.

"Thank you, miss," he said.

"It's Abby."

She didn't know why she said it, other than it seemed proper.

"Abby," he said with a smile. "I'm Arthur."

"Pleased to meet you."

"Likewise."

She backed away from the counter, their eyes still locked, and if she told herself she wasn't smitten, it would have been a lie. She didn't look away until she got to the door. When she finally turned and pushed it open, she was so distracted she knocked into someone on the sidewalk.

"Oh, pardon."

"Abby?"

She was surprised it was Thomas, who had on casual clothes with a bag under his arm.

"What are you doing here?" she asked.

"Ma told me to get Dad's pants."

"She told *me* to get Dad's pants."

"Then I'm off the hook," he said, and she smirked at the pun.

"Why aren't you working?"

"I just quit."

"What...?" she asked, surprised.

"The theater."

She frowned at his deadpan humor. He always liked to tease her, something he had been doing since they were children. Even as an infant, he would pull her hair from behind and scurry off to make her think someone else had done it. When she was eight, he glued the feet of her dolls to the bedroom floor. With everyone else, he wasn't a prankster, rather the most serious one in the family. But they shared a bond, some deep connection that brought out his playful side, a consequence of their twinship.

"Back to the cottage?" she asked.

"Let's go."

They crossed the street as a trolley was approaching, and she opened her purse, hoping she still had some coins. Hearing a shout, they both turned, and it was George. He was parked in front of the pool hall in the delivery truck, forest green with *The Boston Globe* on the side.

Thomas looked over, shrugging his shoulders, and George waved. As the streetcar sat stopped, they had to decide, and a lift home was a lot quicker than a trolley and a bus. So they ran over.

"Hop in," George said, a cigarette hanging from his mouth.

Abby took the passenger seat, and Thomas sat on a bench behind her. The back was empty, but it reeked of newsprint. George beeped to some friends and then made a wide U-turn in traffic, Abby grabbing the door for balance.

"The hell you doin' back in town?" he asked her.

"I had to pick up Daddy's pants."

"You mean *Dad*?"

"What's the difference?"

"Why give those hebes any business?" he asked. "Mangini's is right down the road."

Abby's face dropped, and she was so appalled she would have jumped out if they weren't moving. She could put up with his casual insults, but bigotry was unacceptable. The owner of Gittell's Tailor was Jewish, something her mother had mentioned, and the remark made Abby ashamed for the whole family.

"Maybe she don't like guineas either," Thomas said.

George looked in the rearview, and a smile broke across his face.

"Can you blame her?"

Abby just shook her head. While she always got flustered when George was obnoxious, Thomas either ignored him or egged him on. It was hard to believe George used to bully him, pinning him to the ground when they wrestled, yanking his arm up behind his back. At some point in their early teens all that changed. She was there the first time Thomas overpowered him, throwing him into the side of the shed, and she cheered like it was a victory for mankind. As much as she loved them both—and she did love George, despite his meanness—she always felt safer when Thomas was around.

With George driving, the five miles to Point Shirley only took ten minutes. They sped over the bridge into Winthrop, racing around curves, the truck rattling and spewing black smoke. The only time he slowed down was when a horse cart pulled out from a side street and got in his way.

Abby was relieved when they reached Point Shirley Beach because it meant they were almost home. The heat of the cabin combined with all the swerving was making her dizzy. They were just about to turn onto Bay View Avenue when George hit the brakes, and they skidded to a stop.

"What the hell was that for?!" Thomas exclaimed.

"Hold on."

George put the truck in reverse and backed up. Looking down the dead end, Abby saw Sarah, Noel, and Angela walking up from the water.

"Hey, Abby," Sarah said, squinting in the sun.

After their long morning at Deer Island, Abby couldn't believe they went to the beach afterward.

"Back for more?"

"Noel wasn't sunburnt enough."

When Abby smiled, Noel stepped forward, a floppy hat on her head.

"Is Thomas with you?" she asked.

Abby felt a thud against the seat and got the message—Thomas didn't want her to know he was there. In her striped two-piece suit, Noel looked cute, her breasts pouring from her top. Abby couldn't understand why her brother wasn't interested, but girls liked him enough that he could be picky.

"Are you all going down the pier tonight?" she asked.

"Probably not, I'm wiped."

"There's fireworks tomorrow night for the Fourth of July," Noel said.

As they talked, Angela stepped away and walked around to the driver's side. The weekend before, Abby had seen George with his arm around her, and she wondered if they were now a pair. Nights at the seawall, with all the booze and conversation, were hotbeds of flirtation, and they never ended without at least a few couples vanishing down the beach for kissing and more. She didn't know Angela well enough to warn her, and some girls had to find out for themselves that a guy was a jerk.

"We'll catch up tomorrow?" Sarah said.

Abby nodded with a smile.

"Bring Thomas," Noel said, and Abby waited for another hit to the back.

"He's working."

When her friends walked off, Abby turned and saw George leaning out the window and kissing Angela. It wasn't just a friendly peck, but something deeper and more sensual, and all at once, she was disgusted. Before she could interrupt, they separated, and George wiped his mouth on his sleeve, the crudest show of affection she had ever seen.

"Can we please go?" she asked.

With a smug grin, he put the truck in gear, and they drove away.

"What the hell was all that about?" Thomas said.

"Cool out, brother," George said, glancing back.

"I wanted a lift, not a show."

"What a dish, ain't she?"

As shocked as she was, Abby had to laugh. She couldn't blame George for liking girls. For all his problems, he needed love like everyone else, and maybe, she thought, it would calm him down. Her mother always said that women were the antidote to the destructive ways of men, and as old-fashioned as it sounded, Abby couldn't deny there was some truth to it.

CHAPTER NINE

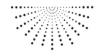

Thomas sat alone in the guardhouse at East Boston Works. Situated directly in the sun, the small structure was stifling, and for the entire shift, he had to lean against the window for air, sweat trickling down his back. He hadn't known what to expect from the job, but it was a rough start, and his only consolation was that they rotated assignments.

Nevertheless, the location was quiet. No one came in the West Gate, most visitors and deliveries going through the main entrance. Across the street was a row of tenements, wood-framed houses with sagging back porches and rotted gutters. Like most cities, the waterfront was the poorest part of town. With the stench of the fisheries and the noise from the shipyards, anyone with the means moved further inland.

A dozen children were playing in the street, stickball and tag, all barefoot and half-dressed. Thomas could tell they were Italians by their dark hair and olive skin, and the area was teeming with immigrants from places like Naples and Salerno. Unlike his mother, he never felt any prejudice toward them, and many of his classmates in high school were Italian. He understood why older residents were wary—it was never easy to be replaced by another group. But change was constant, and as much as his mother reminisced about the old days, he knew East Boston couldn't have stayed Irish forever.

As he stood gazing, he saw a line of women come out a side door in work dresses and overalls. The building had no sign, but he knew it was a factory, and all along the street were small manufacturing firms. As they scattered, he noticed a particular girl, pretty enough that she stuck out from the rest. Standing on the sidewalk, she tore off her hairnet, and a pile of dark curls fell over her shoulders. Something about her shook him from his stupor and he sat up, watching with a curious fascination.

"Nolan?!"

Startled by a knock, he turned, and officer Barrett was at the window. He looked at Thomas and then across the street, where the young woman was now standing alone.

"I see you're honing your skills of observation," he said.

"Yes, sir."

He tore something from his clipboard.

"I suppose you're a Catholic like all these other louts," he said, and he handed a slip to Thomas.

"Pardon?"

"Your schedule. You'll be working Sundays."

"No problem."

"I didn't say it was, son."

Thomas could never tell if he was being curt or just clever. Barrett had the bearing of a soldier, his body stiff and his expression flat, and Thomas wondered if it was from his years in the British Royal Navy or because he was Scottish. Either way, the man was a proud Protestant, something he made clear their first day. But as the sons of Irish or Italian peasants, none of the recruits knew enough about religious distinctions to care.

"I'm off Thursdays and Fridays?" Thomas asked, looking at the slip.

"That's what it says. You can work every day if it suits you."

When he looked up confused, Barrett added, "We're adding

another thirty thousand square feet. Two more berths. We're expecting the new cranes this Friday."

He smacked the side of the guardhouse and turned to go.

"Oh, sir?" Thomas asked, and he stopped. "Would it be possible to have some water?"

Their eyes locked.

"It would be *possible*," he said.

Thomas felt a sudden tension, and he didn't like being ridiculed. Although he had the urge to strike back, he didn't. If his father had taught him anything, it was respect for authority.

"Where's your thermos?" Barrett asked.

"In my locker."

"That's no place for it, is it?"

"No, sir."

The man nodded, chewing the side of his lip, thinking.

"Okay, I'll bring you a jug after I make me rounds."

"Thank you."

The moment he left, Thomas looked back to the street, but the young woman was gone. All that remained were the children, two boys shadowboxing on the stoop, and some girls playing jump rope.

With a yawn, he sat back down in the chair. Looking at his watch, he realized he still had two hours to go, and he dreaded the heat and the boredom. But the job was only temporary, something he kept reminding himself, and everyone had to pay their dues. All his life he had wanted to become a cop, and that dream was now closer than ever.

······

THOMAS and his father got off the bus at Point Shirley Beach. They were still traveling to work together, but it wasn't going to last. The shipyard was extending its operations for the second time that month to accommodate the volume. Boston Harbor was busier than Thomas had ever seen it, ships lining the berths of every dockyard. The traffic was so disruptive that commercial fishermen were even threatening to strike. Just that week, two ships, one with the Free French navy and another British, had arrived for repairs from war damage. After years of inactivity, the Chelsea shipyard had reopened, and there were rumors the Charlestown Navy Yard was building escort ships for the military. If America wasn't at war, it was certainly preparing for it.

As they walked home through the quiet streets, Mr. Nolan didn't say much, stooping forward with his bag over his shoulder. Thomas had offered to take it, but he was stubborn, shaking his head *no* like he was insulted.

His father had worked hard all his life, harder than any of them would ever have to. When he first came from Ireland, he hauled the rocks dug up for the subway extension, a job so lowly there wasn't even a name for it. Later, while in construction, he spent six weeks in the hospital after a boiler exploded in the basement of a building he was working in. After years of manual labor, he applied to be a cop the same month the Boston Police launched one of the biggest strikes in history. They had told him they were hiring replacements, but he wasn't willing to be a scab. So he continued in the trades, working his way up from a stevedore to a crane driver, moving between companies before finally ending up at East Boston Works. Their mother once said that when she first met him, he had so many scars she was surprised to learn he hadn't been in the war.

They came around the bend, and Abby was on the front steps, Sarah standing beside her. Thomas stopped, worried Noel might be lurking nearby. After ten hours in the heat, she was the last person he wanted to see.

"What's got ye?" his father said.

"A foot cramp."

"Well, un-cramp it."

Thomas chuckled and caught up with him. The girls moved to let Mr. Nolan up the stairs, but when Thomas approached, Abby put out her leg. He smirked, and she stuck out her tongue, her cheeks red and chapped from the sun.

THE LAST HAPPY SUMMER

Once inside, he dropped his bag in the foyer, his lunchbox, thermos, and clothing heavy after the long commute. He had considered wearing the uniform to work, but both his supervisor and his father suggested not to. Like most parts of the city, East Boston had some rough areas and some rough people. There were enough criminals to make walking around dressed like someone in law enforcement risky. Cops were safe because they traveled in numbers, but a young man on a streetcar was no match for a gang of hoodlums looking to get even.

After washing up, Thomas came downstairs. His parents were out back at the picnic table. With the windows open, he could hear their conversation, and it sounded tense. The moment he walked out, they stopped talking.

"What's wrong?" he asked.

Mrs. Nolan looked at her husband and then at Thomas. While his father was having his usual cream soda, she was drinking something stronger.

"Your brother," she said, and he got a twinge of dread.

"What about him?"

She pointed at something, and when he came over, it was a newspaper.

"*Social Justice?*" he asked, reading the title. "Doesn't sound so terrible."

"Do you know what this is?"

Her tone was as blunt as an accusation.

"No," he said flatly.

"It's the Christian Front."

Confused, he looked at his father, who could always explain or clarify things when his mother was too upset.

"They're rabble-rousers, son," he said. "They go around talking about the Jews and Communism. Real knackers, they are."

His mother shook her head and took a sip.

"I don't know what's got into him," she said. "Reading such trash."

It was a strange outrage for a woman who could go into tirades about Italians, Republicans, and even Freemasons, an organization

Thomas had never heard of until she mentioned it. He wondered if she was truly disappointed or if it was guilt about her own attitudes.

"Ma, honestly, I don't know anything about it."

She looked up with a trembling smile, her face flushed.

"I know you don't, Thomas. I know."

CHAPTER TEN

As they turned the corner, Abby could hear music, the swing sounds of Artie Shaw blaring in the night. They walked down the dead end to the water, and Sarah stopped to light a cigarette, Noel standing next to her in a dark dress, her hair curled. Abby had invited Thomas, but he said no because he had to work in the morning. And the only reason she told Noel he might show up later was so she would stop asking.

When they came out to the sand, there were bonfires up and down the beach. The houses on the shore were having parties, the smell of beer and grilled seafood in the air. Porches were draped with American flag bunting and streamers, and someone had even made an Uncle Sam mannequin. With the war in Europe, the Fourth of July seemed more significant than in summers past, and everyone was feeling patriotic. People had come from all over to watch the fireworks on Point Shirley, the streets crammed with parked cars from Yirrell Beach to Deer Island.

They started down the beach, past small groups camped out on blankets and sitting on folding chairs.

"Hey, sister?" Abby heard, and they stopped.

Looking over, she saw George at one of the fires. Beside him was

Angela, who gave them all a halfhearted smile. Abby could tell her brother had come straight from work, his trousers soiled and rolled up to his knees. He lived like a vagabond, she thought, going between the cottage and the house, and their mother always worried about where he was.

"Join us," he called.

THEY WALKED OVER, and Sarah and Noel started talking to some girls they knew. Standing by herself, Abby felt uneasy, and she wasn't sure if it was that she didn't know anybody or that her brother was there. When someone handed her a beer, she took a sip and winced. She always preferred the sweetness of cocktails or wine. But even if she didn't like the taste, she liked the feeling. So she had a few more and soon was tipsy.

By nine o'clock, it seemed like the whole beach was drunk, the sounds of laughter and shouting echoing down the coast. The conversation around the fire had become a slobbering exchange of gossip and bad jokes. At some point, George and Angela had drifted away, and Abby was relieved. Still, she looked around for him, more out of duty than concern, but there were too many people.

The fireworks started without warning, launched from a platform on the strand. With Sarah and Noel beside her, Abby heard a boom and then saw a stream of red and yellow shoot into the sky, dispersing in a canopy of tiny flickers. More came, louder and more brilliant, shaking the ground and lighting up the bay.

As she watched, she couldn't help wondering if it was how a bombardment felt. Three thousand miles across the ocean there was a similar clamor, only young men were dying as a consequence. For the past two years, she had suffered through the private anticipation of war, something everyone feared but no one talked about. Their father always said Roosevelt would keep them out of it, but now it seemed like false hope. Thomas told her what was happening at East Boston Works, the expansion of the dockyard and all the cargo going to England, including weapons. For the first time, she felt truly frightened, as much for her country as for the people she loved.

"To hell with Hitler!" someone shouted.

As the fireworks continued, a tingle went up her back.

"Fuck the Krauts!" another cried.

The grand finale came, a burst of red, white, and blue radiance, and the beach erupted in cheer. Somewhere nearby, a group started to sing an old song from the Great War.

Over there, over there,
   Send the word, send the word over there
   That the Yanks are coming, the Yanks are coming

ABBY'S EYES swept the shoreline, and she noticed George standing with Angela down by the water. His friends were there too, a pack of shirtless young men, beers raised and jumping around like wild monkeys. When two guys got into a shoving match, George flicked his cigarette at them, and they all laughed.

Abby could never tell if he was the leader, but she knew he was respected, which was why he hung around with them. Even as a child, he gravitated towards troublemakers, boys who would steal bicycles and pickpockets. She was sure they had done worse things and just hadn't been caught. Like her parents, Abby always thought he would grow out of it, but he seemed no less vicious now than when, at thirteen, he sliced Martin Joyce's arm with a piece of glass because he looked at a girl George liked.

As she watched them, she got a sickening feeling. Whether it was from the alcohol or some deep pity for her brother, she didn't know; her feelings were always a mix of simple and complicated things. But she had had enough of the festivities and decided to leave.

"Where're you going?"

She looked over at Sarah and Noel, who were sitting on the sand, arms wrapped around their knees.

"I'm tired," she said.

"Won't you stay 'til midnight?"

"Do you think Thomas is here yet?" Noel asked, but Abby was tired of answering her.

"See you gals in the morning."

She walked away with her arms crossed, not sure if the chill she felt was from the air or her sunburn. When she got to the street, people were still heading toward the beach, but she wasn't surprised. Fourth of July was the biggest event of the year. It would continue all night, the one time the police overlooked laws about public drinking and disturbing the peace. She remembered as a girl arriving the next morning to see all the debris, the wine and liquor bottles, cigarettes and cigar butts. The bonfires were still smoking, and there were usually a few people passed out on the sand. One time she found a dead jellyfish, which her horrified mother swatted away with an umbrella. Only later did Abby realize it had been a condom.

She walked out to Shirley Street, and three young men were coming toward her. They moved aside to let her pass, and she heard, "Abby?"

Squinting in the dark, she saw the clerk from Gittell's. She almost didn't recognize him in his shorts and polo shirt.

"Arthur?" she asked.

"Did you see the fireworks?"

"Weren't they fabulous?"

He turned to his friends.

"Abby, meet Joel and Steve," he said.

They acted shy, standing in the shadows with their hands in their pockets.

"Hello," she said, perking up. "Are you all headed home?"

"We're from Winthrop."

"That makes us neighbors."

"I live just across the neck. Winthrop Head."

The more they talked, the more she wanted to talk. But it was hard to keep a conversation going with smiles and small comments, and his friends looked eager to go. She hesitated for as long as she could and then said, "It was nice to see you."

"You as well."

As he walked away, he looked torn, and she felt the same hesitation. They watched each other until he reached the corner, and the moment before he turned, he waved, and she waved back.

She continued down the road, smiling and almost giddy. She didn't get that feeling a lot, the last time from a boy who ran deliveries for the bakery she worked at in high school. Unlike Arthur, he was short and not especially handsome, but something about him made her tremble. If she had learned anything about attraction, it was that it was as random and mysterious as love itself.

CHAPTER ELEVEN

A tap at the window woke Thomas. Sitting up, he looked over, and George's bed was empty—he hadn't come home. He didn't know what time it was and had fallen asleep before his parents, which he hadn't done in years. His new job wasn't hard, but the days were long, and sometimes boredom was more exhausting than work.

Something hit the glass again, and he got up. Walking over, he looked out the window and noticed a figure below. As his eyes adjusted, he realized it was a woman. He raised the sash and stuck his head out.

"Noel?" he whispered.

"Thomas. I need to talk to you."

He sighed and turned around, throwing on his pants and groping to find his shoes in the dark. He crept down the stairs, the only sounds his father's snoring and the tick of the clock on the wall. When he walked out the back door, she was standing still beside the tree, arms at her side. He looked around first then went over, lowering his voice.

"What's wrong?" he asked.

"Thomas, I'm in love with you."

He froze.

"Where's Abby?"

Even as he said it, he knew it sounded foolish, a desperate attempt to change the subject.

"She left early."

"Did you see the fireworks?"

"Thomas," she said, peering up. "I mean it. I'm in love with you."

It was obvious she was drunk, her glassy eyes and slurred speech. He got some devious thrill in knowing he could have slept with her, but he knew he would have regretted it.

"Noel," he said.

As she stepped closer, he backed away with a grin. But he was more flustered than amused; he'd never had to fend a woman off before. He was almost at the wall when headlights flashed across the yard, distracting enough that she stopped. Any relief he felt quickly turned to panic when a police van came around the corner and pulled in front of the cottage. He looked at her and then ran to go find out why.

"Thomas!" she yelled, trying to catch up.

He walked over just as two officers were getting out.

"Evening," he said, but neither returned the courtesy.

"Is this the Nolan residence?" the first officer asked.

"Yes."

"Are you Mr. Nolan?"

Thomas shook his head.

"No. That's my father. He's asleep."

"Get 'em," the other officer said.

As Thomas rushed towards the house, the porch light went on and his father opened the door.

"Thomas?" he asked.

"Dad, they want to talk to you…"

Before he could finish, his father came out and walked over to the officers.

"Sir, is George Nolan your son?"

"Indeed," Mr. Nolan said, arching his back like he was trying to look dignified.

His wife came running out in her robe, Abby right behind her.

"What's wrong?! What happened!?" Mrs. Nolan cried.

Her husband put out his hand, and she stopped.

"Ma'am, your son and his friends assaulted some boys at the beach," the first cop said.

"Boys?"

"Young men," his partner clarified.

"Are they alright?" Mr. Nolan asked.

Thomas smiled nervously, touched that his father's first concern was for the victims.

"A little bruised up. But that's not the issue. They yelled racial epithets. Called the boys *kikes*."

There was a dramatic pause.

"Well, were they?" Mr. Nolan asked.

Thomas cringed. Raised in the Irish countryside, where everyone was the same, his father still struggled with the delicacies of race and ethnicity.

"What he means is," Thomas said, "were they Jewish?"

The officers both smirked.

"We've got him in the back," the first one said, ignoring the question. "We're willing to release him to you, but the other boys may press charges."

Mr. Nolan nodded, dropping his head in shame. The cops walked over to the van and opened the back. They helped George out, his hands bound behind his back, and while one man undid the cuffs, the other shut the door. They brought him over, and George was silent, standing with no shirt and no shoes. As Thomas watched him, he was torn between sympathy and disgust, the same conflicted feelings he had always had towards his older brother.

"We don't tolerate this sort of thing out here. This ain't Eastie," the officer said, the slang term for East Boston.

The remark stung, but Thomas understood why he said it. Winthrop was a quiet seaside town whose only curse was that it bordered East Boston. Aside from the summer, it had very little crime, and most of the people who caused problems were outsiders, usually from the city.

"Thank you," Mr. Nolan murmured.

The first cop looked at George.

"Stay outta trouble, you hear?" he said.

George just glared, a reaction that was almost as outrageous as his crime. But the officers didn't notice, or if they did, they didn't care. He probably wasn't the first stubborn assailant they had dealt with in their careers.

They all waited for the van to pull away, and once it was gone, there was an eerie tension, like the silence before an eruption. Without warning, Mr. Nolan turned and smacked George on the side of the head so hard he fell to the ground.

"No, no, no!" Mrs. Nolan shrieked.

Her husband stood over their son, his eyes wide and teeth gritted like a madman.

"You ever dare dishonor this family again, I swear I'll break your neck!"

Thomas had only seen his father that furious twice in his life. Once when a man in a long coat at the park flashed a group of school children, including Abby. The second time was when George was arrested for breaking the windows of a synagogue, an incident that seemed bizarre then but now made more sense.

George lay leaning on one elbow, staring up with a defiant scowl, and Thomas got the feeling he wanted to fight back. As a middle-aged man, Mr. Nolan wasn't as spry as he used to be, and George was the type of person who could sense weakness. But Thomas would crush his brother in an instant if he tried anything, and he gave George a threatening stare just to let him know.

Their father took one last look at his son and then stormed back to the cottage, so upset Thomas could hear him huffing. Thomas walked over and extended his hand to George, who looked at it and got up on his own. The confrontation was over, at least for now, and Abby took her mother up the walkway and front steps.

With everyone back inside, Thomas stood alone, gazing out at the harbor, the dark shape of Snake Island, the lights of the airport beyond. After all the commotion, he was breathing heavily, his body tingling with adrenaline. The scene was peaceful enough that he soon started to relax, and he always loved the ocean at night. Suddenly, he remembered Noel, but when he looked around, she was gone.

CHAPTER TWELVE

George hadn't come home since Friday night. Like her mother, Abby was worried, but she somehow knew he would be alright. An unfortunate fact of life was that bad people survived better than the good. Not that George was entirely bad; she thought of him more as *troubled* than mean or vicious. But he always found a way to make things worse and could never go long without causing chaos or controversy, either at home or out in the world.

Her mother had told her about *Social Justice*, the newspaper she found while cleaning his bedroom. Abby didn't follow politics, but she knew it was founded by Father Coughlin, a crazy priest whose radio show had millions of listeners. Everywhere she went, she saw his followers hawking the publication on street corners. As a girl, she would hear his voice through parlor windows, railing about communist plots and conspiracies, the evils of the New Deal. His views on Jews and other groups were so bizarre that even her mother found them unacceptable. But he seemed to offer answers, especially to young men who were unemployed or frustrated by life, so she wasn't surprised George was involved with the movement.

When she came downstairs, she called out, but no one was home.

The cottage seemed more vacant as the weeks went on, and some days she even felt lonely. She missed those years when the family was always together, something she was reminded of by the picture on the mantle, five of them squished onto the front steps. Someone had taken the photograph, their neighbor Mr. Loughran or maybe their uncle Walter, who had died years before from consumption at age fifty. All the men on Mrs. Nolan's side had died young, which made Abby concerned for her brothers.

The screen door opened, and her mother walked in with a bag of groceries.

"Abby…" she mumbled.

"Hi, Ma."

When she ran over to help, her mother waved her away.

"What plans have you got for today?"

"Dunno. Maybe the beach," Abby said, following her into the kitchen.

"You can't go wrong with the beach."

She put the groceries on the counter and started to unbag them.

"Have you seen George?" Abby asked.

Her mother stopped and slowly turned around.

"I have not."

"I'm worried."

Mrs. Nolan looked down, still out of breath, her day dress ruffled. Her armpits were damp, but Abby didn't mention it because she knew she would be horrified.

"Why don't you go see if he's at the house? I need some baking soda anyway. Pulsifer's Market was out."

"What do I do if he is?"

Mrs. Nolan shrugged her shoulders and wiped her forehead.

"I guess tell him we all say hello," she said.

Their eyes met, and they both smiled, warm sentimental smiles that communicated as much hope as sadness. Her mother had been dealing with George a lot longer than her, and Abby knew compassion had its limits. But they had to care because Thomas and her father did not, and when it came to forgiveness, men were as stubborn as toddlers.

Abby ran upstairs and brushed her hair, pinning it back with a pearl hair comb she inherited from her grandmother. She put on a flowered shirtwaist dress and her good shoes, even spraying on a little perfume.

"Ma," she called down. "Do you need anything done at the tailor?"

"Not at the moment."

If she had to go back to East Boston to look for her brother, she was going to make the most of it, and Arthur was only down the street. But she needed a reason. On a whim, she reached under the bed and got an old blouse. Clutching it in both hands, she tore one of the seams, laughing to herself, even getting a guilty thrill. As desperate as it seemed, she was sure women had done worse things for an excuse to see a man.

......

When she stepped off the streetcar, she was so nervous she dropped her bag, which a kindly gentleman picked up for her. Coming back into the city was always stressful, the noise and congestion, but she also knew going to see Arthur was bold. She had been taught not to chase men, and her mother always said the job of a lady was to let them come to you, say yes or no, and leave the rest up to fate. But things were changing, and women were more independent than ever before. Abby even knew two girls from high school who had moved to New York together, sharing an apartment and working at *Cosmopolitan* magazine.

She walked over to Gittell's, where some teenagers were horsing around on the sidewalk. With their patched clothes and dirty legs, they looked more suited to the tenements of Maverick Square than the respectable neighborhoods of upper Bennington Street. But poverty had been creeping north since Abby was a girl. While her mother blamed it on the Italians, she admitted the Irish were no better when they arrived, living ten to a room and plagued by drunkenness and illiteracy. Her ideas about East Boston were largely from the past when there was still open land, and wealthy merchants and ship captains had homes in Jeffery's Point or Orient Heights. Now it was working-class, people employed by the shipyards or the factories in nearby Chelsea and Lynn. Considering her father was a crane driver, Abby could never understand why her mother was such a snob.

As she approached, the boys moved out of her way and stared. She smiled and turned towards the door, taking a deep breath before going inside. She walked over to the register and took out her blouse, laying it flat on the counter. Looking at the tear, she suddenly panicked that Arthur might know she did it herself, marks from her fingers or some other clue from the nature of textiles.

"Good day?"

She looked up and was surprised to see the older man from her first visit. She never considered that Arthur might not be working.

"Hello. I've a blouse that needs mending."

He ran his fingers along the damaged seam, squinting through his glasses, and Abby got tense.

"Was this from washing?" he asked, his accent sounding like *vahshing*.

"I don't know. It's my mother's."

She cringed; a lie to cover up another lie was always a risk. But he didn't ask any more questions, instead reaching for a ticket and handing it to her.

"Ready Wednesday," he said.

He smiled and turned to go into the backroom.

"If you're not here," she asked, and he stopped, "should I just give this to the young man? The one who was here last week?"

She knew it sounded awkward, maybe even prodding.

"Young man?" he asked, which made her think there was more than one.

"Arthur."

He raised his eyes.

"Ah, yes. My son."

With his fleshy eyes and gnarled hands, he looked too old to be his father, and she had always assumed Arthur was just another employee.

"Oh," she said, stumped.

"He'll be here. He's here every day. He's making a delivery at the moment."

"Okay. Thank you."

With a smile, she headed for the door. The moment she walked out, she felt a sharp pain and winced. When she opened her eyes, the boys were standing around with a guilty silence.

"What the hell was that?!" she snapped.

"Sorry, Miss."

She touched her cheek and looked at her hand, relieved there was no blood.

"Abby?" she heard.

She looked and Arthur was coming toward her. Despite the heat, he wore wool herringbone pants and a shirt with no tie.

"What happened?" he asked.

"I don't know?"

As she stood stunned, her face throbbing, he walked over to one of the boys who was leaning against a mailbox. In a single lunge, he reached behind him and grabbed something, holding it up to reveal a slingshot.

"Hasn't my father asked you to stay away from the front of the shop?"

He circled around, looking each one of them in the eye. Although they kept quiet, they didn't look intimidated, glaring back at him.

"It was an accident," Abby said.

"Now out of here!" Arthur barked. "All of you, before I call the cops."

When they hesitated, he swatted at the boy closest to him, who jumped back but didn't retreat.

"Don't tell us where to go, Jew!"

Abby gasped. Arthur flew into a rage, grabbing the boy by the collar and shoving him so hard he stumbled over the curb. When the others fanned out around him, he pivoted with a fighter's stance, his arms out and ready. But the confrontation didn't last, and Abby was relieved when slowly they started to disperse, snickering at him as they walked off down the sidewalk.

Arthur walked over to Abby, rolling up his sleeves, still winded from the encounter.

"Are you okay?" he asked.

She smiled nervously.

"I believe so."

He took her by the shoulders, crouching to look at her face, and she felt herself blush.

"Probably just a small rock," he said.

"I'm sure they didn't mean it."

"Those kids," he said. "My father asks them every day to leave. Politely. But they never go."

"There's a lot of problems with loitering these days."

He stepped back, his hands on his hips, and looked around. When something caught his attention, Abby followed his gaze. In front of the pool hall were several men, their hats pulled down low, staring over. She didn't know if Arthur knew them, but he seemed to get uneasy.

"Did you need help with something?" he asked, turning back to her.

"No, I was leaving. I dropped off a blouse."

"Let me deliver it to you. Free of charge. For your trouble."

"Really, it was no trouble—"

"I insist."

She nodded, looking up with a shy smile.

"Okay."

"What's your address?"

"Seventeen Bay View Ave."

"I'll drop it off when it's ready."

They lingered a few extra seconds, enough to make her think he enjoyed her company.

"See you then," he said.

With a quick smile, he reached for the door.

"Wait," she asked. "How will you know which blouse is mine?"

He stopped and looked at her with a curious hesitation. She never liked to read into things, but it seemed significant.

"I'll know."

......

ABBY TRUDGED up the front steps, tired from the heat and dying to get out of the sun. Reaching into her purse for the key, she was just about to open the door when she heard a sound. She looked over and saw Chickie in the yard, standing barefoot in a baggy sundress that looked either handmade or secondhand. In her arms, she had a naked doll. Although it was worn out and dirty, she held it with the care of a mother.

"Hello, Chickie," Abby said, leaning over the railing.

"Abby!"

"I like your doll."

Chickie mumbled something she couldn't understand, the doll's name or something about it. Their conversations were always like that, short exchanges of smiles, observations, and one-word comments. It was hard to believe Chickie was twelve because she acted like a girl half her age and showed no signs of maturing. Abby knew she could speak in full sentences because she had heard her, but it was only with her mother or brother and always in Italian.

Suddenly, the Ciarlones' front door opened, and the lady Abby had seen the week before stepped out. She smiled at Abby and then called to Chickie. While a lot of people would have found her sleeveless dress indecent, Abby thought she looked gorgeous. She was just about to compliment her when Chickie ran up to the porch and they went inside, leaving the mystery of who she was for another time.

Abby walked into the house and was met by the stench of sour air.

In the parlor, she saw beer cans and an overfilled ashtray on the table, a sheet and pillow on the couch. As she suspected, George was staying there, which was no surprise because he had nowhere else to go. Her mother would be relieved to know he was safe, but she also would have been outraged by the mess.

"Hey ya, sis?"

Abby flinched and put her hand to her heart. When she turned around, her brother was on the stairs in shorts and a tee-shirt, his hair damp.

"Jesus," she said.

"A little jumpy?"

"Aren't you supposed to be at work?"

He frowned and walked into the parlor, where he grabbed the remains of a cigarette and struck a match. He took a puff and blew out the smoke. With the sunlight coming through the curtains, Abby could see the welt on his face from where their father had hit him.

"What are you doing back?" he asked.

"Ma needed baking soda. The market was out."

She walked down the hallway into the kitchen, and he followed her.

"You sure she didn't ask you to check on me?"

"She's got better things to worry about."

Abby first looked in the cabinets and then went over to the pantry. Behind a bag of flour, she found an open box of Arm & Hammer and smelled inside.

"It doesn't go bad."

She looked up, and he had a sarcastic grin.

"Did you see that woman next door?" she asked.

"Quite a dish, ain't she?"

"Who is she?"

"Probably one of their guinea relatives?"

Abby smirked but didn't respond, knowing it would only encourage him. She whisked by and went upstairs to her bedroom, where she got some clean dresses and underwear, putting them all in her bag. With no dolly tub at the cottage, her mother washed their clothes in the sink. And while doing everyone's at once made it easier, they never got truly clean.

When she came back down, George was sitting on the couch with a beer in his hand. In his shorts, his legs looked skinny, almost fragile, and she could see the scar on his knee from when he crashed his soapbox car as a boy. He seemed anxious, fidgeting with the can before taking a sip, then staring off in a daze. She pitied him the most in moments like this, if only because he looked sad when he was alone.

"I gotta go," she said.

He looked over and nodded.

"Hey, Ab?" he said, and she stopped.

"Are Ma and Dad still mad?"

Their eyes locked, and she paused, thinking. Like everyone in the family, her parents were so used to his behavior that their anger and frustration probably never ceased. But the question sounded sincere, and she thought she even detected a hint of remorse. If he regretted what he had done, she had no reason to make him feel worse.

"I don't think so."

CHAPTER THIRTEEN

Thomas walked along the pier, his nightstick at his side. Although the job had some authority, it was a far cry from being a police officer, something he realized when a group of longshoremen laughed at him because his badge was upside down. In general, the workers were friendly, but it was mostly the normal cordiality between men because he could tell none of them respected the power of the guards.

Nevertheless, they weren't there to monitor the employees so much as the cargo, which was a big target for criminals. A month before, a food service truck was caught leaving with ten thousand dollars' worth of Singer sewing machines that were headed for Brazil. Like any major port, some minor theft was unavoidable when it was civilian shipping. But now that the shipyard had a contract with the Army, responsible for sending munitions as well as supplies to England, they were only one breach away from being replaced by MP's or a Marine security detachment. And no one wanted that.

In the distance, Thomas could see the German tanker *Pauline Friederich* looming in the outer harbor, the Nazi flag flying. It had been stranded in port since the start of the war, more of a curiosity than a threat, the crew stuck in diplomatic limbo.

He continued along his beat to the south side of the yard, where a temporary fence surrounded the new construction site, the sound of drills and diggers constant throughout the day. They were adding a second drydock and two deep-water berths, whose modern winches would be able to load ten tons of freight per hour. Something about the expansion was eerie, like they were preparing for battle, and a lot of people he knew still believed America would stay neutral. Either way, it was keeping men employed, and the waterfront hadn't been so busy in years.

Feeling thirsty, Thomas went between warehouses and headed for the cafeteria. When he walked in, welders and machinists looked up from the tables, their hands greasy and faces red. While it was only midday, they worked in staggered shifts and ate at different times. Thomas took off his hat and nodded, but most of them ignored him. Walking over to the water cooler, he reached for a cup and filled it up.

"Howdy."

He turned to see a guy in coveralls.

"Hello."

"You Barry Nolan's son?" the man asked, and he could hear an Irish accent.

"I am."

"How you gettin' on with the new job?"

Thomas smiled at the phrase *gettin' on*, something his father always said.

"Hotter than I expected."

"Oh," the man said with a wink. "It hasn't even started to heat up."

Thomas gave him a confused look but got distracted when the door opened. Looking over, he watched Officer Barrett poke his head in and wave for him.

"Gotta go," he said.

"Good luck."

He slugged his water and left. When he came out, Barrett was standing away from the door.

"Sir?" Thomas said.

"I need you to work until 10 pm."

"Yes, sir."

"We need extra men on Pier Two. There's some high-security cargo."

Thomas didn't ask what, but he was sure it was weapons or other military equipment. So he nodded, acknowledging the information, not interested in gossip or secrecy.

"Another thing," his boss said. "Don't get too friendly with the workers."

"Sir?"

Barrett looked around and then lowered his voice.

"There's talk of a strike. If it happens, we won't be looked upon too favorably."

......

THOMAS LAY SLUMPED on the bench of the streetcar, his feet sore from standing for fourteen hours. The rumble of the wheels was soothing after a long day and, for moments at a time, he would doze off, worrying he would miss his stop. Along the way, the passengers thinned out, and he noticed a young woman at the front. She wore a headscarf and had a bag at her side. When she turned, he saw her face, and it was the girl he had seen a few days before leaving the factory. She looked as pretty now as she did then with her long hair and red lips, and she reminded him of Vivien Leigh. He wondered if she had worked overtime, or if she could have met someone after work for a meal or drink. He couldn't take his eyes off her, looking away only when she glanced over.

He was surprised when she finally stood up because it was the stop by his house. For a moment, he considered getting off instead of continuing to Point Shirley, curious who she was and where she lived. But he wasn't one to follow women, and after getting pursued all summer by Noel, he knew what it was like.

He watched her as she waited by the door, her fingers wrapped around the handgrip. The trolley stopped, and she got off with a half dozen other people. As they pulled away, he looked out the glass and their eyes met. Then she crossed Bennington Street and was gone.

By the time he got to the cottage, it was dark. He heard a cackle, the sound of his mother's laughter, and went around to the back where he found her sitting with his father, drinks on the table and a candle burning.

"A sight for sore eyes," his father said.

Thomas chuckled and walked over, taking a seat.

"I expect they're paying you well for working so late?" his mother asked.

"There's no overtime until after sixty hours."

His father took a sip of his cream soda and raised the glass.

"That'll change soon if the union has anything to say about it," he said.

"We're not in your union, Dad."

"Even still. We set the standards for everyone."

Thomas smiled; he admired his father's enthusiasm. Of all the things Mr. Nolan valued, fairness was near the top, below honesty and slightly above good manners. But Thomas didn't want to talk about work, especially after what Barrett said, knowing labor disputes could get nasty.

"Has George been home?" he asked.

His mother sighed and turned to her husband. She looked relaxed in her long dress, and Thomas could tell she was tipsy.

"That boy…" she muttered, the closest she was going to get to criticism.

She always defended her oldest son, from the time he ran away in first grade to when he was arrested twice as a teenager. No one in the family understood what made him tick, but she was the most confused because she had given birth to him. Mr. Nolan was different. Like most men, he loved his son, but he had, in some ways, given up on him. As someone who experienced hardship very early on, he saw George's behavior as the height of ingratitude and an insult to God.

Feeling a sting, Thomas smacked the back of his neck. The

mosquitoes were starting to bite, and he had to wash up and find something to eat. As he got up, Abby and Sarah came skipping into the yard, their figures swaying.

"A sight for sore eyes," Mr. Nolan said, looking over.

His wife tapped him on the arm.

"You already said that," she said, giggling.

"I'm getting old. I repeat meself."

Thomas smiled; he was always amused by his parents' small filtrations. Their marriage wasn't perfect, but it was stable and loving enough that he would have wanted the same thing.

The girls came over, their dresses loose and their hair wild from being out all day. Even in the darkness, Thomas could see their red shoulders, the sand on their shins.

"Miss, get some shoes on those feet!" Mrs. Nolan said.

"Sarah has none either."

"I'm not Sarah's mother."

"I'm eighteen."

She reached for her mother's drink and smelled it.

"Gin and tonic?" she asked.

"It's called a highball," their father said. "It sounds more elegant."

When Abby took a sip, her mother grabbed her hand, and the girls burst out laughing.

"You rascal! You may be eighteen, but you're too young to drink."

Abby and Sarah could have been intoxicated—sometimes it was hard to tell with giddy young women. The drinking age had been twenty-one since the end of Prohibition, but no one paid much attention to it. The bars on Bennington Street never denied anybody, and downtown you could get served from the West End to Washington Street if you looked old enough.

"Now, where were you ladies all evening?"

"At the wall."

"The devil's den," Mr. Nolan remarked.

"Stop that," his wife said with a frown. "I spent many fond nights there when I was young."

He raised his eyes.

"Explains a lot."

As she went to swat him, he moved his shoulder, and she missed.

"Did you happen to see your brother?" she asked.

Abby pointed at Thomas.

"He's sitting right there."

Thomas grinned at the joke, but he couldn't ignore its deeper implication. As the youngest and only girl, Abby had suffered more than anyone from George's taunts and trouble.

"Your *errant* brother," her mother added.

"I saw him earlier. He was down at the beach."

After a short pause, Mrs. Nolan looked at Thomas.

"Go see if you can find him. Will you?"

"Leave that boy be," Mr. Nolan grumbled.

Thomas wanted to say no, and not just because he was tired. He had searched for George enough over the years. But when he glanced up and saw his mother and Abby waiting, he knew they were anxious, and he couldn't let them worry.

"Sure," he said, finally.

They both smiled, and their father shook his head. Even Sarah, who had been standing quietly behind Abby, seemed relieved. With a sigh, Thomas got up and walked towards the road.

"Thank you, Thomas," Mrs. Nolan said, but he didn't respond.

CHAPTER FOURTEEN

Abby woke up squinting, the sun coming through the small window and landing on her face. She had only had three beers the night before with Sarah, but her head was pounding. She got up and looked through her dresses, which hung from a wooden peg on the wall. While the ones she brought from home were clean, the others were starting to look shabby, worn out from days at the beach, sitting on the rocks and sand. She slipped out of her nightgown and put on the blue-flowered one, the skin under her arms irritated from falling asleep with her bra on.

As she came down the stairs, she heard a cough. Looking out, she was surprised to see George on the front steps. She wondered if Thomas had found him or if he had come home on his own. Hunched over with no shirt, he looked scrawny, his ribs and shoulder blades protruding. He had always been the thinnest in the family, but now he looked like a skeleton.

He glanced back suddenly like he sensed she was watching.

"What're you looking at?" he asked.

"Nothing much."

When he started to laugh, she laughed too. His remark was more of a greeting than a dig, and they always communicated by sarcasm.

She walked out, the deck hot against her feet, and stood by the railing. It was another beautiful day, the sky clear blue and not a cloud in sight.

"Why aren't you at work?" she asked.

When he turned fully towards her, she could see a dark cut under his eye, and her face dropped.

"George, what happened?"

"Got into a little scrap."

"With who?"

"Doesn't matter."

"Did you start it?"

"No, I didn't *start it*," he said with emphasis. "Someone called Angela a wop."

Abby just pursed her lips; the irony was poignant. In a place where bigotry was rampant, most people learned to keep it to themselves, or at least among their own kind. George never cared, and the only time he refrained from using slurs was around their father, who didn't tolerate prejudice. He was the first person Abby ever heard call a Jewish person a *hebe*, and he even used the word *nigger*, although there were hardly any black people in East Boston

"Hurts, doesn't it?" she asked, finally.

He lit a cigarette and looked up at her.

"The guy who said it hurts."

When he flicked the match, her eyes followed it. In the distance, she noticed a ship at the entrance to Winthrop Harbor, between Deer Island and the airport. It was gray, with guns at the bow and stern, large white numbers on the side. As she stared out, she got a sudden fright, realizing how vulnerable they were. Everyone knew German U-boats were out there, and if America joined the war, the coast would be the first line of attack.

"Is that a battleship?" she asked.

"It ain't no trawler."

"What's it doing?"

George shrugged his shoulders.

"It's been there all morning," he said.

She walked inside and went into the kitchen where she saw three slices of banana bread on the table. Even when she slept in, her mother always left her something for breakfast. But Abby was too hungover to eat, and the sun and fresh air of summer seemed to lessen her appetite. Considering she had put on weight over senior year, it wasn't the worst problem to have. She knew she would make up for it in the fall.

Reaching for a cup, she held it under the tap and drank, the water cold but salty. Through the window, she could see her mother working in the garden, pruning shears in her hand. On the picnic table was a glass, and it didn't look like lemonade. It was too early for alcohol, and even Mrs. Nolan said that drinking before noon was vulgar. But the incident with George had shaken her, and although he was home now, Abby knew she probably needed something to calm her nerves.

Startled by a knock, she glanced over, and Sarah and Noel were at the door. She ran to get it, knowing that the longer they waited, the more time George would have to do or say something rude.

"Hiya, Abby."

"Beach?" Noel asked.

Abby smiled and looked out, but her brother was gone.

"Sure," she said, distracted. "Let me get my things."

......

ABBY LAY on the towel with her eyes closed, listening to the waves. The beach was busy for a Thursday morning and with the tide in, everyone was closer together. Living in East Boston, where the houses were stacked side by side and on top of one another, she was used to being cramped and had learned young how to find solace in a crowd.

"There's Hal Francis," Sarah said.

Abby lifted her head and saw three young men tossing a football down by the water. She knew Hal from high school, and he had been coming to Point Shirley since she was little. The others looked familiar, but over the years so many people cycled through the small summer community that only the regulars stuck out.

"Personally, I'd take Jimmy Dunn," Noel said, filing her nails.

"I still say you should've made it with Ray Lanier," Sarah said.

"Ick. Too short."

"What about Robbie Farrell?"

"With that huge forehead? No thanks."

Abby laughed to herself at their girlish gossip, hearing the names of people she had known all her life. They acted like teenagers, which they all still technically were, but it seemed silly now that they had graduated. Either way, she was glad Noel was talking about other boys because it would take the focus off Thomas. At first, she couldn't understand why her brother had no interest in her. But the more Abby got to know her, the more she realized how annoying she was.

"Aren't they quite a pair," Sarah said, nodding.

Abby looked over and saw George sitting on the wall with Angela. With them were three other guys, their shirts unbuttoned and hair slicked back. She didn't recognize them, so she assumed they were from East Boston. They were passing around a paper bag, cold beer or maybe wine. The cops sometimes overlooked public drinking at night, but never during the day, and it made Abby nervous. Knowing her brother had been arrested before, she didn't want to see it happen again.

As she watched them, Angela took a sip and spilled some. Wiping her lips, she giggled, and George and the others laughed.

"I don't know what she sees in him," Abby mumbled.

"Your own brother?"

Abby rolled over onto her stomach, her eyes still on them.

"I'm just being honest."

"Where's Thomas today?" Noel asked.

Abby frowned.

"With his fiancée," she said, and when Noel gasped, she added, "Just kidding. He's at work."

"I thought he was off Fridays?"

Something hit the ground and sand went flying. They all moaned, dusting off their arms and shaking out their hair. When Abby sat up, she saw a football on the ground.

"Sorry, ladies."

She looked over and it was Hal Francis, swaggering towards them in tight swim trunks, his shoulders dark from the sun. He was handsome, and he knew it, but Abby never liked boys who were prettier than her.

Reaching for the ball, she tossed it to him, and he caught it in one hand.

"Thanks, Abby," he said. "How's Thomas?"

Abby smiled, but inside she felt sad. Whenever she ran into people she knew, they always asked about Thomas and never about George.

"He's working at the shipyard. But he's waiting to get on with the police."

Hal's expression changed, and she knew why. In their freshman year, his father, who was a cop, had been shot and killed in the South End while responding to a bank robbery. After his mother had a nervous breakdown, he and his seven siblings were sent into foster care until she recovered. With his good looks and charm, people probably mistook him for a pompous jock, never realizing the tragedy he had suffered.

"You ladies wanna play catch?" he asked.

Noel peered up, her lashes fluttering.

"I don't know how to throw a football," she said in a girlish voice.

"Then I'll teach you."

Sarah looked over at Abby, who shook her head.

"I'll play," she said to Hal.

They both got up, still wiping off sand, and went down to join Hal's friends. Abby was glad because she preferred to be alone, and she could only listen to Noel's chatter for so long. She rolled onto her back, shut her eyes, and began to dream.

"Abby!"

Startled, she leaned up. She knew that voice. When she looked over, she was surprised to see Chickie waving in the distance.

"Hello, dear," she said, waving back.

Chickie ran towards her, a small shovel in her hand, her knees scuffed. She wore a yellow swimsuit, and her hair was tied back.

"Abby! Abby! Abby!" she said, laughing.

"What are you doing here?"

She had never seen Chickie outside of East Boston—she never saw her outside of her yard. For working-class families, the beach was an easy escape from the congestion of the city, but some couldn't even afford the dime for the trolley and bus.

"Concetta," Chickie said, pointing.

Abby looked over and saw the woman who was staying with the Ciarlones. She sat on a towel with a basket beside her, her thick dark hair flowing in the breeze. In her red swimsuit, she looked even prettier than in a dress, her long legs and thin waist more striking than any of the girls Abby knew.

"Who is that?"

Chickie gave a confused look.

"Concetta," she said.

"Is she a relative?"

Chickie curled her lips and shrugged her shoulders, and Abby could never tell if she understood her.

"Abby play?" she asked.

When the woman glanced over, Abby waved, but she didn't see her.

"Sure. Let's play."

CHAPTER FIFTEEN

Thomas stood beside the fence in the blistering sun, sweat seeping down his forehead from his wool cap. He watched as the construction crew worked, wondering why they had posted five guards on the site when no one could steal cranes or the heavy hardware required to build them. But it wasn't just about theft, something he realized the night before when they caught six boys wandering through the south yard with firecrackers and slingshots. With so many immigrants, the area around East Boston Works was swarming with children who had no place to play. They were bound to explore, and nothing was more fascinating than a shipyard.

"Nolan?"

Barrett was calling from the security office, a small brick building next to one of the warehouses. In the hours of dull repetition, Thomas often lost track of time and as he walked over, he loosened his tie, relieved the shift was over.

"Don't get too comfy," Barrett said.

"Sir?"

"We're meeting in the assembly room."

Thomas continued into the building and first went to his locker, taking out his thermos and slugging some water. At the back of the building was a room for training and meetings. When he entered, men from the day shift were seated around a long table, and more were coming in. With all the chairs taken, he stood against the wall and waited, nodding to guys he knew.

Finally, Barrett arrived, marching in like a general. He walked to the end of the room and stood in front of a large chalkboard.

"Gentlemen," he said, "As many of you may already know, the *Industrial Union of Marine and Shipbuilding Workers* has been in negotiations with management. We're told that they're unable to come to an agreement. As such, we believe the union is preparing to strike. If that happens, we'll need all available resources to keep order. Now, any questions?"

Someone in the back raised his hand, and Barrett pointed.

"Sir, will we get time and a half?"

"Under the provisions of your employment contract, no overtime pay will be granted during periods of compulsory shifts that are the result of internal labor disputes."

Everyone groaned. The sentence was a handful, but they all understood what it meant.

"Anyone else?" he asked, head raised and looking around.

Aside from a few grumbles, everyone was too tired to argue or complain.

"Very well," Barrett said, and the meeting was over.

By the time Thomas had changed and got his things, his father had already left. As he walked out the main entrance, he stopped and looked down towards the West Gate. Except for some kids playing on the sidewalk, the street was empty.

He couldn't stop thinking about the girl from the factory. What started as mild interest had turned into a fascination, and even if she was married or engaged, he had to know who she was. There weren't many women who got his attention, and Abby always said he was a snob. But something about her was different. Throwing his bag over his shoulder, he headed to Maverick station.

......

The bus stopped at Bay View Avenue, and there was a line waiting to get on. It was the end of the day, people leaving Point Shirley Beach to go home, their hair frizzy and faces red. As Thomas got off, he saw Abby coming up the side street from the water, a towel under her arm, purse in her hand.

"How's the water?" he asked.

"I only dipped my toes in. But cold. How was work?"

"Long."

"I saw Chickie today."

"You went home?"

"No, at the beach. She was with a woman. A gorgeous woman."

Thomas raised his eyes, and they started to walk. He didn't know if she was exaggerating, but she always liked to tease him about girls. In high school, he had dated one of her friends, and although it didn't last, Abby never stopped talking about her.

They came around the bend to the cottage, and there was a car out front. Suddenly, Thomas heard two people arguing, a sharp exchange of words. He ran to see what was happening, and when he got to the yard, George was shouting at someone. The man was tall, dressed in a suit, and he had a bag in his arms. He looked flustered, holding out his hand and backing away.

"Arthur?!" Abby exclaimed.

Thomas didn't know who it was, but he ran over and got between them.

"What the hell's going on?"

"Stay out of this!" George said.

Seeing Abby take the man's hand, Thomas realized they knew each other, and any sympathy he had for his brother was gone. He dropped his things and went at him, grabbing him by the shirt and shoving him back.

"Don't tell me to stay out of anything!"

George tried to resist but couldn't, and it wasn't only because he was drunk. Years of boxing had made Thomas stronger and quicker,

THE LAST HAPPY SUMMER

and he could have knocked him out if he wanted to. But his brother had already been humiliated once on the lawn that summer by their father, and Thomas wasn't cruel enough to do it again.

"Here, here!"

When he looked over, their father was coming down the front steps. Thomas let go of George, and they stood facing each other, seething and out of breath.

"What's this all about?"

"Ask him," Thomas said, and their father looked at George.

"What?"

"You tell *us* what!" Thomas snapped. "I come home and you're threatening some guy?"

"Yeah, the Jew who snitched on me last week!"

Thomas was outraged until he saw the car pulling away and knew the man hadn't heard it. Abby stormed towards them across the yard, the bag in her hands. She ran up to George so fast he flinched, and then she pointed in his face.

"You're a bastard!"

George scoffed, but he didn't strike back. Instead, he stood quietly fuming, his hands on his hips and body swaying. Mr. Nolan walked up and looked him straight in the eye.

"Son, 'ave you been drinking?" he asked.

George hesitated, gazing down with a smirk.

"Who cares?"

"I care, goddammit!"

Thomas shuddered. His father was a gentle man, but when he got mad, it could make the earth shake.

"Who was that man?"

He looked over at Abby, who seemed on the verge of tears.

"He's from Gittell's tailor," she said, her voice shaking. "He was dropping off my blouse."

Mr. Nolan nodded and then looked back to George.

"What's your problem with him?"

Their eyes locked and George stared back with a stubborn pout. Thomas realized then it was the same man his brother and his friends had fought with the week before, an unfortunate coincidence for everyone.

"You go to that shop tomorrow after work and apologize."

"I ain't apologizing to anybody."

Mr. Nolan stepped closer, his jaw clenched, and Thomas stood ready in case it got physical.

"What did you say to me?"

"I said *I ain't apologizing to anybody.*"

Their father licked his lips, shook his head, looking around. All at once, his rage subsided and his expression softened. He almost looked sad.

"You're to leave here at once."

"Just let me get some of my things," George said.

He whisked by Thomas and went toward the front door.

"Son," Mr. Nolan said, and George turned around. "You're not to go to the house either. Give me the door key."

Thomas glanced at Abby, who looked back with similar shock. George had gotten in trouble a lot over the years, but somehow this seemed more serious.

"It's under the mat."

......

THE COTTAGE FELT different with George gone, which was strange because he was never there much anyway. He had been kicked out before, but he always had a place to go. If he misbehaved in the summer, he would stay at their house in East Boston; at other times of the year, his father would send him to the cottage, which was punishment enough because it had no heat. Nevertheless, it was always a soft eviction that made Mr. Nolan feel like he was disciplining his son without putting him at risk. For the first time, George was banished from both places, and he had never been homeless before.

"Pass the corn, please," Mrs. Nolan said.

When Thomas handed her the bowl, he knocked over her glass, and she jumped up.

"Oh for heaven's—"

"I'm sorry, Ma," he said.

He grabbed all the paper napkins, but they weren't enough.

"I'll get a towel," Abby said, getting up and running into the house.

All evening, Thomas had thought his mother was drinking lemonade, but as he sopped it up, he could smell the alcohol.

"An accident's an accident," Mr. Nolan said, and his wife frowned.

"Well, you could at least help."

"You're doing fine yourself."

Thomas smiled, but it wasn't their usual playful bickering. Everyone was upset by what had happened, although no one would have said George didn't deserve it. All his life he had gotten more than his share of sympathy, whether it was from teachers, family, friends, or neighbors. As a child, Thomas got jealous, not realizing there was a difference between good and bad attention.

Once the mess was cleaned up, Mrs. Nolan poured another drink. Despite the tension, it was a beautiful night, the harbor calm and the last rays of sun fading behind the city. Over at the airport, Thomas saw an Army plane taxiing, a heatwave rising from the tarmac around it. With its large twin turbines, it looked like a cargo aircraft, but he was never interested in military things like his brother. When they were boys, George would play for hours with his toy soldiers, creating elaborate battles in the dirt pile behind their shed. Thomas knew he wanted to enlist and had probably already tried. But with flat feet and bad eyesight, he would have been quickly rejected.

They finished eating, and the women got up to take everything in. Thomas handed his mother the casserole, careful to avoid another mishap; there was still enough for leftovers. She called the dish of ground beef, onions, and potatoes *cottage pie*, but it was really her own invention. They had been eating it once a week since he could remember, usually at room temperature in the summer.

With Abby and their mother inside, Mr. Nolan reached under the chair for his pipe. He never smoked around his wife, which Thomas assumed was some Irish custom because she didn't mind.

"I saw the second crane going up today," Thomas said.

By now, it was dark, and he couldn't see his father's face until he lit the match. The sweet smell of tobacco reminded him of their uncle who used to come to visit from Maine when they were kids.

"There's talk of a third once the drydock is done," Mr. Nolan said.

"There'll be overtime until Christmas."

His father shrugged his shoulders and blew out the smoke.

"Perhaps," was all he said.

It was a strange fact that people who took their work the most seriously talked about it the least. His father had been at East Boston Works for over two decades, and Thomas was twelve before he even knew what he did.

"Dad," Thomas said, speaking hesitantly. "Is it true they might strike?"

His father took the pipe out of his mouth.

"*They* is me. And the answer is yes."

"Why now?"

"Why not?"

"The Navy Yard is building ships. Bethlehem Steel can't even find welders. There's more work than ever."

His father nodded, tilting his head like he was considering the point. But he had been in the union longer than his children were alive, and Thomas knew he was only being polite.

"If things aren't improved when times are good, they'll never be when they're not."

"Could it get confrontational?"

"I suppose."

"Should I be worried…as a guard?—"

They were interrupted when the women came back out. Thomas had a feeling his father didn't want to talk about it anyway. At the shipyard, guards and workers were cordial, but they were also adversaries, something supervisor Barrett had warned their first day. It was never a problem when operations were smooth, but a strike could change all that, and Thomas was surprised his father never mentioned it.

"I smell smoke," Mrs. Nolan said.

Her husband lowered his pipe so she couldn't see it.

"Maybe you're on fire."

When she giggled, everyone smiled, a moment of humor in an otherwise somber night.

"I want something sweet," Abby said, skipping over the grass.

At some point between clearing the dishes and cleaning them she had changed her dress, and Thomas wondered why girls were always so fickle.

"Why don't you go down to the ice cream shop?" Mr. Nolan suggested.

"Are they still open?"

"They close at nine," their mother said, taking a seat. "But don't be late, you gotta get your books in the morning."

Any mention of Abby going to college always left everyone stumped, if only because none of them had gone. They were all excited for her, but for their mother, it was a particular source of pride. Since the day her daughter got accepted, she couldn't stop bragging about it, whether in church or at the market. It was so bad that even her husband told her she was acting *highfalutin*.

"Wanna come?"

Thomas didn't realize Abby was talking to him until his mother said, "Go on, Thomas. Blow away the cobwebs."

He nodded and got up, his back sore from standing all day. He didn't want to go, but he knew Abby was still upset by what happened and needed company. Besides, they didn't hang around together like they used to, and as children, they'd been the closest thing to best friends that two siblings could be. In the summers, they would spend every day at the beach with their friends, coming home burnt to a crisp. At night, they would venture down to the seawall, always turning back because they were intimidated by all the older kids. One year, George got a job at the ice cream shop where he would hand them free cones when his boss wasn't looking. Thinking back,

Thomas got a twinge of longing. He was never really sure if those were happier times or if he just liked to think so.

"Would you get me a small vanilla?" Mrs. Nolan asked as they walked away.

"They only have one size, Ma," Abby said.

"And extra sprinkles."

Thomas looked at his sister, and they both smiled.

CHAPTER SIXTEEN

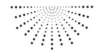

Abby leaned towards the small mirror on the wall, a lock of hair between her fingers. Positioning the scissors, she closed them with a snap, and a piece of her bangs fell to the floor. She continued down the sides and then the back, taking off no more than an inch, the ends brittle from the sun and saltwater.

When she was younger, her mother would cut her hair—she cut the whole family's hair—and Abby had only been to a stylist two times, once for her First Communion and again for Confirmation. Her father said they didn't have money for such things; her mother insisted fashion and grooming were wasteful extravagances. Abby never felt poor, but that wasn't hard in East Boston, which had enough tenements and flophouses to make anyone who owned a home feel like gentry. Her mother always described them as *lower-upper-middle-class*, a made-up term that seemed to reveal more about her own insecurities than their economic status.

"Abby?"

She quickly brushed her hair and grabbed her purse and sweater. When she went down the stairs, her mother was waiting at the bottom, a cold drink in her hand.

"Don't you look darling!" she beamed.

Abby smiled shyly, looking down at her flowered shirtwaist dress. She hadn't worn it since the night she went out after graduation, and it fit better now that she had lost a few pounds.

Her mother faced her, fixing her collar, wiping off a bit of lipstick.

"Do you have change for the bus and streetcar?" she asked.

Abby nodded.

"Be polite, *sirs* and *ma'ams* always. *Madam* if it's an elderly woman," her mother continued.

"What if it's an elderly man?"

"Then it's *Old Geezer*."

They both laughed, and her mother leaned forward, kissing her on the cheek, the most affection she had shown her in months. Abby thought she smelled liquor, but it could have been from the boysenberry scones she made that morning.

"Now, go get 'em."

"Thanks, Ma."

She walked out and went across the lawn, waving to Mr. Loughran, who was repairing something on his ham radio antenna. When she got to the end of Bay View Avenue, a bus was arriving, the door opening to a crowd of passengers carrying bags, beach towels, and picnic baskets. The last to exit were two older ladies, speaking Italian to each other and wearing patterned dresses. Abby got on and found a seat at the back. As they pulled away and drove across the strand, she looked out at the water, a stretch of clouds floating on the horizon.

She caught the streetcar in East Boston then the subway at Maverick Square, which crept eerily through the tunnel under the harbor. Despite living so close, the city always seemed like a foreign place, full of excitement and activity but also danger. She had been going there all her life and was still amazed.

At Scollay Square, she got off to change lines, pushing through the crowds, her purse tight to her side. She knew people who had been robbed, and women were always easy targets, especially downtown. She never felt at risk in East Boston, which had twice the crime, but where everyone knew each other.

As she waited on the platform, she saw a group of young GIs in khaki uniforms. With their smooth chins and eager eyes, they looked more like boys pretending to be soldiers. Just the sight of them made her nervous, the threat of war growing each day. A week before, a convoy of military trucks had gone down Shirley Street, confirming rumors that the Army was building a battery on Deer Island.

"A dime to save America?"

Turning, she saw a young man in shirtsleeves and a tie, his hat tilted to one side. He was holding out a newspaper, and across the front, it said *Social Justice*, the same one George had been scolded for having.

"No. Thank you," she said.

"You seem like a nice gal."

She smiled and looked away.

"You know the communists are trying to take down America?" he continued.

"That's news to me."

When he stepped closer, she wished she hadn't said anything.

"It's true. Roosevelt is controlled by the Jews. They wanna start another global war."

The word sent a shiver up her spine. She hadn't felt so uncomfortable since, two years before, a homeless man followed her and her friend six blocks when they came into the city to go shopping.

Hearing a bell, she looked over and was relieved to see a streetcar pulling in.

"Here," the young man said, shoving the newspaper into her hand. "It's free."

She pushed it away and he scowled, his teeth yellow and uneven. When the trolley doors opened, she ran to get on and didn't look back.

······

ABBY WALKED UP and down the aisles of the university hall, tables covered with books and other academic materials. The room was packed, the echoes of hundreds of students, mostly men but more women than she had expected. It was the first time she had ever been inside a college, and the high ceilings and arched windows were elegant.

She kept her sweater wrapped around her arms, stopping at the different stations and browsing the textbooks. She tried to look calm, but inside she panicked because she didn't know where to begin. Along with her acceptance letter, she had gotten a note telling her to come to the fair to get her books for the fall semester. She didn't know if she had to buy or borrow them, and even her mother said it wasn't clear. In her purse was the eighty dollars she had saved from working at Betty Ann Bakery all through high school. It was the most money she ever had, but she worried it wasn't enough.

"Are you taking Biology 1?"

She turned around to see a young woman, dressed in a blue halter, her blond hair in rolls.

"I…I'm not sure," Abby said.

"Did you get your handbook? It will have all your classes."

Abby hesitated, embarrassed that she didn't know. She was tempted to lie, but her father had taught her that, in moments of crisis or confusion, honesty was always the best way.

"I did not."

"Come. I'll show you."

The girl took Abby's hand, and they maneuvered through the crowd.

"I'm Frances," she said, glancing back. "Call me Fran."

"Abigail—Abby."

"Abby? Really? I had a cat named Abby."

Abby chuckled.

"And I had a parakeet named Frances."

And it was true. When she was ten, an elderly woman on her street died, leaving behind a bunch of pets. Most were distributed among the neighbors, and Abby got the parakeet, which came in a round wooden birdcage. It lived in their parlor for two years until a coal shortage sent the house temperature plummeting, and she came down one morning to find the bird dead.

They reached a long table where university staff sat fielding questions from students.

"She needs her handbook," Frances said, pushing her way to the front.

A woman looked up, her glasses hanging at the end of her nose.

"Name?" she asked, coldly.

"Abigail Nolan."

She looked through a metal box, flipping through the files.

"Freshman?"

Abby nodded.

"I don't have you in here. Check with the bursar."

"The bursar?"

"To confirm your tuition payment."

"I'm on scholarship," Abby said.

"Partial or full?"

"Full."

The woman raised her eyes and stood up.

"Mr. Gordon," she said, calling to a man at the end of the table. "We've got a full scholarship student. She needs her handbook."

Some students looked over, and Abby got self-conscious. Since the day she got the acceptance letter, she had been proud of the scholarship. But seeing her new classmates, all of them cheery, confident, and well-spoken, she felt like she didn't deserve it.

"Over here, dear," the man said.

When she walked over and said her name, he immediately found her file.

"These are your required courses," he said, pointing with a pen. "You're entitled to the textbooks but not any accompanying materials. Those you'll have to buy. Can you afford it?"

The question felt insulting, but she knew he didn't mean it that way.

"Of course."

"Very well. Life sciences are the first two rows. Arts and humanities, including poetry, are along the back wall."

He gave Abby the booklet.

"Thank you," she said.

The man smiled and quickly went to help another student. When she stepped away, Frances waved, and they walked over to a quiet corner.

"My," Abby said, her face flushed. "This is hectic."

"Wait 'til first day of classes."

Abby looked at her, confused.

"You've been already?" she asked.

"I went to boarding school. Academy of the Assumption in Wellesley. It's sort of like college."

Abby smiled, relieved to know Frances was a Catholic, who her mother said were the only people she could trust. When Mrs. Nolan was a girl, Protestant Yankees still controlled the city, looking down their noses at the Irish and other groups.

"Do you know your room number?" Frances asked.

"My room?"

"Your dormitory room."

"Oh. Actually, I'll be commuting."

"Where do you live?"

"East Boston," she said, somewhat ashamed.

While their section was tidy and mostly middle class, others weren't, and East Boston had a reputation for being gritty.

"The airport," Frances said, the most many suburbanites knew about the area. "We flew out to Bermuda in April."

"Must've been fabulous."

"The beaches were lovely. But it's like the Dark Ages. No automobiles, only horse buggies."

Abby listened with a smile, but inside she felt inferior, and the farthest her family had gone was Maine. It was something she had feared more than the schoolwork, meeting people with the money and experiences she didn't have.

They stood for a moment in friendly silence. Now that she had her classes, Abby was more relaxed, but the commotion still made her uneasy, and she was sweating.

"Listen," Frances said, putting down her bookbag. "I'm almost done. Father is picking me up. But let's meet for tea before the semester begins…"

She got a notepad from her purse and scribbled something down.

"Call me," she said, tearing off the piece and handing it to her.

Abby looked to see a phone number, Duxbury 624, one of the wealthiest towns on the South Shore. Still, she was glad they met, and Frances didn't seem like a snob. There was no telephone at the cottage, but Abby knew she could always go home or use the payphone at the post office in Winthrop center.

"I'll do that."

"Terrific!"

She gave Abby a quick wave and then turned to go.

"Fran," Abby said, and she stopped.

"Yes?"

"Thank you."

CHAPTER SEVENTEEN

Thomas had his lunch in the locker room of the security building, a cold ham sandwich and some boysenberries his mother had picked that morning. He had been eating by the pier, but the sun was too hot and the noise from all the construction was annoying. With tensions rising between the union and management, the cafeteria was now off-limits to guards, which was unfortunate because it was the coolest place in the yard aside from the storage freezers. The day before he had made the mistake of walking in and was met by the hostile stares of a dozen welders. Thomas had taken the job hoping it would prepare him for the police department, never expecting to be in the middle of a labor battle.

As he closed the lunchbox, his supervisor walked in.

"Nolan," Barrett said, his face damp with sweat. "I need you at the West Gate for the rest of the afternoon."

Thomas just nodded—it was never smart to show any preference for an assignment. While he knew the guardhouse would be stifling, he might also get a chance to see the girl from the factory.

"Yes, sir."

Barrett came closer, squinting at him. Reaching out, he brushed the side of Thomas' chin and made him flinch.

"Watchman, you know what clean-shaven means?" he asked.

"Yes, sir."

"It doesn't appear so."

"Sorry, sir. We're staying at our summer cottage. I forgot my blade sharpener."

Barrett frowned, his fat cheeks scrunching up, revealing the lines of middle age.

"Summer cottage? You're a regular noble, are you?"

Thomas responded with a hesitant grin. With Barrett, he could never tell if it was friendly joking or antagonism.

"It's really nothing more than a shack, sir," he said, which was how his mother always described it.

"Good. Then you'll feel right at home in the guardhouse."

When Barrett walked away, Thomas frowned. He put his lunchbox in the locker, grabbed his thermos, and left. He walked along the pier, where a merchant ship had just come in, its lines tied and its massive gangways down. Men were starting to position the winches to hoist one-ton pallets from the freight lot.

With white seaspray on the hull, Thomas knew it had come across the Atlantic, not just up the coastal waterways. He wondered if it had been with a convoy because with the threat of U-boats, few ships made the crossing alone anymore. Hitler had been careful not to provoke the Americans, but with so much cargo going to help Great Britain and other allies, the line between which ships were neutral and which were not was getting blurrier by the day.

"Hey, watch it!"

Thomas was so lost in thought he walked into two longshoremen.

"Sorry."

"You'll be sorry if you get in our business," one of them said, his voice gravelly.

Thomas could always respect authority, but he wouldn't take intimidation.

"Yeah? What the hell's that supposed to mean?"

"It means what it means."

So far, he hadn't had any problems with the workers, aside from occasional glares or hard looks. He understood enough about unions to know it was part of the game, and they had to play tough. But he wasn't willing to be bullied in the process.

Seeing their tags, he realized they were in the wrong location. Pier Two was restricted.

"Go on," he said. "You're not supposed to be over here."

They scoffed and walked away, giving him some small feeling of satisfaction.

As he came around the corner of the warehouse, his father was walking out of the cafeteria, his hardhat under his arm and lunchbox in hand.

"Dad," he said, relieved to see someone he knew.

"Thomas."

"I'm working the back gate. Should we meet at Maverick Station?"

Mr. Nolan smiled, his cheeks red and lips dry. The day was only half-over and already he looked drained.

"Not today, son. We've got a meeting after work—"

When one of the foremen called, they both looked over.

"Tell your mother I'll be late."

"I will."

"Another thing. Could you stop at home and get the key under the mat?"

Thomas nodded sadly, and not just because the house was his brother's last refuge. At one time, no one on their street locked their doors.

"Of course, Dad."

He watched his father as he walked away, lumbering across the pavement like an elderly man. But he wasn't that old, having just turned fifty-two, and it was mostly from working hard all his life. Mrs. Nolan was three years younger, and they had started a family late. When she had George at twenty-nine, she feared she wouldn't be able to conceive again, which was strange considering women now had babies after thirty all the time.

Thomas continued across the yard, and when he got to the guardhouse, the previous watchman was waiting to leave. He relieved the man and then walked inside, writing his name in the ledger and putting down one o'clock even though it was a few minutes after. Even with both windows wide open, the space was roasting, so he fanned himself with an envelope. Rolled-up sleeves weren't allowed, but he did it anyway, loosening his tie too. With four hours to go, he leaned back on the stool and tried to get comfortable.

Sometime later, a loud horn sounded.

Opening his eyes, he was horrified that he had dozed off. He jumped up and looked out, hoping no one was around. The horn blared again, and he looked around to see a Boston Globe truck waiting outside the fence. He walked over, opened the gate, and waved the driver through.

"Afternoon."

"Why didn't you go in the front?" Thomas asked.

"It's clogged up. I guess they're trying to get a crane boom through."

Thomas reached in the guardhouse window for the clipboard.

"You work with my brother?" he asked as he wrote down the plate number.

"Maybe. Who's your brother?

"George Nolan."

The man's expression changed.

"I know George. He was let go last week."

······

THOMAS LEANED AGAINST THE WINDOW, the trolley packed in the Friday evening rush. Beside him sat a sharply dressed man wearing too much cologne, and somewhere behind him, a baby was crying. At the front, a group of teenagers was swearing and acting rowdy. He was tempted to tell them to shut up, but he would have been a hypocrite because he was once the same way. And it wasn't that long ago. Almost nineteen, he felt he had aged a decade since adolescence, and nothing made you old faster than the fears and stresses of adulthood.

With his stop approaching, he got his things and stood up. The car had thinned out, the only passengers left a few old people who looked as tired as he felt. He wanted nothing more than to continue on to Point Shirley, but he had to get the house key and, more importantly, his blade sharpener. Barrett's remarks earlier were a warning, and Thomas didn't want to be caught with a scruff again.

He got off, and the streetcar pulled away. As he waited to cross, he saw several men in front of the pool hall. Dressed in suits, they stood with cigars in their mouths, joking around and waving to people they knew. Bennington Street was always lively at night, the bars full and kids on every street corner. His mother would have grumbled about *the Italians*, but it was really a mix of people, and far less territorial than places like the North End or Charlestown.

As Thomas approached his house, he heard sobbing and stopped. Next door, he saw a figure crouched on the front steps.

"Miss?" he asked.

When she looked up, he was surprised to see the woman from the factory.

"Hello."

"Are you alright?"

She nodded, biting her lip. Even in the darkness, he could see her face, and she was beautiful.

"Yes. Thank you."

He waited to see if she would say more.

"I live right there," he said, so she wouldn't be scared. "But we're at our cottage for the summer."

"Cottage..." she said with a strong accent.

"In Winthrop. Just down the road."

"Ah, yes. The beach."

"You were there with Chickie," he said, remembering what Abby had told him.

"You saw us?"

"My sister did."

She smiled and wiped her eyes with a napkin. After a brief silence, he asked, "Are you here for long?"

"I arrived three weeks past."

It wasn't what he meant, but he blamed it on the language barrier.

"From Italy?"

"Yes. That is correct."

"Your English is good."

She glanced down, fidgeting with the napkin.

"Thank you. I...I worked at the American Consulate in Rome until..."

She trailed off, and he understood why. The war was a hard topic, especially for Italians in America, testing their loyalties and making them objects of suspicion. While most were patriots, Thomas had heard about a social club in Maverick Square that closed because members were split over those who supported fascism and those who supported democracy.

"I saw you last week," he said, changing the subject. "I work at East Boston Works."

"I am a seamstress at the moment."

In her voice, he could detect a hint of sarcasm, maybe even shame.

"And I'm a guard *at the moment.*"

She looked up with a grin, and he got a warm exhilaration. Suddenly, the front door opened, and it was Mrs. Ciarlone, Chickie standing behind her in pajamas. She leaned out and said something in Italian, the softest Thomas had ever heard her speak. After the young woman replied, she closed the door, either ignoring Thomas or unaware he was there.

"I'm sorry. I must go."

When she took the railing and stood up, he got flustered because he didn't want her to leave.

"I'm Thomas," he said quickly.

"I'm Concetta."

"If you ever need anything…I stop by the house a couple times a week."

Tilting her head, she looked at him and smiled.

"Thank you, Thomas."

CHAPTER EIGHTEEN

Abby kept her schoolbooks under the bed, laying each one flat against the floor because there wasn't enough room to stack them. They had been in the corner, but the room was so small she kept tripping over them, and she even spilled nail polish on her calculus textbook. While most had been included in her scholarship, she had to buy a biology lab kit as well as math instruments: a protractor, a compass, and a ruler. After getting pencils, pens, and notebooks, she only had half of her savings left. But forty dollars was enough for a couple of dresses and some shoes. And with the women's shop on Bennington Street just across from Gittell's, she had every reason to stop by and apologize to Arthur.

When she came downstairs, her mother was working in the garden as usual. It was getting to the point where Abby couldn't tell one day from another, and sometimes she had to check the calendar. She used to love getting lost in the endless routine of summer, but now it made her anxious. College loomed over her in the same way the war loomed over the country, and as awful as it was to compare the two, she couldn't deny it would be some relief to finally get either one started.

As she reached for an apple, she saw the housekey on the sill and was reminded that George no longer had a place to live. If he had been younger, she would have worried more. But he had a job and friends, and despite all his failures in life, he was a survivor.

Hearing a knock, she went out to the foyer, and Sarah and Noel were at the door.

"Hiya, Abby," Sarah said.

Noel just smiled, her hands clasped behind her back and her bosom protruding like she knew it and was proud.

"I just got up."

"Lazy girl," Sarah said.

"What time is it?"

"After nine."

"We're heading down to the beach. You coming?"

Someone coughed, and she looked back to see her mother, leaning in the kitchen doorway with a drink, her forearms streaked with dirt.

"Need any help, Ma?"

"I'm fine," she said, catching her breath. "You go. But can you pick up some vinegar for dinner? I'm making potato salad."

"Sure."

Abby held up her finger to her friends and ran upstairs. Summer days were always easy to prepare for and required only six things: a bathing suit, a hat, a coverup, a towel, her purse, and sandals. Often she went barefoot, but she had cut her heel two days before, and it was sore. After running a brush through her hair, she grabbed her things and was gone.

When they got to the beach, the tide was out, the sky clear to the horizon. Abby started to put her towel down, but Sarah stopped her, and she realized why when she saw Hal Francis and his friends throwing a football around in the shallows. So they continued another twenty yards and found a flat stretch of sand.

"Is this a better view?" Abby joked.

"Indeed."

"I could use another lesson," Noel said.

"You've got Jimmy Dunn."

"I haven't seen him yet this summer."

Abby didn't recognize the name, but it was the second time they mentioned him, and she was sure Noel had had a fling.

As she went to sit, Sarah called to someone, and Abby turned to see Angela coming toward them. With her tangled hair and sunken eyes, she looked ragged. Abby had never seen her before that summer, and all she knew about her was that she was from East Boston too, which didn't mean much because forty thousand people lived there. Except for high school, where kids from every neighborhood mixed, Abby could have gone her whole life without meeting her.

"Join us," Sarah said.

Angela gave a faint smile.

While Abby knew she had been seeing George, she wasn't sure if it was steady. But she was curious, as well as concerned, because she hadn't seen him now in four days. She was just going to ask about him when Sarah saved her the trouble.

"Where's your flame?"

"Fishing," Angela said.

"Catching lunch?"

"Or dinner."

They all chuckled, but Abby was confused. George didn't fish, and he didn't own a reel and rod.

Angela stood quietly for another minute, staring out in a daze. With her arms crossed and hips tilted, she probably looked good from a distance, but up close she was in rough shape.

"I gotta go," she said, finally.

With a feeble wave, she plodded off down the beach, her feet dirty and her suit bottoms loose. She looked like she hadn't bathed or changed in days, but then everyone got straggly after a few weeks on Point Shirley.

"Is she alright in the head?" Noel asked.

Sarah sat up, watching Angela like she was waiting until she was out of earshot.

"She's got it tough at home," she said.

"How do you mean?"

"Her father's a drunk. A damn tyrant."

"How do you know?" Abby asked.

"They were here last year. They rent a cottage at the end of Otis Street."

"I don't remember her."

"You were too busy with Jack what's-his-name."

Abby responded with a poignant smile. They had met at the ice cream shop after she bumped into him and knocked the top off his cone. Embarrassed, she bought him another, and they spent the night by the wall with Sarah and some other girls, talking and flirting. He and his younger sister had come from North Dakota to stay with their grandmother, who she learned later was the mother of his stepfather.

They walked the beach at night, kissed in the shadows, and Abby even let him feel her breasts, the first time ever. He left Point Shirley before her with an emotional farewell not far from the spot where they first saw each other. At the start of school, they exchanged a few letters, but like everything good or worthy about summer, it didn't last, and the frenzy of senior year helped her get over him.

"Jack Ellsworth," she muttered.

"What?"

She looked over at Sarah, who was rubbing oil on her shoulders.

"His name was Jack Ellsworth."

"Have you seen him?"

"No. I think they were here for just last summer."

"A pity, isn't it?"

"Sarah!" someone yelled, and it was Hal Francis.

When he waved, Sarah got up, fixing her top before waving back.

"You gals ready for some football?" she asked.

Noel was standing before she could finish, but Abby didn't move.

"Aren't you comin'?"

Abby just shook her head.

"Suit yourself."

They walked off down to the water, and Abby lay back on the

towel and closed her eyes. With the hot sun on her face, she smiled to herself thinking about Jack Ellsworth, all the excitement and angst.

She hadn't felt that spark again until Arthur. After the awful incident at her house, she didn't know if she could make it up to him, but she was willing to try. With his quiet charm, he wasn't like other young men she had met, and he was kind without being weak, a rare combination. Still, she understood the hazards of romance and had seen it sidetrack a lot of young lives. Two girls in her class had gotten pregnant, both of them dropping out, and a guy Thomas knew from the movie theater had killed himself after a hard breakup, jumping into the path of a train in Orient Heights.

Despite all the distractions, Abby was determined to stay focused on September and the great hope of college. She had worked all her life for it, studying late and on weekends while her friends were out having fun. Even her mother, who was almost more eager than her, had said *slow down on those books, young lady*. Abby didn't know where it would take her—she didn't even have a career picked out. But she had seen what happens without a dream, and her neighborhood was filled with people who had settled for less, slogging away at menial jobs on streets they never left.

······

SOMETIME LATER, she woke up. She was glad someone had put the coverup over her because she would have been scorched. Sitting up, she stretched her arms and adjusted her hat, gazing out at the water, the tide now halfway up the beach.

"The princess has awoken."

Squinting, she looked over at Sarah, who was chewing a piece of taffy.

"Did you get me some?"

"Hal gave it to me."

"He also gave her a kiss," Noel said, tinkering with her ankle bracelet.

"More like a peck."

"Looked like a kiss to me."

Abby smiled. There was something special about waking up in the comfort of friends. But it was getting late, and she had to go, knowing her mother would be waiting for the vinegar. So she stood up, wiped the sand off her legs, and gathered her things.

"Where're you going?" Sarah asked.

"I've had enough sun."

"We saw a whale," Noel said.

"Meet down the wall later?"

"Maybe," Abby said, waving. "Bye for now."

As she walked away, Sarah called to her, and she turned. She tossed a piece of candy, and even with her towel, purse, coverup, and shoes in her hands, Abby caught it. It was squishy from the heat, but she hadn't eaten all day and was hungry.

"Thanks."

"See ya," they both said.

She walked up the beach to the road, where she cleaned off her feet and put her sandals on. As she came around the corner to Bay View Avenue, she stopped. Standing in front of Pulsifer's Market was a man, leaning over a trash barrel and digging through the trash. He had no shoes on and his shirtless back was deep red. While she stood watching, the owner came out and confronted him. The man turned, and Abby gasped when she saw it was George.

Instantly, she ran over to him.

"What's the problem here?" she asked.

The owner looked at her, hands on his hips and his gut protruding.

"Problem? I can't have vagrants in front of my shop. That's the problem!"

"I ain't no vagrant!" George shouted.

She got between them and held out her arms, knowing no decent man would risk hurting a woman. George looked terrible, his face gray and a cut above his eye. Even if he was tough, the owner was twice his size and would have the law on his side.

"Come, George," she said. "Let's go."

She put her arm around him, and he stank of booze. To her surprise, he didn't argue or resist. He glared at the man and then walked with her down the street.

"What the hell was that all about?"

"Aw, Abby," was all he said.

He shook his head, struggling to form the words, and she couldn't tell if it was because he was drunk or something else. When they stopped at the corner, he had to hold the street pole for balance.

"Where are you living?" she asked.

"Stayin' with friends."

"Where?"

"East Boston," he said with a hiccup.

"Everyone's been worried to death about you."

Although no one had said it, she knew it was true. In the Nolan family, they could laugh, joke, gossip, and complain, but they could never talk about serious things.

"Really?"

"Of course. Why wouldn't they be?"

"Then why'd Dad kick me out?"

Their eyes locked. She could have mentioned the incident with Arthur, but she didn't even want him to know his name.

"All the trouble you cause," she said.

He responded only with a guilty grin, but at least he didn't deny it.

"Maybe you should apologize," she added.

"Never."

Suddenly, a car pulled up, a Buick convertible about a decade old. The whitewall tires were worn, the wheel wells rusted, and it spewed black smoke.

"Georgy!"

In it were three young men, their shirts open and wearing sunglasses. And if any of them were familiar, it was only in the way that all George's friends looked the same.

"Hey, fellas," he said.

Walking over, he leaned against the door, and someone gave him a cigarette. Abby stood on the corner with an annoyed smirk, and the guy in the backseat winked. Moments later, George looked back at her and waved, and she knew she had to let him go. Instead of opening the door, he tried to hop over, and they pulled him in, smacking him on the ass and laughing. The driver put it in gear, and they sputtered off down the road.

CHAPTER NINETEEN

Thomas knew it was going to be a difficult day when he saw a crowd by the main entrance. It was barely 7 am, the harbor immersed in a light mist, two tugboats passing on their way to bring in some merchant or military ship that had arrived the night before. A few dozen men stood out front holding signs and sipping coffee. It wasn't rowdy or contentious; there were no police or reporters. If he didn't know about the strike, he would have thought it was a shift change.

As he crossed Border Street, he got a few curious stares, but no one said anything. He never wore his uniform to work and was glad he didn't, especially today. He continued to the side gate where a guard stood checking IDs. Just because the workers were on strike didn't mean everyone else was. The shipyard had lots of non-union employees, from secretaries to janitors and, of course, the security staff.

He showed his card, and the man looked through his bag, giving him a quiet nod of comradery before waving him through. Security had always been high at the facility, where in peacetime millions of dollars in cargo passed through each week. Now it was like Fort Knox, trucks arriving every day with food and other supplies for allied countries, England mostly but Russia and Free France too. With so much artillery being transported, everyone was worried the Army would take over the security, and they would all be out of jobs.

As he headed across the yard, he heard a commotion and looked back. A guard he knew was getting heckled, and he wasn't surprised because the guy was carrying his uniform and hat. It was the first sign of trouble, and Thomas knew there would be more if the politicians didn't step in to help.

Supervisor Barrett stood at the entrance, his arms crossed and face stern.

"Into the boardroom," he said as men from the first shift arrived.

Thomas went to his locker and quickly changed. When he got to the room, the seats at the table were all taken and people were leaning against the walls. He found a spot at the back, and Barrett walked in with two other supervisors.

"Gentlemen," he said. "It should be obvious by now that the union has chosen to strike. Any questions?"

He looked around, and everyone just shook their heads.

"In normal times," he continued, "this would lead to a temporary cessation of operations…"

He paused dramatically.

"But these are not normal times. Now, in terms of freight, we're fortunate that all transatlantic activity is being held up in Maine until a Navy escort convoy returns from the U.K. We can suspend our shipping obligations for about one week…"

There was momentary relief, the hope that they wouldn't have to defy the strike. But it didn't last.

"The dockyard expansion project cannot wait, however. So the company has opted to bring in temporary workers, welders, chippers, et cetera."

"Scabs," someone said.

"Replacements!" Barrett barked.

Whether they supported the union or not didn't matter because it wouldn't change their own work situation. The pay for a watchman was low, but except for Barrett and the other supervisors, no one seemed like they were there for a career. As Thomas looked around, everyone was about his age, young men who were just out of high school or had lost their jobs, doing this until a better one came along.

"No incitement," Barret said. "The workers will do a dog and pony show, try to get you riled up. Remember, you are not their enemy."

"But the scabs are!"

The room erupted in cheer, and Thomas felt a wave of unity. He didn't know what the workers wanted, but he saw what the union had done for his family. Even if the strike didn't last long, men would lose pay, and that included his father.

"Gentlemen!" Barrett shouted, and everyone shut up. "This shipyard has been contracted to provide services for the government of the United States. Not only have we been sending crucial supplies, but soon we'll have the capacity to repair all classes of warships and other vessels damaged in combat..." As he spoke, the mood changed, men looking around at one another. "Every minute we're down means another minute of suffering for our friends overseas. Every minute we lose getting these ships loaded and on their way means more time for Hitler to get a foothold in Great Britain. And if that happens, America stands alone against Nazi tyranny."

The room went silent. Then someone clapped, and the rest joined in. As gruff as Barret was, he had made the dull life of shipyard work seem like a sacred mission. And it was ironic that it took a Scotsman to inspire in them feelings of pride and patriotism.

"Now, Mr. Cooper has your assignments."

Everyone started to get up, putting on their caps and fixing their belts. Thomas didn't know if there would be trouble, but he made sure his baton was hitched right. He waited in line, and when he got to the desk, the supervisor asked his name. The man looked through the roll and then said, "West Gate."

Thomas sighed, and the assignment was a relief for two reasons. He would be away from the picket line and close to where Concetta worked. He filled up his thermos in the hallway and walked out into the morning sun.

Two new ships were in port, one from Holland and another from the Canary Islands. Men were standing on the deck smoking. Except for emergencies, crew members of foreign ships were no longer allowed onshore, the government fearing spies or defections. He had heard about men jumping off in the night so they wouldn't have to go back to war-torn Europe. When he waved, one of them waved back, and he sympathized with their isolation.

Crossing the yard, he heard loud chanting and saw a line of workers coming through the front entrance. Even from a distance, they looked nervous, and he had no doubt they were the replacements. Some blacks were among them, an unusual sight because the facility was almost all white. And yet he heard more racial slurs in the course of one workday than he did in months on the streets of East Boston.

He got to the guardhouse and relieved the man on duty, who looked tired and anxious to go. Thomas sat down and got comfortable. With a breeze off the harbor, the structure wasn't as hot as earlier in the week. There had been talk of a summer storm, but the sky was clear, and rain never bothered him anyway.

The hours passed by more slowly than usual, the drag of his anticipation. In the background, the noise of the picket line blended with the buzz of drills and saws and the creak of winches. He was so happy to be away from the activity that he didn't even take lunch.

Sometime in the late afternoon, he heard voices. When he looked up, women were leaving the factory across the street. He walked out and went over to the fence where he searched for Concetta. She was one of the last ones, stepping out and lighting a cigarette like she had been waiting all day for it.

"Concetta," he called, not sure if he pronounced it right.

She waved with a smile and came over.

"It's Connie," she said.

"Connie?"

"My friends told me. It sounds more American."

Thomas laughed.

"Okay, Connie."

Startled by a bullhorn, they both turned.

"What is it?" she asked.

"A strike."

"A strike?"

"The workers want more money," he said, the simplest way he could explain it.

She stared down the road, but the entrance was out of view. When she turned back, she seemed less concerned.

"How is your house on the beach?" she asked.

"The nights are pleasant. The mosquitoes are not."

"Mosquitoes?"

"Little bugs. They bite, suck your blood."

"Ah," she said, muttering something in Italian that sounded like a translation.

Taking a final drag, she dropped her cigarette on the sidewalk and stamped it out. In other parts of town, it would have been rude, but in the industrial backstreets of the harbor, with litter and trash everywhere, it was perfectly appropriate.

They stood facing each other through the fence like an inmate and visitor. She was easy to be around, her expression gentle, her silence as charming as her words. He wondered why she had been crying the night he saw her on the steps. The world was a hard place, and after ten years of depression and war looming, everyone had something to be sad about.

"I'm sorry. I must get the train—"

"Nolan!"

Cringing, he looked back, and it was Barrett. She whispered *goodbye* and turned to go, probably worried she was getting him in trouble.

"Concetta," he said, and she stopped.

"Connie."

"Connie. How'd you like to see a movie?"

"A movie?"

"Yeah, like at the theater."

"Nolan?" his boss called again, getting closer.

"When?"

"Saturday?"

She hesitated, her eyes darting, and he could tell Barrett was making her uneasy.

"But I work until six."

"Me too. We could meet here. After work."

"Okay," she said, smiling. "Saturday."

She scurried off, glancing back with a little wave. Thomas walked over and met Barrett at the guardhouse.

"Guard duty doesn't mean cavorting with the locals."

"She was asking directions, sir."

"And I'm sure you obliged her," he said with a smirk. "I need you to work this weekend."

"This weekend?"

"That's right. Both days. Morning and night."

Thomas contained his disappointment, but it was the worst possible luck. When he glanced over to the street, Connie had already turned the corner and was gone.

"Yes, sir."

......

By the end of the shift, Thomas could tell from the noise that the picket line had grown, and he knew it wasn't just workers. Strikes always attracted a variety of rabble-rousers, from members of other unions who came out for support to political activists who used it to draw attention to their own causes.

For the entire afternoon, not a single truck or person had come to the West Gate, and he wondered why they even had it. But he didn't complain, and as uncomfortable as the guardhouse could be, especially on hot days, it was the best-kept secret in the facility.

He was relieved by an older guard who showed up five minutes late and then had to use the bathroom. Once the man returned, Thomas made the long trek back to the locker room, changing his clothes and punching out. He crossed the yard with a quiet dread, wishing he could leave another way but knowing that all employees had to go through the main gate.

He passed through security and came out to the street where a hundred men stood in a line, another hundred lingering on the sidewalks. Local residents had gathered to watch, sitting on stoops and leaning out apartment windows. Cops were on every corner, and there were even some police horses.

Keeping his head down, he walked out with the other employees, hoping to avoid any attention. But immediately, they were met with shouts and jeers.

"Fuckin' scabs!"

Two officers waved them through, shouting at them to keep moving. Like a panicked child, Thomas looked around for his father but didn't see him. When he felt a hot splash, it took him a moment to realize someone had thrown a coffee cup. He was almost through the crowd when he was shoved from behind and stumbled forward. Turning around, he saw a stocky guy with dark hair, his arms out and scowling.

"Scab!" the man yelled in his face.

Thomas stopped, his temper surging, and it took every ounce of self-control not to hit him. But he wasn't foolish enough to fight there, and with tensions so high, the situation was only one altercation away from becoming a riot.

"Go, man, go!" a cop screamed.

Thomas hurried through the line, and when he got to the other side of the street, he felt like he had just escaped the eye of a storm. Shaken and out of breath, he ducked around the corner and took a minute to calm down. Reaching into his bag, he grabbed a napkin and wiped the coffee off his neck, feeling humiliated. Then he headed to Maverick Station to catch the train.

CHAPTER TWENTY

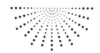

*A*bby leaned into the mirror, her forehead tanned and her cheeks dry and peeling. In the past, she didn't worry about her looks like other girls, but she had reached an age where beauty was as much about dignity as it was about attraction.

Using her fingernail, she scraped her skin gently, pulling off any dead pieces. Weeks of sun had brought out her freckles, something she never liked about herself, and her brothers used to call her *tomato face*. Considering she had brown hair, she didn't know where they came from and had only seen them on redheads.

She felt the floor shake and knew someone was coming up. Moments later, her mother peeked into the room, a damp apron around her waist.

"Where'd you put the vinegar, dear?" she asked.

"I didn't get it."

Before her mother could ask why, she said, "I saw George. He was digging through a trash bin."

Mrs. Nolan's face dropped, but it was probably more from sadness than surprise because nothing George did shocked anyone anymore. She bit her lip, nostrils flared like she was trying to hold back her emotion. She always took her son's failings the hardest.

"Where?" was all she asked.

"In front of the market."

She nodded once and then turned to go.

"Why won't Daddy let him back?" Abby asked, and her mother stopped.

"IF HE WANTS to pick fights with people because of their race, he won't do it on our property."

As noble as it sounded, it was dishonest because she was more prejudiced than anybody. Growing up, Abby listened to her gripe about the Jews, the Italians, or the Yankees. At one time, there were even "gypsies" on their street, a family so looked down upon that every other group was united in their scorn for them. Only years later did Abby find out they were actually Armenian.

"Dinner's almost ready," her mother said. "Get some shoes on. I saw yellowjackets earlier."

"Do you have any cold cream?"

Mrs. Nolan examined her face.

"In the bedroom, beside the washbasin," she said.

"Thanks."

"But not too much. It's expensive."

Abby smiled, and her mother walked away.

When she came downstairs, Thomas was walking in, and he looked aggravated. She wanted to ask why, but she knew he wouldn't tell her. For all his confidence and charm, he was very private and never talked about his feelings.

She went into the kitchen and saw a half dozen lobsters on a platter, deep red and still steaming. Like George, she didn't care for the fish, one of the few things they had in common.

"How's that face?" her mother asked.

"Throbbing."

Mrs. Nolan held out a bowl of potato salad, and Abby took it outside. Her father was seated at the table, his work clothes on and a glass of cream soda in front of him. She smelled smoke but didn't see the pipe, knowing that her father always kept it hidden.

"Hello, love."

"Hi, Daddy," she said.

Her mother brought out the lobsters, and they waited for Thomas. When he finally came out, his hair was wet, and he had on clean slacks. He acknowledged everyone with a cold nod and then sat down, pouring some water from the glass pitcher.

"How was work?" Mrs. Nolan asked, putting lobster on the plates.

"Maybe you should ask Dad."

Their father just grunted, raising his eyes.

"I'm asking you."

"The union went on strike today. I had to walk through a mob to get out of there."

"Mind your tone, son."

Abby looked at her father then Thomas, fearing they were going to argue.

"I wish you had told me before I took the job."

"I didn't know."

"What's all this have to do with you?" Mrs. Nolan asked her son.

"Guards are the enemy."

Mr. Nolan put down his glass and looked across the table.

"Watchmen are not the enemy," he said. "Strikebreakers are another story. And if I could make a suggestion, wear your uniform when you leave so they know you're not one of them."

Abby listened, but she didn't know much about shipyards, unions, or strikes—most women didn't. Any job that involved confrontation didn't interest her, and she was glad to be going to college.

The conversation ended, and they began to eat, the only sound the cracking of shells, the clink of dishes. In the distance, the sun was descending behind the city, and there was a breeze in the air. Over at the airport, Abby watched a small plane land, kicking up dust on the tarmac. As much as she loved her afternoons at the beach, dusk was always her favorite time of day.

"What's in this?" Mr. Nolan asked, a chunk of potato on his fork.

"Corn oil and lemon juice. We were out of vinegar."

When her mother glanced over, Abby ignored her.

"I saw George today," she said.

At first, no one said anything, a pointed silence that only revealed everyone's mixed feelings about him.

"In the truck?" her father asked.

"No, at the market."

She could have said more, but she didn't want to embarrass George or more importantly, her mother. Thomas put down his utensils, loud enough that they all looked up.

"I was told he lost his job," he said.

Everyone stopped eating.

"By who?" Mr. Nolan asked.

"A Boston Globe driver. He was making a delivery at the shipyard."

Again, more silence. Abby looked across to her father, and just his expression was enough to get her choked up. She felt as sad for her parents as she did for her older brother. They had always tried with George, overlooking things they would have punished Thomas and Abby for. Although she resented it at the time, she now understood it was only out of love and concern. But George's problems went deeper than childhood mischief and being easy on someone was no way to redeem them.

"Let's all keep him in our prayers," her father said.

......

ABBY WALKED ALONE through the dark streets. All around, she could smell the smoke from grills and hear people talking on their porches. When three kids rode by on bicycles, the youngest one smiled and rang his bell. Crickets chirped, and every couple of minutes, she would hear a mosquito buzzing in her ear and swat it away.

Coming out to the beach, she saw dozens of young people at the seawall, talking and laughing. There was a bonfire on the sand, and another one in the distance. As a girl, she always got nervous approaching a crowd, but she no longer had the same apprehension, and most of them were just kids anyway.

"Ab?" she heard.

She looked over, and Sarah was standing by the fire with Hal Francis and his friends. In his polo shirt and pleated shorts, he looked even more handsome at night than in the day, and she wondered why she never noticed him more at East Boston High.

As she walked over, Sarah gave her an urgent wave, and they stepped away from the others.

"Everything alright?" Abby asked.

Sarah looked around and lowered her voice.

"I saw your brother."

"George?"

"I think he's been sleeping on the beach. Angela too."

Abby's expression sharpened, and she felt defensive.

"And why do you think that?" she asked.

Sarah paused.

"Because someone told me."

"Then you don't *think*. You know!"

"I'm sorry, Ab."

They heard hollering and looked down the beach. While the seawall was mostly people they knew, the group farther down was rowdier, and even her mother used to tell her to avoid them. Away from the houses and hidden by shadows, they could raise hell and escape if the cops came. It was also the place where Abby knew George would be.

"I've gotta find him," she said.

"Then I'm coming."

"No."

Abby started walking, and Sarah followed. With her fists clenched and huffing, she felt like an outraged parent. But George was no child, and the most she could do was let him know she was worried about him.

She approached the fire and saw a ragtag bunch, young men in scruffy t-shirts, barefoot girls with too much makeup.

"Hey toots," someone said.

She walked up to the nearest guy, who had a beer in his hand and a cigarette behind his ear.

"Where's George?"

"King George?"

"George Nolan!"

He put up his arms, spilling some of his drink.

"Cool down. I ain't seen him."

She looked around at the others. Even in the darkness and smoke, she could tell some of them were smirking, and it only made her angrier. Her eyes landed on a short guy with a cigar in his mouth and a petite blonde standing beside him.

"You," she said. "Have you seen George Nolan?"

He hesitated a moment, then pointed with his thumb.

"Down at the rocks."

When someone made a sarcastic comment, everybody laughed. But she was too upset to be bothered by insults or ridicule. Her mother used to warn her about people who were low-class, from *swamp Yankees* to *shanty Irish* to Italian *cafones*. Abby always thought she was just being a snob, but now she understood why because there was nothing worse than a lout.

She gave them all a bitter look and stormed off, Sarah chasing after her.

"Ab," she heard, but she didn't answer.

She reached the end of the beach, the narrow strand that marked the boundary of Point Shirley. At one time, it was a bridge connecting Deer Island to the rest of Winthrop. Over the years, it had been filled in by machines and shaped by the tides, and now it looked like a natural extension of the peninsula.

When Abby was young, it was the farthest she was allowed to venture, and she remembered standing by the road with her friends and gazing at the prison, its granite walls and barbed wire fence. Her mother once said that George would end up there if he didn't change his ways, and Abby never doubted it—some of his friends had already done time. He was hardly a gangster, but on the streets of East Boston, it didn't take much to turn a young man with no skills or direction into a criminal.

Soon the flat sand ended, and the beach grass began. Abby stopped and stared out at the bluff, the only sound the waves and the faint laughter of the gatherings behind them. She noticed a flicker, the glow of a cigarette, and went towards it, her heart pounding and sweaty all over.

Finally, she came over a dune and saw a figure in the darkness.

"George?"

"Abby?" she heard, relieved that it was him.

There was someone else too, and as her eyes adjusted, she saw Angela. They were huddled around a small campsite with sleeping bags and blankets, a canvas duffel bag, and cans of cheap beer.

"George. Please come home."

"Go away."

"Please."

"We're happy here," Angela said.

"Mind your business!" Abby snapped.

As she stepped closer, Angela got up, dressed only in baggy pants and a swimsuit top.

"Don't tell me to—"

"Stop, Ange," George said.

Abby ignored the girl and focused on her brother. Seeing his bomber jacket on the ground, she went to pick it up. As she did, Angela tried to stop her. What came over Abby, she didn't know, but she turned and punched her right in the jaw.

"Ow!"

Angela charged at her, shouting and swinging. Somehow Abby stayed calm, remembering what Thomas had taught her in the backyard, arms raised and feet out for balance. But girl fights never had the discipline of boxing.

Angela grabbed her hair and started to pull her down. When Abby kicked her in the knee, she shrieked and let go. They wrangled in the grass for half a minute, kicking and swiping. Angela slapped her, and Abby dug her nails into her neck.

"Knock it off!" George shouted.

He ran over and forced them apart.

"That...that's my brother," Abby said, straining to speak.

"And that's my boyfriend."

"He needs to come home!"

"Your father won't let him!"

As furious as she was, Abby couldn't deny it, and she was even ashamed. She stood gasping for air, her face sore and her dress ripped. With George between them, they had both stopped swinging, but tempers were still high. Abby hoped it didn't start up again because she wasn't sure she could fend her off a second time.

"Go!" George shouted at her, pointing.

Their eyes locked, and she shook her head, so disappointed she wanted to scream. But she didn't. Instead, she glanced back at Sarah, who stood at the edge of the grass, wide-eyed and stunned. Abby waved to her, took one last look at her brother, and they walked away.

CHAPTER TWENTY-ONE

*A*s Thomas walked the five blocks from Maverick Station to the shipyard, he got some uncomfortable stares. They weren't threatening, but he knew people in this part of town didn't like cops, and in his security uniform, he was easily mistaken for one. The area had always been tough, the narrow streets crammed with rundown wooden homes and brick buildings. There was a barroom on every corner and pool halls where unemployed men hung out front smoking cigars, up to no good. If the depression had done anything, it had turned street hoodlums into full-time crooks.

While Mrs. Nolan always complained about the Italians, the bad areas were a mix of cultures, and poverty didn't discriminate. In high school, Thomas knew two Lithuanian brothers who lived in a tenement across from the Bethlehem Steel facility. The oldest, Lukas, was killed his sophomore year while trying to scale the high-voltage power lines near the railyard. At the time, his younger brother was doing time at Deer Island for stabbing an off-duty policeman during a robbery.

And those weren't special cases. Thomas knew dozens of guys who had been in trouble with the law, which was why he was never shocked by George's behavior. For all the tidy homes and church-going people of their neighborhood on upper Bennington Street, East Boston was overall a gritty place. And it was hard to ignore the fact that after four generations in the country, his mother's side of the family hadn't gone too far.

As he came down the street, the crowd by the entrance was twice what it had been all week. Each day, management tried to bring in the replacements earlier, and each day the workers would be there to confront them. The buses they arrived on had been stoned, and the police had brought in more horses to keep order. Thomas had been showing up an hour before his shift started to avoid any trouble, but he always got a few snickers as he walked in. His father had stopped waiting for him in the morning, and Thomas couldn't escape the feeling that the strike was drawing a wedge between them. Mr. Nolan didn't say anything—he never said much about work—but Thomas knew it was wearing on him.

Holding his breath, he crossed the street and went around the picket line, not making eye contact. But when someone shouted directly at him, he couldn't help but stop. Glancing over, he saw a heavyset guy with dark hair, the same one he had clashed with earlier in the week. Thomas sized him up in a flash, knowing how he would approach him and where he would strike. In any conflict, strategy was as important as physical skill. He hadn't been in a ring in six months but still thought like a boxer, something his coach Mr. Fidler had instilled in him at East Boston High.

By the time he got to the gate, there was a line. As he stood waiting, he felt exposed and got uneasy.

"Hey, Pinkerton!" someone yelled.

Thomas didn't know if it was an insult or a mistake because they were private and didn't work for the famous agency. When he looked, it was the same man again, standing at the edge of the picket line heckling him. Between them was a police officer, who looked at Thomas with an expression of mild contempt. Cops never liked security guards, seeing them at least as clumsy amateurs and at most as a threat to their jobs.

"Keep walking, scab!" the worker yelled.

Thomas could no longer take his insults. Looking over, he raised his middle finger and the guy's face went purple. Thomas dropped his bag, and the man ran at him. They were just about to fight when two cops jumped in their way.

"Enough, boys!" one of them barked.

A few more officers ran over, some with their billy clubs out. Thomas had tried to make a quiet entrance, and now he felt like the whole workforce was watching. He turned away to hide his face and was relieved to see he was next in line. The guard quickly searched his bag and waved him in, and Thomas ran across the yard, trembling and out of breath.

He went to the office and got his assignment, disappointed it wasn't the West Gate. For the past two days, he had been looking for Concetta, but their schedules didn't align. With everyone working extra shifts due to the strike, he couldn't take her to the movies, and he had to tell her. It would be a bad night anyway, which made him feel less guilty about canceling. A summer storm was coming, the sky a sheet of gray, and his mother had been taking in the wind chimes when he left. Barrett had handed out parkas, but the rain wasn't expected until later.

Thomas stood by the tall wooden fence separating the main yard from the addition. By now, the foundation for the drydock had been poured, the keel blocks set. Replacement workers were installing retractable ramps and putting the final touches on a maintenance building. Next to it were the two new cranes that would be used for ship repair and loading cargo. While in normal times their booms would be painted white or light beige so planes could see them, they were now dark gray for camouflage.

At one time, the idea of an air attack sounded farfetched, but with German forces now deep in Russian territory, Hitler seemed unstoppable, and no one knew what to expect. The Army had already started construction on a new base on Deer Island, and Thomas had heard from sailors that coastal defenses from Narragansett to Casco Bay were being built up.

At noon, he was relieved and went to have lunch before starting his next patrol. Before the strike, he couldn't eat in the cafeteria because things were tense between the guards and workers. Then management decided that, even after the labor dispute was settled, they would have to use separate facilities. Some of the men thought it was because they weren't in a union, but Barrett's explanation made more sense. With so much sensitive freight leaving the port, it wasn't smart to let the two groups get too friendly.

Aside from the construction, the shipyard was quiet for a Saturday. The loading area was full of cargo, stacked up in rows behind a barbed-wire fence. It looked like food and other supplies, and the fact that the crates were unmarked meant they were probably going to England. Thomas hadn't seen much military equipment in the past week, but he was sure it was there. A guard had told him they were loading artillery and other weapons at night so civilians wouldn't see it.

By six o'clock, his regular day was over, and his extended shift began. With the overcast sky, it was darker than usual, and the temperature had dipped just enough to make it feel like an autumn evening.

As he started down the side of the warehouse, he heard a loud hum and stopped. Looking over, he saw three fighter planes drop from the clouds over Castle Island, headed for the runway at East Boston Airport. They flew directly over the sequestered German tanker *Pauline Friederich*, a scene that was as chilling as it was ironic.

Someone called, and Thomas turned around. One of the supervisors was running towards him, an eager look on his face.

"Strike is over," he said.

"Over?"

"An agreement has been reached. Work resumes tomorrow at 6 a.m."

Thomas didn't know how to react, so he just smiled and said thanks. He never really felt strongly either way and hadn't been on the job long enough to understand the disagreement. But if he had to pick, it would have been the employees because that was where his father stood.

The man hurried to the next post, and Thomas continued along his beat. He passed a yard filled with hundreds of barrels of oil, gasoline, and chemicals. When he came to the front of the shipyard, he looked toward the main gate. There was a handful of people out front, policemen and bystanders, but the picket line was gone, and the crowd had dispersed. He was glad it was over, and if he had known how much the guards were disliked, he probably would have stayed at the movie theater.

As he circled around to the security office, he veered from his route and went in. At the end of the corridor, Barrett's door was open, and the light was on. Thomas took off his hat and approached, knocking once.

"Come in."

When he entered, his boss looked up from his desk, glasses on and a pen in his hand.

"Nolan," he said.

"Sir, I hope I'm not interrupting—"

"You are."

After a tense few seconds, Barrett smiled, and Thomas smiled back.

"I'm happy things have been settled."

"We all are."

"I...I was wondering..." he said, stumbling. "If we don't need the extra—"

"You'd like to be relieved early?"

"If possible, sir."

"It's Saturday night, and you've a date."

Thomas didn't know if it was a question or statement, but it was remarkably perceptive.

"Yes, sir."

Barrett nodded and reached for a ledger. Opening it, he ran his finger down the schedule and then looked up.

"You're lucky," he said. "We've got sufficient coverage. But I need you in tomorrow. We've got a backlog now and need to get four ships out of port before this storm."

THE LAST HAPPY SUMMER

"Thank you."

Thomas left the office and rushed to his locker to change. With his bag over his shoulder, he ran across the shipyard, tightening his belt and fixing his shirt as he went. When he finally got to the West Gate, he slid to a stop by the fence and his heart sank. The street was empty —the factory girls had already left.

Just as he turned to go, he heard a soft voice. Looking over, he saw Concetta leaning against a car smoking a cigarette.

"Connie," he said, still catching his breath.

"You need to get out?" someone said.

He turned back and a security officer was looking out the guardhouse window.

"Do you mind?"

The man came out, reaching for his keys as he lumbered over.

"No problem," he said, unlocking the small door beside the gate. "Now the strike is over."

Thomas thanked him and walked over to Connie, excited but also embarrassed for being late.

"I'm sorry," he said.

"I thought there was trouble."

"Trouble?"

"With the strike," she said, taking a final drag and tossing the butt.

"It's over."

She stood up straight and smiled.

"What better news," she said.

......

By the time they got to the theater, the line was out the door. *Caught in the Draft* had just been released, and everyone loved Bob Hope. Connie looked disappointed until Thomas approached the doorman, who lifted the cordoned rope and let them in. Having worked there throughout high school, he knew everyone, and the employees always helped each other out. Thomas bought some popcorn, and they were lucky to find seats because the theater was packed.

After a short advertisement for Defense Bonds, the show started. The movie was a comedy, the story of a film star who was terrified of getting drafted. Thomas was more entertained by Connie, who put her hand to her mouth each time she laughed. She was always reserved, almost somber, so it was fun to watch her giggle. Of all the girls he had ever met, she was the most interesting, and he loved her modesty and quiet charm. But she also seemed wounded, a pain he could sometimes see in her eyes when she daydreamed or was thinking. As he wondered about it, he got the urge to put his arm around her, and it was only to comfort her, not for romance.

The film ended with applause, and the lights went on. As they walked out, Thomas nodded to people he had known all his life. He saw the younger sister of a guy from middle school, now grown up enough to wear lipstick. By the ticket booth, a group of Abby's friends stood in bright-colored dresses, their hair primped.

"You are a popular man," Connie said.

Thomas grinned.

"East Boston is a small place."

When they came out the front doors, there was already a line for the late show. They strolled down the sidewalk, the street bustling in the summer warmth, and he felt silly carrying his knapsack. But Connie was in work clothes too, a dark dress and low-heeled shoes, and she didn't seem like the kind of girl concerned with first impressions.

They approached an ice cream shop, where people were sitting out front on benches.

"How about some ice cream?" he asked.

At first, he thought she was going to say no, but she always hesitated before answering.

"Ice cream," she said, staring at the neon sign in the window.

It was close enough to a *yes* that he opened the door, and they went in. They ordered two cones, both chocolate with sprinkles, and he reached in his bag for his wallet. While there was one empty table, the shop was too loud, so once they got their cones, they left. They passed some guys speaking Italian, and Thomas noticed her look over at them.

"You never told me why you came to America," he said.

"Doesn't everybody want to come to America?"

"Not everyone. There wouldn't be any room left."

She chuckled, wiping her lips with a napkin.

"Maria is my aunt," she said, and when he frowned in confusion, she added, "Maria Ciarlone."

"I never knew her first name."

"She wrote to me and said I should come now before America gets involved..."

Before America gets involved. The words were unsettling, and it was a phrase everyone used, as if it was a business venture. Like a lot of people, Thomas still clung to the hope that the country would stay out of it. But the more activity he saw at the shipyard, the more he realized they were already, in some ways, at war.

"I was working at the American Consulate," she went on. "So I got a visa. Otherwise, it would not have been possible. Quotas are quite limited."

"Did you come for work?"

"As a seamstress? No. I came for sanity."

He raised his eyes and took a long lick of his cone.

"I'm not sure East Boston is the place for that," he joked.

She smiled but didn't laugh, and he got the feeling she had more to say. And he was right because when they got to the corner, she stopped and turned to him.

"Thomas," she said. "My husband was a soldier. He was killed in Greece three months ago."

A chill went up his back, and for the first time, he was at a loss for words. He didn't know what surprised him more, that she was a war widow or that she had married so young. As they stood facing each other, he felt some drops, and it started to sprinkle.

"I'm so sorry."

She responded with a faint smile like she had been told so many times before it had no effect.

"I never met my aunt before," she said, speaking dreamily. "She came here before I was born. I know her husband died building a dam. So we are partners in grief, I would say."

"We don't know the family too well...except Chickie."

Her face brightened.

"Chickie. A magical little girl."

"A real firecracker."

They both chuckled, a moment of humor in an otherwise grim conversation, something only a child could evoke.

Thomas finished his ice cream and tossed the cone in a barrel. The sprinkle quickly turned to rain, the pitter-patter of droplets on awnings and car roofs.

"Come," he said. "Let me take you home."

"No. I can walk."

"Connie, I can't—"

"I insist, please. You have to take the streetcar."

As she said it, he heard a bell, and a trolley was coming up Bennington Street. He only agreed because he could tell she wouldn't change her mind, but he didn't feel good about it. Of all the life lessons his father had taught him—and tried to teach George—courtesy towards women was near the top.

"I had a—"

Before he could finish, she leaned forward and brought her lips to his. They kissed under the lamplight, and when he put his hands on her waist, she didn't resist. It only lasted a few seconds, and he would have enjoyed it more except that he got self-conscious. Out in public and around so many people he knew, there was bound to be gossip.

They pulled apart, and he looked into her eyes, overcome by a tender yearning that made leaving her even harder.

"I'll see you again?" he asked.

"I'd like that very much."

With a breathless nod, he threw his bag over his shoulder and ran to catch the trolley.

CHAPTER TWENTY-TWO

Abby crept into the pantry, a canvas bag in hand. She took a loaf of Wonder Bread, a week old but still good, and a box of Arnott's biscuits her mother sometimes had with tea. She tiptoed up the stairs and opened the linen closet, taking out a blanket and an old pillow no one used. Then something creaked behind her, and she froze.

"What are you doing?"

She spun around and it was Thomas, shirtless and wearing only underwear. They had finally reached an age where it was inappropriate, but no one in the family cared about modesty except their mother.

"Just needed some things," she said.

He glanced down at the bag.

"For what?"

She looked at him, pausing for a moment before deciding that there was no point in lying.

"For George."

"What do you mean *for George*? What the hell happened to your eye?"

She touched her face, the bruise from her scuffle with Angela. No one had noticed until then because she had been covering it with foundation. Either way, it wasn't unusual to have injuries, and as kids, summers on Point Shirley were always full of scrapes, scratches, and bumps.

"He's living on the beach," she said, her voice cracking.

"How do you know?"

"I saw him. Angela is with him too."

Thomas squinted in confusion.

"She's from Eastie," she added. "You met her."

"What's her last name?"

"I don't know. She's got long, dark hair."

Even as she said it, she knew it was too vague. East Boston was full of swarthy girls, the daughters and granddaughters of immigrants, mostly Italians.

"Did you tell Ma and Dad?"

She shook her head. When she found out that George was living on the beach, she had been afraid to tell anyone. Her mother always had been more sympathetic to him, at times even protective. But her father, while hardly a tyrant, was the disciplinarian of the family. As someone who had been on his own since age twelve, he had little tolerance for a young man who had been given dozens of chances and blown them all.

"We have to tell them, Ab. We gotta help him."

She smiled warmly, appreciating his concern.

"I am…helping."

He looked down at the bag again.

"That's not gonna help. You know we're getting a storm?"

She just nodded.

"We gotta tell Dad. He's gotta let him back home."

Abby agreed but only because she had his support. As fair as her father was, she never felt like he truly listened to her unless she had one of her brothers on her side, and usually, it was Thomas.

"I heard the strike is over."

"Yeah, it's over," he said.

He walked away, and she shut the closet door, just in time because she could hear her parents returning from church.

As she came downstairs, her mother walked in wearing a wide-brimmed hat and linen dress, her grandmother's pearl necklace around her neck. Her father looked stylish in his gray jacket and pants, the only suit he owned. With the sky dark and overcast, they both had umbrellas, but the rain hadn't started yet.

"You missed a lovely sermon," Mrs. Nolan said, winded from walking.

"Something about war and the resilience of God's children," her husband mumbled.

All their lives, they attended Mass on Sundays as a family, getting ready and walking the three blocks to St. Mary's. Even George went, which aside from having a job, was the one thing their father insisted on after he quit high school. In the summer, their parents were less strict, and the only time they made them go was on the Feast of the Assumption. But Abby and her brothers were getting older too, and while their mother was devout, even their father had remarked they were at an age where they could decide for themselves.

Mrs. Nolan put her pocketbook on the table and looked in the mirror.

"Where're you off too?" she asked, glancing over.

Abby hesitated. If she was too afraid to say anything about George, some part of her hoped her mother would ask about the bag and force her into an admission. But she didn't, instead taking off her hat and fixing her hair.

"To the beach," Abby said.

"In this weather?"

"Just for a bit."

"Well, get a hat on that head."

"Yes, Ma."

Abby grabbed her hat off the rack and walked out the door.

......

By dinnertime, it was raining, gusts coming off the water and shaking the cottage. Everyone sat around the kitchen table while Mrs. Nolan got the ham out of the oven and mashed the potatoes. The window over the sink had been open, but she shut it after the wind knocked over one of the potted plants.

Once everything was ready, she made a drink and sat down. After a quick prayer, she handed the tray to Abby, who took a couple of slices and passed it to Thomas.

George had now been gone a whole week, and with the family holed up from the storm, Abby felt his absence even more. When she went to the beach that afternoon, she had found his campsite in the weeds, but he and Angela weren't there. She left the bread and biscuits, scattering them among their things so they wouldn't realize someone had left them. Like most people, George was too proud for charity.

"What's this?"

Abby looked up, and her father was holding out his glass.

"Cream soda," her mother said.

"It tastes funny."

"They were out of Barq's, so I got White Rock."

Abby glanced over at Thomas, and they both chuckled. Mr. Nolan wasn't a hard man to please, but he was specific about his favorite drink. He stood up and went over to the cabinet, where he got a clean glass and filled it with water, his wife watching with a smirk.

"Has anyone heard from George?" she asked.

The room filled with an uncomfortable tension. The longer George was gone, the less his name was mentioned. It pained Abby to think he had been forgotten or forsaken, and two days before, she woke up with tears after dreaming he had been washed out to sea in a storm. But she was old enough to understand her parents' dilemma, and she respected the hard choice her father had made. No one could say they hadn't done everything to help their eldest son.

"George is living at the beach," Thomas blurted.

Mrs. Nolan put down her knife and fork, and her husband looked up.

"What did you say?" he asked.

"He's living there," Abby said, struggling not to cry. "I saw him. His girlfriend too."

As she spoke, the wind shook the windows. Her father rubbed his chin, something he only did when he was troubled or confused.

"We have to do something," Mrs. Nolan said, looking across at him.

He wiped his lips with a napkin.

"Which beach?" he asked Abby.

"Point Shirley. At the end."

"Which end?"

"Deer Island."

Without another word, he returned to his meal, and everyone else did the same. But it was obvious he was upset, and Abby was glad because it meant he would do something. As the one who had kicked George out, he was the only one who could invite him back home.

They finished dinner, and Mrs. Nolan got up, pouring another drink before clearing the table. There was a gloomy silence in the cottage, and it wasn't just the stormy night. Abby could tell everyone was thinking about George. While she helped her mother clean up, her father and Thomas left the kitchen, and she heard them whispering in the parlor. Throwing down her dishrag, she ran out to them.

"I'm going."

"Dear—" his father started.

"Please! I can show you where he is. He trusts me."

She didn't know if it was completely true, but she was less threatening than anyone else. When her father got distracted, Abby looked back and saw her mother in the doorway, a mop in one hand and her drink in the other.

"It might be good to have her come along," she said.

Mr. Nolan consented with a nod, and Thomas didn't seem to care either way. They were both capable, but Abby knew that having too many men in a tense situation was a recipe for conflict.

As the only one with a raincoat, Abby's father handed her an umbrella, and Thomas wore a light jacket. At their worst, summer storms were a nuisance, and no one ever froze or got sick. Mr. Nolan looked at his wife and then his children, holding his coat closed by the collar and reaching for the door. Walking out, Abby got some tingle of pride or elation, realizing it was the first time they had ever gone out together to try to help George.

CHAPTER TWENTY-THREE

They walked down the steps to the sand, and Thomas was surprised to see the beach so empty. In his teens, the youth of Point Shirley would come out in any weather. The biggest bonfires they ever had were during thunderstorms; some of the best times swimming were after hurricanes. It seemed another example of how things had changed, both there and in the world, and sometimes he thought kids now had none of the guts of his generation.

The sea was dark and choppy, and across the sound, Nahant lay hidden in the gray haze. Thomas couldn't see any boats, but he could hear a foghorn, its drone echoing down the coast. Despite the tumult, it was peaceful, and he always loved the rain. As a boy, he would sit by the window during storms and gaze out, thinking about baseball, boxing, or girls while his brother read comic books by candlelight. George never had the same sense of wonder, fascinated only by things he could see and touch, and Thomas imagined that life was dull when you couldn't dream.

"I didn't see an ocean until I was thirteen," their father said out of the blue.

"I thought Ireland was an island."

"And I lived in the middle of it. Longford. Then Offaly for a few years."

Thomas glanced over at Abby, who held the umbrella with two hands, and they both smiled. Their father never talked about his childhood, and almost everything they knew of it was from their mother, who had gleaned bits and pieces throughout their twenty years of marriage. Thomas never resented him for it, although every child yearned to know their parents' pasts. But considering he had been orphaned young, his siblings scattered to various institutions, it was a brutal introduction to the world, and Thomas understood why he never spoke of it.

Soon the flat sand ended, tapering off into a wide stretch of beach grass, the lights of the Deer Island Prison beyond. Suddenly, Thomas heard voices and saw three men in a small clearing. He could tell they were angry or agitated, something about their posture; boxing had taught him how to read people.

As they got closer, he was shocked to see George, standing across from them without a shirt, his head sunken. He heard sobbing too and noticed a girl behind the men, her long hair blowing in the wind.

"George?"

"Who the hell are you?"

"Gentle, son," his father said to him quietly.

"That's my brother," Thomas shouted.

"And that's my sister!"

Thomas went towards them, his father and sister following behind. As his eyes adjusted, he saw the longshoreman from the picket line who had harassed him, unmistakable with his big head and wide shoulders. He stood soaked in a t-shirt with his arms out, but Thomas wasn't intimidated. He was only there to get his brother.

"George, come home."

"He ain't going nowhere!" the guy said.

Beside him was an older man, who had a flat cap pulled down over his eyes. He said something in Italian that seemed to provoke the other two, and Thomas realized then it was a father and his two sons.

"C'mon George," Mr. Nolan said, a tinge of sadness in his voice.

George looked up and started toward them, swaying as he went. Thomas didn't know if it was from drunkenness or despair, but he walked over to the campsite to meet him.

"I said, *he ain't going nowhere!*"

Thomas ignored them, waving his brother on with an encouraging smile. When he went to put his arm around him, the longshoreman ran at them. In a flash, Thomas pivoted and swung, punching him so hard he thought he broke his hand. Without a gasp or a grunt, the young man fell on his back and was out cold.

The girl screamed. When her other brother charged, Thomas was ready. He jabbed him in the abdomen, knocking the wind out of him, then a direct hit to the eye. The guy didn't go down, but he was stunned enough to back away and put up his hands. Still, Thomas wasn't a fool, and he had fought enough thugs to know you had to hit them twice as hard and twice as much. So he lunged at him, and the man tripped over a rock. Thomas was just ready to get on top and put him in a chokehold when his father yelled, "Thomas!"

Staring down at the guy, Thomas hissed and made him flinch.

"Let's go, please," Abby said.

When she touched his arm, he jumped, so full of adrenaline that his body twitched. He looked over at the Italian father and his daughter, who were huddled together, watching to see what he would do next. Thomas had seen the girl around town, her lanky figure and long hair. She was as ragged as George, and it was obvious they had been living outside together. In some ways, he was more disgusted with her than with his brother. Men were always wild and unpredictable, but he expected more civility from a woman.

The longshoreman crawled over to his brother, smacking his face and trying to rouse him. Thomas took George by the shoulder, and they went over to their father and Abby, who stood quietly panicked.

"I'm sorry," George mumbled.

When he spoke, Thomas could smell liquor.

"It's alright, son," Mr. Nolan said, patting his son on the back.

"I lost my job."

"There's more to be had."

"Is Ma okay?"

"She's fine. Let's get you home."

The way they spoke, like a father to his young son, was poignant, and Thomas got so emotional he had to look away. For the first time in years, George was remorseful, and Thomas wondered if the experience had changed him.

They started down the beach with the breeze in their faces, the rain now just a sprinkle. Thomas looked back a couple of times to make sure the two brothers weren't following. While he won the battle, he worried he had started a war. He didn't know who they were, other than that the stocky one worked at the shipyard, and he was sure he would see them around Point Shirley. But he wasn't scared, and he would fight them again. If his father had taught him anything, it was that family was most important, a lesson he understood now more than ever before.

CHAPTER TWENTY-FOUR

Thomas sat in the guardhouse, the rain tapping against its thin metallic roof, the wind whipping debris across the yard. With a pencil in hand, he made doodles on the copy of the Boston Herald the earlier guard had left behind. He sketched the buildings across the harbor, the Custom House Tower and the brick tenements of the North End, all blanketed in fog. As a boy, he loved to draw and would spend hours on gray days like this, capturing the shapes of the world around him. He even kept a book of his pictures under his bed until George found it and tore them to pieces. Even though they were just boys, Thomas still resented him for it.

All afternoon had been quiet, but there was never much activity at the West Gate. When a delivery truck pulled up, Thomas told him to go to the main entrance, too lazy to let him in. In between drawing, he would gaze over at the small factory across the street, thinking about Connie. With the strike over, his work schedule was back to normal, but he hadn't seen her in a few days. Considering she was his neighbor in East Boston, he knew he could always stop by her house.

A gust came off the water and shook the small structure enough that Thomas looked up. The moment he went back to his sketch, a massive boom shook the ground. At first, he thought either some munitions had detonated, or that a ship had hit the pier.

Then suddenly, the facility alarm went on.

He quickly got up and walked out, pulling the hood of his parka over his head. Nearby, two men were taking a lorry out of a storage shed.

"What the hell was that?" one of them asked Thomas.

"I don't know."

They dropped what they were doing and followed Thomas out to the dock area. Everything seemed to have stopped midmotion, workers standing by the deck hatches of a merchant ship, cargo nets hanging in the air. As a guard, Thomas had every reason to be concerned. His job was as much about safety as it was about security, and they had been trained in gas explosions, oil fires, and all the hazards of commercial shipping.

He started down the pier where, in the distance, he saw people rushing into the shipyard annex. He ran towards it, splashing through puddles, and as he got closer, fire engines burst through the front gate. They raced across the yard and stopped at the fence, men jumping out and getting their gear. Thomas followed them through the gate where he saw smoke, but it wasn't from fire.

"Nolan!"

When he turned, Barrett was coming toward him through the crowd.

"Sarge?" Thomas asked, the first time he ever used the title.

"Son," was all he said.

"What happened?"

Barrett took off his cap, shaking off the drizzle and wiping his forehead. He hesitated a moment, then looked at Thomas.

"The boom of the Hyde crane collapsed and fell back into the boiler shop."

Their eyes stayed locked for what felt like an hour. Thomas didn't know the lingo, but he knew it was bad.

"Is anyone hurt?" he asked.

"They're trying to get him out now."

"Who?"
"Your father."

......

Abby stepped off the streetcar on Bennington Street. She had an umbrella in her hand, but she didn't need it because the rain had died down. East Boston looked gloomy in the aftermath of the storm, the streets and buildings gray, water dripping from rusted downspouts. She hadn't been back in over a week, and already the noise and congestion grated on her nerves. As a child, she didn't like the city, although she loved her home. Once she asked her parents if they could move to Point Shirley forever, but at the time, the cottage didn't even have heating or plumbing.

Crossing over to Gittell's Tailor, she saw a gang of boys on the sidewalk, young enough that they still wore knickers. As she approached, they all went silent. They looked like urchins, one of them holding a dirty baseball, another trying to light a cigarette butt with wet matches. She gave them a polite smile and reached for the door.

When she walked in, the shop was empty. She went over to the counter, looking around, her heart racing. She hadn't seen Arthur since the incident with George and was still upset about it. Hearing footsteps coming up the basement stairs, she tried to stay calm. All her anxiety faded when Arthur's father walked out from the back.

"Good afternoon," he said.
"Hello."
She stood frozen.
"May I help you?" he asked, prodding her with a smile.
"Oh, pardon. Is Arthur here?"
He shook his head.
"He left on Monday, I'm afraid."
"Left?"

"The Army. Randolph Field, Texas."

The way he said it, rolling the "r," was charming, but it did nothing to lessen the brunt of the news. Abby was stunned. Arthur never mentioned he had joined the military. But they had only spoken a few times, so she knew she had no right to feel jilted.

With the old man waiting, she suddenly perked up.

"I wish him well then," she said.

She turned to leave and was almost at the door when he called to her.

"May I ask who inquires?"

"Abigail Nolan."

Walking out, she got a sinking feeling in her stomach, which she told herself was menstrual cramps and not heartache. The truth was she had hoped for something more with Arthur, whether it was romance or just friendship, and she wished she had come to apologize for George's actions sooner. The older she got, the faster things changed, and it was a tough lesson about procrastination.

She walked up the hill to the house, and there was a milkman parked across the street. When he waved, she realized it was Timothy Enright, a classmate from high school who had bought the business from his father the day he graduated.

"Abby!"

Startled, she looked over and saw Chickie on the porch. She was sitting on the lap of the Ciarlones' guest, the woman combing her hair in long, gentle strokes.

"Abby," Chickie called again.

Abby smiled, and the woman peered up and smiled back. But she didn't interrupt them, knowing that Chickie never got much attention. She went up the front steps, reaching into her purse for the keys, and as she approached the door, she stopped. They were still on Point Shirley for another three weeks, and she knew if she went inside now, it would only make her worry about everything she had to do to get ready for the semester.

She reached for the mail instead, which aside from going to see Arthur, was the only reason she had come back to East Boston. There were only a few pieces; a sweepstakes bulletin, a church newsletter from St. Mary's, and something from the coal company, which probably wasn't a bill because they didn't use any in the summer. Finally, there was a letter, plain white, the edges damp from the rain. When she turned it over, she saw *Thomas P. Nolan* typed across the back. In the corner, the return address was Boston Police Department Headquarters.

A shiver went up her back, and she filled with excitement. She kept the letter in her hand and shoved everything else into her bag. Waving to Chickie and the woman, she ran down the hill, stopping only when she got to Bennington Street. A trolley was coming, so she hurried across to catch it. It screeched to a stop, and the doors opened. But at rush hour, dozens of people had to exit first.

As she stood in line to get on, her eyes swept the windows, and Thomas was looking back. With a big smile, she held up the letter, mouthed the words *Boston Police*, the news he had been waiting for. But he didn't react, staring out with a blank expression that gave her a creeping dread. As his twin, she knew him so well she could almost feel what he felt, and by the time she reached the door, she was trembling.

CHAPTER TWENTY-FIVE

September

ABBY RAN down the stairs so fast she slipped, and she blamed it on her new shoes, the soles smooth and the leather stiff. She had grabbed the banister just in time, but it was loud enough that her mother came running out of the kitchen.

"What happened?"

"I tripped is all."

Mrs. Nolan looked her up and down.

"Get a sweater on," she said. "It's brisk out there."

Abby turned around and went back upstairs. At the end of the hallway, Thomas was standing in a t-shirt and underwear, his hair matted from sleeping.

"Good luck today," he said, scratching his head and then going into the bathroom.

"Thanks."

She walked into her bedroom and got a pink sweater from the dresser, picking off the pills and other imperfections. She had had it since freshman year in high school, a Christmas gift sent from her aunt in Maine who had since passed away. Of the four sweaters she owned, it was the least worn out but still looked shabby.

She put it on and stood in front of the mirror, trying out several different button combinations before finally settling on the top two. Knowing how fussy her friends were about fashion, she worried the girls at Boston University would be even worse.

As she ran her fingers through her hair, she glanced down at the picture of her father and froze. The pain was like that, she thought, hitting her in waves, subsiding for minutes and sometimes hours at a time, always to return. She had learned to control it, or at least delay it, and the only thing that helped was staying busy.

He had been gone five weeks now, barely a second in the loss of a loved one. Most mornings, she awoke thinking he was still alive, a fleeting illusion that hurt but didn't last. It was a hard break for a girl her age, but she didn't blame God, humanity, or even the shipyard, knowing that bitterness was no remedy for grief.

"Abby?" she heard.

"Coming, mother."

"You're gonna be late!"

"Be right there."

She picked up the frame, closed her eyes, and kissed the glass. Then she put it back on the dresser like she was resting a baby, whispering a silent prayer.

She ran back down and went into the kitchen, where her mother was standing by the stove. On the table was a plate of bacon and fried potatoes. She sat down and picked at her food, mainly out of respect for her mother because she had no appetite. With her father's death and school starting, she had been anxious for weeks, and her mother said she looked as *thin as a stick*.

When Abby got up, her mother glanced over.

"That's all?" she asked.

"I ate half."

Mrs. Nolan took the plate and put it on the counter. In better times, she would have thrown out the leftovers, but Abby knew she would save them for Thomas or George, or to make a soup. The family had gotten some compensation for Mr. Nolan's death, but it in no way made up for the loss of his income. And it seemed a sin that, after losing a loved one, they now had to worry about money.

Abby went out to the foyer and got her backpack, lifting it over her shoulder. With nine textbooks and other materials, it was heavy, and she hoped they had lockers at Boston University. Her mother came out to say goodbye, wiping her hands on her apron.

"Be a lady," she said, straightening out Abby's sweater.

It wasn't the most heartfelt advice, but her mother was always more concerned about appearances.

"I will."

"Do you have change for the streetcar?"

Abby held up her purse.

"He would be so proud," Mrs. Nolan said, putting her arms around her.

The way she said it, using *he* instead of *your father*, was some indication of her hidden sadness. At the funeral, she barely cried, standing with her back arched, as proper as a duchess. She had always been less emotional than other women, but Abby knew it was more out of concern than stubbornness. She was only trying to be strong for her family.

When they pulled apart, they were both teary. Abby smiled and reached for the door, and the moment she walked out, she felt free.

……

SHE REACHED Bennington Street as a trolley was pulling away and had to wait for the next one. At Maverick Station, she caught the subway, which crept along in the darkness under the harbor. Halfway through they stopped, and she felt a slight panic until she realized they had to let an oncoming car pass before continuing. She kept her eyes on her watch, timing the trip she would have to make five days a week. Her

THE LAST HAPPY SUMMER

scholarship was generous, but it didn't include housing. While her father had once mentioned helping her get an apartment after *she proved herself*, that was no longer possible; one more in a thousand lost hopes.

When they finally got to Scollay Square, it was ten minutes later than she expected. The station was chaotic, with people rushing in every direction. She ran for the stairs, and when she got to the top, she stopped. Ahead on the platform, she saw dozens of soldiers, dressed in khaki uniforms, rucksacks and rifles at their sides. Some train employees had formed a line in front of them, and when she walked over, one of them said, "Miss, you're gonna have to wait."

"But I have to get to class."

"I'm sorry. The next two cars are express."

She dropped her bag, dizzy and out of breath. The first trolley rolled into the station, and half the men got on. By the time the second arrived, a crowd had gathered. Even with America still neutral, there had been more and more military activity, and the sight of soldiers wasn't unusual. She just couldn't understand why they had to travel during rush hour.

Finally, the unit was gone, and an empty car pulled in. Considering she had been there the longest, she fought to keep her place at the front. She got on and found a seat near the door so she would be ready to go. It was already 8:45 a.m., and her first class started at nine.

The streetcar rolled into the darkness, around long, winding bends, the screech of metal against metal. Abby was making good time until they breached into daylight at Kenmore Square and traffic was at a standstill. It took another ten minutes to go up Commonwealth Avenue, and by the time she got off, she knew she was late.

She took out the map she got on book day and looked around, but the campus was overwhelming, the buildings all scattered. Scurrying up the sidewalk, she found the address, a five-story structure with a stone façade and arched windows. She took the stairwell up to the third floor, and when she finally reached the room, the door was closed, the class underway.

She nervously grabbed the knob and opened it. All the students looked up at once, most of them men, and she felt the blood rush to her face. The professor glanced over, a thirtysomething lady in a gray suit with a pleated skirt, and Abby was surprised because she had only ever seen women wear dresses.

"May I help you?"

Abby swallowed and held up her curriculum.

"English Romantic Poets?"

"Name?"

"Abigail Nolan."

"Take a seat," the teacher said coldly.

Abby nodded and went down the first row, finding a desk at the back because all the others were taken. Unzipping her bag, she took out her textbook and notebook. But when she looked for something to write with, she realized she had forgotten all her pens and pencils.

Someone tapped her shoulder, and she flinched. Turning, she saw a young man holding out a pen. He was handsome, with a pinstripe suit and dark hair slicked back. She smiled and took it.

By the time the bell rang, Abby had three pages of notes, but she didn't understand any of it. She put her things away and as she went to get up, the young man beside her extended his hand.

"Harold," he said.

They shook, and she gave him his pen back.

"Abby."

"I know."

When she squinted in confusion, he added, "You already announced it to the class."

"My train was late."

"You don't live on campus?"

"I'm...I'm living at home presently."

They walked together up the row, stopping near the door.

"Listen, Abby," he said. "If you'd ever like to grab a drink, listen to some jazz, even just talk, I'm only a short jaunt away on Bay State Road."

"Is that a dormitory?"

As he spoke, she noticed his teeth were perfect.

"No. My own place. I prefer the solitude of—"

"Miss Nolan?"

They both turned, and the professor was calling her.

"Time to answer to the authorities," Harold joked.

With a quick wave, he smiled and dashed out. She walked over to the teacher, who was wiping off the chalkboard. By now, the room was empty, making Abby even more anxious.

"Madam?" she asked, remembering what her mother had told her to say.

"You were late to my class."

"I'm sorry. My train was late."

"You're a commuter?"

"Yes."

The woman paused, and her expression softened. It was the second time Abby had been asked and although she wasn't ashamed, she preferred not to reveal anything that would make her seem different.

"Have you chosen your extracurricular activity yet?" the professor asked.

"Activity?"

"Yes. Required for all incoming freshmen. It's in your handbook."

Abby got flustered. So much paperwork had come with her admissions packet that she hadn't read it all.

"I have not," she said.

"Have you considered volleyball?"

When the teacher looked at Abby's arms, it made her uneasy. But she understood why she did, and after swimming and roaming outdoors all summer, she had more muscle tone than most girls.

"I've never played before."

"We welcome novices. We train twice each week. Tuesday and Thursday evenings. I'm the coach. We meet in the gymnasium on St. Botolph Street."

She spoke in quick, direct sentences that at first seemed unfriendly. But the more they talked, the more Abby realized it was just her personality.

"Yes. I'd love to," Abby said.

"Very well, Miss Nolan. I'll put you on the roster. The first practice is next week."

"Thank you, Madam."

"It's Ms. Stetson."

"Ms. Stetson," Abby repeated.

As she turned to leave, she remembered something.

"Oh, Ms. Stetson," she said, and the professor looked over. "Are there any lockers available?"

"First floor, across from the cafeteria. But you'll have to see the bursar to get a key."

"Thank you."

Abby adjusted her bag over her shoulder and headed for the door.

"And Miss Nolan…"

Abby stopped and turned around.

"That, too, is in your handbook."

Their eyes locked, and Abby thought it was a subtle admonishment until the woman smiled.

CHAPTER TWENTY-SIX

Thomas walked through the shipyard, hands in his pockets and his jacket buttoned up. It was only the second week of September, and already there was a chill in the air, especially by the harbor. With the annex now open, the pier wasn't as crowded, but the shipyard was operating around the clock. Two merchant ships, one with an American flag and the other Panamanian, were being loaded, and over in the drydock sat a British frigate that had been shelled by a U-boat, luckily escaping its torpedoes. It was the first major repair in the new yard, and the fact that it had been damaged by the Germans made it a spectacle. The construction fence was still up, but men peeked through as they passed, and the guards had been instructed to keep everyone away.

As Thomas made his rounds, men nodded, and some even said hello. Although the summer strike had been tense, relations between the longshoremen and security were back to normal and had even improved. But that wasn't the only reason the workers were so friendly.

Mr. Nolan's death on the job had earned his son the respect of the entire union. Management had been generous, covering the cost of the funeral and giving Thomas a week of paid leave. They even offered George a job, which was a surprise because he had a criminal record. But with a labor shortage, firms were more lenient with background checks, and Barrett had commented that they were now taking *crooks and conmen*. Thomas wasn't crazy about his brother working there, but his mother was happy about it, and that was more important.

As he approached the cafeteria door, George was coming out with his lunchbox. On his hardhat was written BHN - 8/4/41 with a cross over it, Mr. Nolan's initials and the day he died written in black marker. All the men did it, a tribute to their fallen coworker, and although Thomas appreciated the honor, he didn't like being reminded about it every day.

"Hey, brother," George said.

Thomas just nodded. George had been friendlier since their father's death, but Thomas still got tense around him. They had clashed all their lives, and even a family tragedy wasn't enough to erase those years of conflict and bad feelings.

"What time you out?" George asked.

Thomas looked at his watch.

"A couple hours."

George lit a cigarette and looked over at the freighter in the distance.

"You know that jalopy is headed to Russia?" he asked.

"I don't keep track."

"And loaded with guns."

Thomas smiled. He had been working there long enough to know gossip was dangerous.

"Then I guess the Russians need our help."

George curled his lips and took another drag. He had put on weight since the summer, but his skin was clammy, his eyes bloodshot. As boys, people said they looked identical, and now they could have been from different families.

"Catch ya later," George said, patting him on the shoulder.

He flicked his cigarette and walked off, and Thomas went into the cafeteria. It was on his beat, but he was also thirsty, and stopping by was more convenient than carrying around his thermos.

As he stood drinking by the water cooler, one of the workers walked up.

"I saw you talking to George Nolan," he said.

Thomas took the cup away from his mouth.

"He's my brother."

"Are you a friend of Father Coughlin too?"

Thomas hesitated. He didn't know much about Coughlin other than that he was some kind of celebrity priest. But if he was controversial enough that even his mother, who had her own bizarre theories, didn't like him, then Thomas knew he was trouble.

"I'm not religious."

"The Father is about more than religion, son."

Thomas crushed the paper cup and tossed it in the basket.

"I'm sure he is," he said, walking away.

Once outside, he continued past the storage area, which was piled high with crates and barrels. With East Boston Works operating as a government contractor, all cargo was confidential, and only the highest-ranking officers were told what was inside. But everyone knew most of it was from the U.S. Army, supplies for Great Britain and Russia. And the forklift operators would have had to be aware of the weapons and explosives, otherwise one mistake could blow the whole place up.

Thomas finished his patrol and got back to the security building right when his shift was ending. After standing for roll, he went to the locker room, changed into his regular clothes, and left. Walking across the yard, he glanced over at the annex where engineers were finishing the repairs on the second crane. Not only had its collapse killed his father, but it had taken out two buildings and a digger. It even started a fire, something Thomas learned from the newspaper report, not from being there.

The truth was, he didn't remember much about that day other

than the chaos and shouting. Barrett had told him his father was in the wreckage, but Thomas didn't realize he was dead until later. Police officers arrived at the cottage the next morning with two representatives from the company. Seeing their grim faces, Thomas knew before they came up the front steps, although his mother held out hope until she heard the words. She took the news with a somber dignity, making the men tea and then asking some questions.

Abby was the only one who got hysterical. After coming back from the beach, her mother met her at the door and told her. She screamed, dropped her things, and ran off. Thomas and George went after her, splitting up and each taking a side of the peninsula. It was almost dark when Thomas finally found her, sitting on the rocks by the seawall, staring out at the horizon.

The entire community had come together in support, reminding Thomas that despite all the changes, Point Shirley was still like one big family. The service was at St. Mary's in East Boston, but after the burial, everyone came back to the cottage. Their neighbor, Mr. Loughran, surprised them with a fully catered spread, including tables, place settings, and a buffet. Considering Mrs. Nolan hadn't had time to prepare anything, she burst into tears at the sight of it, the first time she cried since hearing of her husband's death.

Thomas walked around back to the West Gate where a guard sat half asleep in the guardhouse, his hat tipped back. When he waved, the man got out and unlocked the gate. The timing was perfect because across the street the factory was getting out.

Thomas waited on the sidewalk, one hand in his pocket and his bag over his shoulder. Finally, he saw Connie, who was always one of the last ones out. When their eyes met, they both smiled. She ran towards him, and he ran to her, and they met in the middle of the street. But it was too public for any show of affection, so he just took her hand and they started to walk.

"How was your day?" he asked.

"I cut my finger."

She held up her hand, and there was a bandage around her thumb. Taking her wrist, he gently kissed it.

"That should help."

"It's better now," she joked.

The moment they turned the next corner, she grabbed his arm and pulled him into an alleyway. They embraced against the wall, kissing passionately, arms flailing. When he squeezed her ass, she moaned, and he got the urge to lift up her dress.

"Hey, you!"

Instantly, they separated. Glancing up, Thomas saw an old woman leaning out a tenement window, her face gnarled, a hairnet on her head.

"This ain't no flophouse!" she barked.

When he looked at Connie, she put her hand to her mouth and giggled.

"Sorry, dear," he yelled back. "We must be in the wrong place."

He took Connie's hand, and they walked out to the street. Now he was aroused, tingling with angst. They had talked about sleeping together for weeks but had no place to do it. While her aunt sometimes went out, Chickie was always at home, and since her husband's death, Mrs. Nolan only left for groceries or church. Thomas knew when George worked, but Abby's class schedule was too unpredictable to plan around. When he suggested they get a hotel room, Connie called it *common*, which he took to mean degrading.

······

BY THE TIME they got off the streetcar, it was almost dark. As they walked past the pool hall, Thomas could feel the stares of the men out front. He hated the hoodlums on Bennington Street, whether they were street kids or older guys, and he knew he would have to deal with them once he was a cop. He didn't start training for another month, and the only reason he stayed at the shipyard was to help his mother.

When they got to their street, they stopped at the corner and kissed goodbye. Connie went first, leaving Thomas behind, and he watched her as she strutted up the hill. She didn't want her aunt to know about the relationship, and he understood why. Her deceased husband was Mrs. Ciarlone's half-brother, younger by twenty-six years, the product of a second marriage. Thomas didn't care, but the neighbors were gossipy, so it was better for both of them if no one knew.

After she was gone, he continued up the street. When he walked into the house, he smelled something cooking. Abby was sitting on the couch in the parlor, a book on her lap.

"What's that?" he asked, hanging up his coat.

She held it up, and he saw *Volleyball: Rules & Techniques.*

"You can't learn a sport from a book."

"I have to start somewhere."

Their mother came out from the kitchen with a spoon in her hand.

"I told her she needs to focus on her studies," she said.

"I can do both."

Mrs. Nolan looked up the stairway.

"George!" she shouted, then she turned to Thomas. "Get your brother, please. Tell him dinner's ready."

Thomas yelled up the stairs, and moments later, heard footsteps. George came down barefoot, still dressed in his coveralls from work. His face was red, and it wasn't just from working outside because Thomas could smell booze. All the workers drank, stopping at Sonny's in Maverick Square after each shift, and even his father used to go for the conversation. Mr. Nolan was probably the only one at the shipyard who was dry except the owners who, as his wife claimed, were more moderate in their habits because they were Protestants.

Everyone went into the dining room and sat down. Mrs. Nolan brought in a pot of stew, resting it on a wooden trivet at the center. Once she was seated, they bowed their heads, and she said some words about family, gratitude, and love. She still couldn't mention her husband, but the prayer had all the implications of grief and loss. And his absence was always felt the most when they were all together.

For Thomas, there were brief moments each day when he didn't think about his father, which gave him some hope for the future. He always thought he was tough, and boxing had taught him more about handling the challenges of life than about defeating an opponent. But he was weak when he was tired, especially after a long day. When their mother finally finished and everyone looked up, he saw Abby's face and got choked up.

CHAPTER TWENTY-SEVEN

*A*bby crossed the railyards behind Copley Square and went down a side street, the campus map in her hands. The neighborhood was mostly residential, with blocks of brick townhouses with black shutters and window boxes. Some even had bars on the basement windows. The area didn't look rough, but she had spent so much of her life between East Boston and Point Shirley that the rest of the city was a mystery.

When she came around the corner, she saw a building in the distance, *Boston University Gymnasium* in huge white letters on the side. It looked more like a warehouse than a sports hall. She walked in the rear door and went down a long, dark hallway, following the muted sound of voices and footsteps. Finally, she opened a door and squinted in the light.

"Miss Nolan?"

Standing on the sidelines of a wide, open gymnasium was Professor Stetson. She had on a sleeveless shirt and shorts and socks halfway up her calves.

"Madam…" Abby started before saying, "Ms. Stetson."

"Have your outfit?"

Abby nodded.

"Good. Changing rooms are in the back."

Abby smiled and headed towards them, staying close to the wall and off the court. The gym had two nets, and practice games were underway. She changed into shorts, a top, and her tennis shoes, which were worn after a summer of long walks and beach days. When she came back out, she got goosebumps, and it wasn't just from the cold. Her classmates all had on more modern attire, and she was self-conscious in her shabby clothes.

A whistle blew, and the girls came off the court.

"Abigail?" she heard.

When she looked over, it was Frances, the girl she met on book day.

"Fran," she said, relieved to see someone she knew.

"You chose volleyball?"

Abby thought for a moment. It hadn't really been a choice because the professor had put her on the spot.

"I figured, *why not?*"

"I'm so glad!"

They walked over to the team, where the players were huddled around Ms. Stetson. The professor circled as she spoke, looking everyone in the eye. After going over the rules of the game, she discussed strategy. Lastly, she talked about comradery and the importance of good sportsmanship. She had the confidence of a leader and was much more than the stiff academic Abby met on her first day of class.

Once she was done, she ordered the girls into groups, and they did calisthenics. Abby stretched and twisted, following Mrs. Stetson's orders, straining to touch the floor with both hands. All her life, she had been active, including two years on the track team in high school. But she never thought of herself as athletic, at least not in the way her brother Thomas was.

They trained for over an hour, including volleying with the ball, and at one point she and Frances were opposite each other. When the whistle finally blew, Abby was sweating and out of breath. Ms. Stetson pointed, and everyone headed for the changing room, some girls running.

"Wasn't that a joy?" Frances said.

"I feel like I'm thirty."

"You did swell."

They walked over to the lockers, and everyone started to undress. Abby hesitated, having never changed around people she didn't know before. In the distance, she heard water go on, and when she looked, a line of bare asses rushed past her toward the showers. Being from the city, she never considered herself a prude, but they were all so comfortable in the nude. And while she always thought suburban girls were more modest, she now wasn't so sure.

"You gonna wash up?" Frances asked, holding a towel over her naked body.

"I...I'm gonna take a bath at home."

Frances smiled.

"See you Thursday then?"

Abby nodded, anxious but trying not to show it.

"Yes. Thursday."

Frances walked away, and Abby started to change. Alone in the locker room, she heard something and glanced back. Standing by the door was Ms. Stetson, a clipboard in hand and looking over with a vague expression.

"Did you not bring a change of clothes, Ms. Nolan?"

"I did not," Abby said, and it was a good excuse why she wasn't showering with the rest.

"Before the gates of excellence, the high gods have placed sweat."

Abby smiled awkwardly and turned away.

"Hesiod," the professor said.

"Pardon?"

"The quote. It's Hesiod, the Greek poet."

"Oh."

She finished putting on her dress and tied her shoes, feeling embarrassed with Ms. Stetson in the room. When she had everything in her bag, she went towards the door, the professor standing beside it like a sentry.

"Good evening, Ma'am," she said.

"Good show of effort today, Ms. Nolan."

"Thank you."

......

WITH RUSH HOUR OVER, the journey home was easy, and by the time the trolley reached her stop, it was dark out. Abby was exhausted, but she still had homework, and she worried about how she would manage both volleyball and school. Many of her classmates took on even more, several sports and social organizations, the etiquette club, the debating society, and sororities. One girl she met was in the choir, which met five nights per week and traveled twice per month. For now, Abby's only job was school, but she knew she would have to work again, even if it was only part-time. Her mother had mentioned her going back to the bakery, more of a suggestion than a demand. But with her father gone, Abby knew money would be tight.

She stepped off the streetcar and crossed Bennington Street, the lights of all the shops still on. When she reached the sidewalk, a tall figure walked out of Gittell's Tailor. She thought nothing of it until he turned and came toward her, and something about his posture was familiar. Her heart began to race, and the moment he stepped into the lamplight, she gasped.

"Arthur?"

"Abigail?" she heard, and it was him.

He had on a full Army dress uniform, with a pointed cap tight around his head. Even in the dim light, she could see bars and badges gleaming on his jacket. He hadn't been away long enough to earn any medals, so she assumed they were standard.

But Abby didn't know much about the military. On her mother's side, their family had been in the country for over a century, and no one had served. It had been a source of mild embarrassment for her father and brothers and shame for her mother, especially in a neighborhood with so many veterans from the Great War.

"So nice to see you," he said.

"You're back?"

"For a couple of weeks."

"The Army?" she asked, although she knew.

"My father said you came into the shop."

Abby hesitated, not wanting to seem too eager.

"Perhaps. These last few weeks have been a whirlwind."

"I imagine college is demanding."

She looked up with a sad smile.

"Actually, Arthur, my father died in August."

She watched his face drop, which was no small consolation for her grief. She never asked for sympathy, but sometimes it was nice to know people cared.

"At the shipyard," she explained before he could ask. "A crane accident."

He took a deep breath and looked around.

"I am so sorry."

She raised her eyes, a casual acknowledgment that was sometimes the only defense against her anguish.

"These things happen," she said. "Life goes on…as they say."

She didn't believe it, and she could tell by his reaction that he didn't either. But a street corner in the dark was no place to reflect on the tragedy and hardships of life. She owed it to him and to herself to stay optimistic.

"Do you need anything?" he asked.

"Just a warm bath."

She knew it sounded suggestive, but she didn't care. Under her mother's watch, she had always been proper and polite, but if the girls at school could run around with their fannies out, she didn't mind being a little sassy.

"Abigail—"

"Abby," she said. "My mother calls me Abigail. And the priest at St. Mary's."

The mere mention of church seemed to highlight their differing religions. But she never considered such things, which she saw as the petty prejudices of her parents' era.

"How'd you like to see a movie this weekend?" he asked.

"A movie? I'd love to."

She changed her stance, leaning back on one leg, trying to look sexy despite her sweaty clothes and faded makeup.

"How about Friday night?"

"Friday night it is."

"I'll pick you up."

"I'll be ready."

Slowly, they backed away from each other, and she didn't want to be the first one to turn. When she gave him a cute wave, he waved and went back to the shop. She was surprised because he had been leaving, and it made her think he had been looking out for her.

She headed home, so excited she had the urge to skip. As she approached her street, she saw a couple embracing on the corner. They kissed and then parted, the woman continuing up the hill. Moments later, the man went in the same direction. It seemed scandalous, like a lovers' rendezvous, and after her encounter with Arthur, Abby was intrigued.

She walked behind him and thought it might be Salvatore, Mrs. Ciarlone's son. But when he went up the front steps of her house, she realized who it was and rushed to catch up.

"Hey, lover boy," she said.

Thomas turned around.

"Shhh!"

"Who's the doll?"

"A friend."

"She sure is," she said, giggling.

Thomas frowned and opened the door. When they walked in, Abby immediately smelled something burning.

"Ma?"

She ran into the kitchen, and smoke was coming out of the oven. Turning it off, she noticed a chair tipped over in the corner. And there beside it was her mother.

"Thomas!" she screamed, but he was right behind her.

He threw the table out of the way, and they both knelt next to her.

"She fell," he said, feeling around her head.

"Ma," Abby said, trying to hold back tears.

Thomas shook her, and she flinched but didn't wake up. He put his arms under her, and when he lifted her, rosary beads fell from her hand. Abby picked them up and followed him into the parlor where he rested her on the couch.

"Get some ice," he said.

Abby hurried to the kitchen and looked in the icebox, but it was empty. When she came back out, the front door opened, and George walked in.

"What happened?" he asked.

"She fell."

"There's no ice," Abby said.

Instantly, her mother's eyes popped open.

"Ice in September? Who buys ice in September? It's so pricey."

Abby let out a nervous sigh and glanced over at Thomas and George, who looked as relieved as she felt. Before, their mother always had her husband to look after her and vice versa. Now that he was gone it left a hole in the family they couldn't fill. Abby still had four years of college, but at some point, she wanted her own place. Thomas would be on the police force by Christmas, another step towards independence. Even George had talked about moving out. For the first time, the roles of the family had flipped. Abby and her brothers were now responsible for the care and safety of their mother, a heavy obligation for any son or daughter.

George brought in a glass of water and gave it to her. As she drank, her hand was jittery, her fingers frail. Everyone knew grief was hard on the body, but it didn't explain why she was barely fifty and looked a decade older.

"Ma," Thomas said, crouched on one knee. "You have to see a doctor."

She frowned, waving her hand like she was shooing away a fly. But it was obvious she was shaken, and she still couldn't look anyone in the eye.

"I'm fine," she said. "It's not the first time I've fallen."

CHAPTER TWENTY-EIGHT

Thomas was worried about his mother, but he was also angry. The night she fell, she had been drinking. There was a bottle of gin open on the counter and a broken glass in the corner. She always drank, although in varying degrees, and alcohol was as much a part of her life as her quirky humor and excessive pride. But it had gotten worse since her husband died, and her evening highball had turned into two or more. He could always tell she was drunk by her short, breathless words and her glassy eyes. Her personality changed too, and although she rarely got confrontational, she was annoying with her gossip and strong opinions.

Mrs. Nolan had refused to see a doctor, probably out of embarrassment. She had tripped on the chair and fallen back, hitting her head on the cast iron radiator, knocked out cold. Needing ice, Thomas had gone across the street to ask the McNultys. But he didn't tell his mother, knowing she would have been horrified. For all her talk about community, she never accepted help from neighbors or anyone else. She always blamed the Ciarlones for being unfriendly, yet never even greeted them when they moved in. The family had been living next door for over five years, yet the only person Mrs. Nolan would acknowledge was Chickie.

Thomas walked his beat, his collar up and eyes squinting from the cold breeze. In the distance, the leaves on the few, scattered trees along Border Street were starting to turn, the smell of autumn in the air. It was hard to believe that only weeks before, he had been sleeping without sheets and sweating in the guardhouse.

As he passed by the freight area, the door of the tool shed was open. Peering inside, he saw shadows moving around in the back. He pulled open the door, and the sunlight flooded in to reveal two longshoremen.

"What're you doing in here?" he blurted.

They both turned. Thomas kept a straight face, but inside he was surprised. One of them was the stocky guy who had taunted him during the strike, the brother of the girl George was living with at the beach. Thomas hadn't seen him since the fight that night and always worried about when he would run into him.

"A hook broke on the cargo net," the man said coldly. "We need clamps."

"This area is for foremen only."

They stared back with dry smirks.

"How'd you get in here?" Thomas asked.

"It was open."

Thomas frowned and waved them out.

"Let's go," he said.

When he started the job, he was too easy on the workers, and Barrett had even accused him of being timid. Now that he was going to be a cop, he had to be firm, and there was no better place to practice.

"Recognize me?" the guy asked as they walked out.

"Stan Musial, right?"

His friend chuckled, but the sarcasm wasn't a stretch. With his big ears and crooked smile, he did resemble the baseball player.

As they parted in the lot, Thomas glanced at the man's shirt and saw V. Labadini on his pocket. He didn't expect trouble, but he wanted to know who he was in case there was any.

The two workers walked towards the pier, arms swaggering, and probably feeling insulted. The longshoremen thought they owned the place, and their ability to stop work gave them a confidence they too often mistook for power. They had made some gains in the strike, but with the Department of Defense now overseeing operations, they were losing control.

The shipyard was now on a *wartime footing*, which was unusual considering the country wasn't actually at war. It was the phrase Barrett had used a week before in a special meeting with the whole security staff. With almost eighty percent of the cargo passing through the facility now from the Army or civilian contractors, barbed wire had been installed around the entire perimeter fence and alarm boxes put in some locations.

As Thomas walked past the annex, he peered between the slats of the fence and saw a ship in the drydock. A tricolor flew from its bow, blue, white, and red with a cross in the middle—the flag of the Free French Navy. South of Iceland, it had been attacked, outrunning a German U-boat but blowing out one of its steam engines in the process.

Thomas had been thinking a lot about the war lately, and not only because it was getting worse for the Allies. The more time he spent with Connie, the more he wanted to know about her. He wondered about her past, imagining her family and home life and what she was like as a little girl. He worried she had seen awful things in Italy, but he was too polite to ask. Even with her husband deceased, he couldn't help feeling some tinge of jealousy in knowing someone else had loved her first.

"Nolan?"

Startled, he turned around and Barret was walking toward him.

"Sir?"

"Sticking around for some sightseeing?"

"Sir?"

"Your shift ended ten minutes ago."

Thomas glanced down at his watch, cringing when he realized he had dazed off. But he was more panicked than embarrassed because Connie was getting out, and he had to meet her.

"Sorry, sir," he said, flustered.

"Don't run, son. She'll be waiting."

Barrett gave him a warm smile. He had been kinder to Thomas since his father died. And although he still spoke with the force of a disciplinarian, his voice was somehow gentle, and he overlooked things that before he would have scolded Thomas for.

Thomas grinned and headed to the security building. He quickly changed and ran across the yard, which even in the early evening was bustling. Men now worked around the clock, loading freight and making repairs. At one time, a large merchant ship would have been a big deal, but now they were commonplace, staying only one or two days. Supplies were arriving so fast that deliveries were even coming in the West Gate, and when Thomas got there, a guard was waving a semi-truck through.

He was supposed to be signed out and searched. One of the new rules imposed by the Army was that watchmen and workers were to be treated no differently. But the officer was too busy to bother, so when Thomas looked over at him, he just told him to go.

Across the street, some girls were jumping rope in front of a stoop. The factory was closed, but he didn't have to look far for Connie, who was sitting on the curb. She stamped out her cigarette and stood up, smoothing out her dress.

"Sorry I'm late," Thomas said.

She leaned forward and kissed him on the lips.

"I don't mind to wait," she said in her clumsy English. "Happy birthday."

He smiled.

"Thanks. It's not 'til tomorrow."

Facing each other, she looked up into his eyes.

"I have a gift for you."

She reached into her pocketbook and took out a small box tied with a white ribbon. He thought she was going to give it to him, but instead, she took his hand.

"Come. Let's walk," she said.

They turned at the next corner, a narrow street of brick

rowhouses. They went a few more blocks, and Thomas was curious because it was in the opposite direction of Maverick Station. He could tell she was looking for an address, and when she finally found it, she stopped and handed him the box.

"What?—"

"Open," she said.

He untied the ribbon, opened it, and found a tarnished key inside. When he looked up, she had a mischievous smile. She took the key from his hand and unlocked the front door, and they walked into the vestibule. Putting her finger to her lips, she waved him on, and they went up to the top floor. She opened a door, and they entered a small apartment.

Before he could ask, she turned around and said, "A girl from work stays here."

He paused.

"And where is she?"

"Out until late."

Staring into his eyes, she giggled, and all at once, he understood. He laughed too, the quiet laughter of secret pleasure. She let her pocketbook fall to the floor, and he dropped his bag. In an instant, they embraced and began to kiss. At first, she was more aggressive than him, but it didn't last, and his weeks of pent-up arousal won over.

She pulled her dress over her shoulders, and it slipped off like a sheet. He reached around and undid her bra, sucking her breasts while she groaned. Somehow they made it to the bedroom, a tiny space with a window overlooking the harbor. While she laid down, he tore off his clothes and crawled beside her. Groping and writhing, he got on top and was inside her in seconds.

"It's not safe," he said, stopping midway.

"I've a womb veil."

He frowned, confused.

"A...ah...diaphragm," she added.

She didn't pronounce it right, but he knew what she meant. So he continued, pulling her close and rocking his hips. He had only had sex with two women before. One was a girl he was steady with his junior year in high school, and the other was one he met the previous summer at Point Shirley. Each time was short, awkward, and risky; the fear of pregnancy or disease was enough to stifle any passion. But he was an adult now, experienced enough to enjoy it and accept the consequences.

He moved faster and faster, the bed creaking beneath them. In one final burst, he shut his eyes, and his body froze up. With a muted grunt, he rolled off her and onto his back, gasping and out of breath.

"That was beautiful," she said, snuggling beside him.

Too winded to reply, he just looked around the room, its white plaster walls, bare and cracked. Aside from the bed, the only other furniture was a bureau. In the corner, some plain skirts hung from a rusted nail. When they arrived, Thomas had been too stunned and too excited to notice, but he realized now it was nothing more than a tenement.

"Who did you say lives here?" he asked.

"A friend."

"From work?"

"She's from my town."

"Rome?" he asked, and she shook her head.

"I worked in Rome. I'm from a small village."

"Where is it?"

"It's…in the South," she said.

He nodded and said no more, frustrated but not willing to ruin the moment. They had been together for weeks, and he still felt like he didn't know her. He couldn't blame it on the language difference because her English was decent, and she wasn't shy because she could talk for hours. But whenever he asked about her life, her expression changed, and she gave long, vague replies that said much but revealed nothing.

For the next hour, they lay curled together naked, the only sound their breathing and footsteps in other apartments. As she played with his hair, he stared into her face, seeing the subtle lines around her eyes, her skin youthful but not young. All his other relationships were with girls, and she was the first real woman he had been with. He always suspected she was a few years older, but he never asked because he knew he wouldn't get an honest answer.

He could have held her all night, but it was getting late, and he worried her friend would come home. As he got up and started to dress, she leaned on her elbow and watched him.

"Are you coming?" he asked.

"I have to clean up."

Looking around, he raised his eyes. There wasn't much to clean.

"I can't leave you here."

"You go," she said. "Marta is expecting me. We might have tea."

"And tell her about your dalliance?"

With a distracted smile, she reached into her pocketbook for her cigarettes.

"What means *dalliance*?" she asked, lighting one.

"This."

She blew out the smoke and sat up, holding the sheet over her breasts.

"You Americans have words for everything."

"Maybe we just have a lot to say."

He leaned over and kissed her, the taste of tobacco on her lips. Fixing his jacket, he put his bag over his shoulder.

"See you tomorrow?"

She looked up, her eyes glistening, and gave him a little nod. He felt guilty leaving her alone, but he had no choice. Standing at the door, she blew him a kiss, and he smiled. Then he turned around and walked out.

CHAPTER TWENTY-NINE

Abby stood by the door in her red dress and white sweater. She had tried her hair three different ways and settled on pin curls, swept to the side. The light lipstick she used when she had a summer tan was now too pale, but she didn't have any to match. As she fretted in front of the hallway mirror, George came down in his t-shirt and slacks, got a beer from the pantry, and walked back up without a word.

After work, he spent most of his time in his bedroom. What he did up there was a mystery, but at least he wasn't out getting into trouble. Abby knew he was still under the spell of Father Coughlin because she had seen some copies of *Social Justice* in his bag.

The priest had been taken off the air a year before by the government for spreading propaganda. Using the newspaper, he continued his fight against President Roosevelt and the 'international bankers' he said were trying to drag America into another war. Aside from his political rants, he talked about the struggle to get ahead, which resonated with a lot of frustrated young men. It was a surprise that Mrs. Nolan, who had her own quack ideas about things, forbade George from talking about Coughlin in the house, even threatening to kick him out if he did.

In the parlor, Abby's mother sat listening to *Gene Autry's Melody Ranch* on the Philco radio, the sound of fiddles and banjos in the background. She had been drinking since dinner, highballs without ice because there was none. By now, she was tipsy, but Abby never minded as long as she was in a good mood. When she wasn't, her behavior was unpredictable, and she was still healing from her fall.

"You would think you have a date with Prince George of Wales," Mrs. Nolan said.

Abby smirked but didn't look over.

"Maybe I do."

"Who is this boy again?"

"Not a boy. He's a man."

"Dear, at my age, anyone under forty is a boy."

"I told you. He's from Winthrop. He's in the Army."

Headlights came up the street, and Abby saw a black Buick pull in front of the house. Arthur stepped out, and she got a slight panic, hoping her mother wouldn't remember him from the incident at the cottage. Even if she did, George was really the one she worried about. When she warned him, he said, "I ain't got nothing against the Jew," and she believed it. Since their father's death, he had mellowed, and although far from pleasant, he was easier to be around. Abby wondered if, in some ways, he blamed himself for what happened or if he regretted all the problems he caused, realizing it was too late now to apologize.

Hearing a knock, she licked her lips and then opened the door. Arthur stood on the porch in his military uniform, a bouquet of roses in his hand.

"Hello," she said.

"Hi, Abby."

She looked at the flowers, and he took one out.

"This one is for you," he said, handing it to her. "The rest are for your mother."

The gesture was so touching she got teary.

"Mother," she called, and Mrs. Nolan came over.

"Madam," Arthur said, taking a slight bow, "please accept my condolences for the loss of your beloved husband."

She took the flowers and looked at Abby, so moved she couldn't speak. Her cheeks were red, but she wasn't drunk enough yet to be an embarrassment.

"Why, thank you," she said, her voice trembling.

Abby made quick introductions and got her coat. They said goodbye and left, Mrs. Nolan shutting the door behind them. As they walked down the steps, someone was coming up the sidewalk.

"Abby?" she heard, and it was her brother.

"Thomas, this is Arthur."

As they shook, Thomas didn't seem to recognize him or if he did, pretended not to. Considering all that had happened since, Abby knew the altercation between George and Arthur was like another lifetime ago.

"Where're you two off to?"

"To see a film," Abby said.

"Really? Which?"

"*A Yank in the R.A.F.*," Arthur said.

"I hope it doesn't ring true."

Abby smiled at Arthur, who looked dashing in his uniform.

"The U.S. Army for now," he said.

"Nice to meet you. Have fun."

With a tired wave, Thomas walked up to the house. He was always friendly, but he had a glow on his face and a calmness to his voice that made Abby suspicious. As his twin, she knew him better than anyone and was sure his dreamy mood had something to do with love.

She was so busy thinking about it she didn't realize Arthur was holding the door open.

"This is some machine," she said, scurrying over.

"It's my father's."

It was beautiful, a two-door Buick Coupe with a gleaming chrome grille and whitewall tires, sharper than any car in their neighborhood. She got in and the vinyl seats were smooth against her legs. As they pulled away, she noticed a curtain move across the street, Mrs. McNulty snooping as usual.

......

THE MOVIE GOT out at ten, and when they left the theater, Bennington Street was busy. As they strolled down the sidewalk, older couples nodded to Arthur, acknowledging his service, while younger people didn't seem to care. A generation that hadn't grown up with war didn't have the same respect for soldiers.

"How about some ice cream?" Arthur asked.

"Sounds like a dream."

They walked into the shop, and it was much quieter than in summer. Arthur ordered vanilla, and Abby had the same, which she took as some small sign of their similar interests. They sat in a booth by the window, the cool night air radiating off the glass.

"Why did you join?" she asked.

Arthur smiled.

"To be truthful, mostly for my father."

She tilted her head, looking at him with a warm curiosity.

"He's very patriotic about America," he explained. "He left Russia as a boy. Most of his family died in the pogroms."

"I'm sorry," she mumbled, not sure how to respond.

"It was long before I was born. I only hear stories."

"So when do you go back?"

"A few weeks. I don't have the exact date."

When she found out he had enlisted, she never expected him back so soon, and it was a surprise. But it still sounded short, and she felt a sense of urgency. Abby wasn't as sentimental as other girls, who thought they were in love after one date, but she wanted to get to know him better.

"Do you worry about war?" she asked.

He shrugged his shoulders.

"I worry about a lot of things. But yes, war is one of them."

She smiled at his honesty. He had none of the bravado of other young men she knew.

"Where do you go...?" she asked. "Next."

"Maybe back to Texas. I don't know yet. My unit hasn't been assigned a battalion yet."

"Overseas?"

"Possibly. I hope to stay stateside for now so I can come back to visit my father. He's alone."

"Do you have siblings?"

He nodded and ate the last of his cone, wiping his lips.

"A brother in college in San Francisco. But he's no use. Our mother died five years ago."

The clerk called from the counter, and they both looked over. The shop was closing.

"Perfect timing," Arthur said.

They got up to leave, and he helped her get her coat on. They walked out and started down the sidewalk towards the car. Standing by a lamppost were two young men, both wearing caps and baggy clothes. When Abby and Arthur passed, one of them held out a newspaper.

"Social Justice!"

"I prefer The Globe," Arthur snickered.

Abby laughed, but Father Coughlin's followers always made her uncomfortable. She saw them everywhere: at the subway stations and on street corners. For a while, they were harassing people at Boston University until the administration kicked them off the campus.

"Hey soldier," one of them said, and Arthur stopped. "You know Hitler isn't the enemy?"

"You sound pretty sure."

"I'm damn sure."

"Tell me, then. Who is?"

"The Communists."

"The Je..." his friend said, but the slur was drowned out by a horn. Arthur stood frozen, his expression sharp and staring over. Abby recognized that look before men were about to argue or fight, something she had seen all her life. She was relieved when he shook his head in disgust and continued walking. She knew he wasn't afraid—she had seen him defend himself before. So she assumed he did it for her.

"They're crazy," she said as they approached the car.

He got the door and turned to her.

"They're more than crazy. They're dangerous."

CHAPTER THIRTY

Sitting in the guardhouse, Thomas leaned against the window and tried not to yawn. He hadn't worked a Saturday in weeks. The night before, he had taken Connie to see the Andrews Sisters at the RKO Theater downtown, then to a seedy bar in Scollay Square that didn't check IDs. They didn't get home until after two a.m., walking the mile and a half from Maverick Station because it was too late for a streetcar. The weather was mild, and they held hands the whole time. When someone called for quiet from a second-floor window, Connie yelled back in Italian, and they laughed. Along the way, they passed a public park where they ducked into the shadows to kiss and grope. At one point, he thought they would make it. But even as a horny nineteen-year-old, he liked her too much to dishonor her, and screwing in a public park was no start to a courtship.

Connie was different from any girl he had met before. At times, she was mysterious, almost gloomy, while at others, she was wild and carefree. She was always willing to go out, and he didn't know if it was because she liked him so much or because she didn't have many other friends. Either way, he cherished their time together and hoped it would continue. There was nothing more agonizing in a new romance than the fear it wouldn't last.

With only twenty minutes before his shift ended, he reached for a copy of the Boston Globe someone had left behind. Across the front, the headline was *U.S. TANKER SUNK; 18 SAVED*. The news from Europe had been bad for months, but places like Vilnius or Lwów didn't mean much to people whose forebears came from Ireland or Southern Italy.

Now the war was getting closer, and eight American merchant ships had been sunk by U-Boats. Earlier that week, Thomas had talked with some sailors headed to Brazil, and they were nervous, knowing German submarines were prowling up and down the coast and in the Caribbean. The Russians had stopped Hitler's advance at Stalingrad, and the British were finally striking back with air raids over German cities. But the Wehrmacht still had momentum, and everyone believed America was only months, maybe weeks away from declaring war.

"Thomas Nolan?"

When he looked up, a guard was standing at the window.

"Yeah?"

The man didn't look familiar, which wasn't unusual now. With the increase in operations, the shipyard had been hiring watchmen as fast as workers, and the crew had doubled since he started over the summer.

"Barrett wants to see you in his office."

Thomas nodded and got his coat. They walked between the warehouses and crossed the yard where, in the distance, two tugs were guiding a ship toward the pier. They went into the security building, and he followed the man to the end of the hallway. When Thomas walked into the office, Barrett was behind his desk, and seated around him were three men, one a Boston Police officer and two in civilian clothes.

"Nolan," he said.

"Sir?"

Barrett looked up at the guard.

"Shut the door," he said.

The moment it closed, Thomas got nervous.

"This is Detective Dyson with BPD. And this is agent Taylor and Heinz." After a dramatic pause, he added, "Federal Bureau of Investigations."

At first, Thomas wondered if it had something to do with the men he found scrounging through the tool shed. But he knew the feds would have no interest in a box full of mallets and augers.

"Are you the brother of George L. Nolan?" Taylor asked.

"I am."

"Are you aware of his involvement in the *Christian Front*?"

"The *Christian Front*?"

"It's a political organization associated with Father Charles Coughlin. Do you know who he is?"

Thomas looked at Barrett, then back at the men, feeling slightly defensive.

"Of course. Who doesn't?" he asked.

Taylor accepted his reply with a long nod.

"The *Christian Front* has been highly critical of our president. And they're virulently anti-Semitic."

He looked over to the cop, who Thomas realized was a lieutenant detective by his stripes.

"They've committed a number of attacks on persons of Jewish ancestry," Officer Dyson explained. "Last weekend, they assaulted a group of students in Franklin Park."

The prejudice Thomas experienced growing up was harsh but evenhanded—every group was wary of the other. And while adults were mostly cordial, kids acted out that hatred in a thousand different ways. When the first Italian shop opened up on Bennington Street, an Irish gang burned it down. The owner of a Chinese laundry had been robbed by local teenagers, who yelled *filthy chink* before running out. So it was no surprise that when George and his friends got caught vandalizing a synagogue, people assumed it was adolescent mischief and not bigotry.

"Was my brother involved?" Thomas asked.

"No," Taylor said. "But he's been handing out *Social Justice* at work, trying to recruit his coworkers to the organization."

There was a short silence, and all the men looked at each other.

"Mr. Nolan," agent Heinz said, speaking for the first time. "The *Christian Front* is spreading fascist propaganda at a time when we're on the brink of war. We're monitoring their activity across the country…"

Standing with his hat in his hands, Thomas felt like he was on trial.

"Public places are one thing," he went on, "but we can't have any political unrest at facilities providing defensive support for the United States Government. Not now. Not ever."

"I understand," Thomas said.

"We need you to keep an eye on your brother."

"How do you mean?"

"Just like it sounds," Taylor chimed in. "Let us know if you see any suspicious behavior, here or at home. Report anything to Barrett at once."

It sounded more like an order than a request, and Thomas felt insulted.

"I'm not responsible for what he does," he said.

It was a bold reply, but it was also true.

"Mr. Nolan," Officer Dyson said, a hint of irritation in his tone. "You've been selected for the upcoming police class, have you not?"

Thomas cringed. When he looked over, Barrett sat with his arms crossed, his eyes raised. Thomas hadn't informed the shipyard he would be quitting, and he could tell his boss wasn't pleased.

"That's right."

"We would expect any candidate fit for the department to also be compliant in such matters as regards national security. Wouldn't you agree?"

If it wasn't a threat, it was a strong warning, and the implications were clear. With a bitter smile, Thomas nodded and looked at the officer.

"Yes, sir."

THE LAST HAPPY SUMMER

......

When Thomas stepped off the trolley, the wind hit him, and he shivered. He loved the evenings, but he didn't like that the days were getting shorter because it meant the cold was coming. Winters were long in Boston, the snow starting in late November and staying until April. As a boy, it was fun, and the weather never seemed to get in the way. He remembered snowball fights on their block and building igloos on the flats along Chelsea Creek. One year, the harbor froze, and he and some friends walked the ice over to the North End, only to be turned back by a gang of knife-wielding Italians.

Now the colder months were mostly gloom, or maybe he was just feeling down. The conversation at work left him anxious and confused. But more than anything, he was disappointed because, since their father's death, George's attitude and behavior had improved. During the week, he usually went to his room after dinner, and if he did go out, he was always home before midnight. He had been good to their mother, helping her with the laundry and even with the dishes on nights Abby stayed late for volleyball practice.

Thomas didn't know much about his activities, but if the FBI was involved, they had to be serious. Before Father Coughlin was taken off the air, lots of respectable people listened to him, including the McNultys across the street and the Loughrans, their neighbors on Point Shirley. At the peak of his popularity, Thomas was barely in his teens, too obsessed with baseball and girls to care about politics. But if their father had called the man a *knacker*, the closest he ever got to using profanity, then Thomas knew he was trouble.

As he started up the hill, he noticed a dark shape ahead. Hearing the groan of a woman, he ran towards it.

"Ma?"

Mrs. Nolan was lying on the sidewalk, her arms flailing and trying to get up. Beside her was a torn paper bag, apples, pears, and potatoes scattered around it.

"Ma, what happened?" he asked, kneeling down.

"I tripped."

Her words were slurred, her balance unsteady. He smelled alcohol, but now wasn't the time to discuss her drinking. Taking her by the arm, he lowered her onto the steps, where she sat with her hand over her eyes, dizzy and disoriented.

Headlights came up the street, and when a black car pulled over, Abby burst out of the house.

"What happened?!" she cried, running down the front steps.

"She fell," Thomas said, out of breath.

Abby crouched and put her arm around her mother.

"Ma? Are you hurt?" she asked.

"I'm fine."

"Is everything okay?" someone asked.

Thomas looked up and saw Arthur, dressed in a gray suit, flowers in his hand. The porch light went on next door and moments later, Connie, Chickie, and Mrs. Ciarlone came out.

As Thomas helped his mother up, he didn't acknowledge them. Glancing over, he could tell Connie was concerned, but for now, their relationship was still a secret. With her husband so recently deceased, she told Thomas she didn't want her aunt to know, afraid she might be upset or, even worse, disown her.

"We have to get you to the hospital," Abby said.

"I'm fine."

"I'll take care of her," Thomas said.

"I can take care of myself," Mrs. Nolan mumbled as they walked inside.

Thomas looked at Abby, who stood in a dark dress and coat, her hair done up. Arthur was waiting on the sidewalk like he wanted to help but didn't know how to.

"Go," Thomas said firmly.

With a quick nod, Abby turned around and left.

CHAPTER THIRTY-ONE

Abby ran down the corridor, ten minutes late for her German class because she had gone to the wrong building. Before she entered, she stopped to compose herself, but she was more frustrated than flustered. After a month of college, she still couldn't get organized. Whenever she arrived to class on time, she would forget one of her books; whenever she had all her books and homework, she would show up late.

The week before, she had missed a biology practicum because she didn't know about it. Another time, she turned in a handwritten English paper on Lord Byron that was supposed to be typed. The only thing going well was volleyball, but if she didn't end the semester with all her grades over a C, she couldn't stay on the team. The rule only applied to female students, something she found obnoxious. But she was in no position to challenge it, knowing the administration wouldn't take seriously any student who was failing three classes.

She wanted to blame her academic struggles on work, but she had only been back at the bakery for a week. With money tight, her mother had threatened to sell the summer cottage, their family legacy and a place they all loved. After a short discussion between Abby and her brothers, they agreed to pitch in for the groceries and bills. With everyone now employed, there was no excuse not to, and when they told their mother, she was so happy she cried. Even George was cooperative, promising to buy all their coal that winter from a friend who had a fuel company. Abby's only hope was that it was legal and not stolen, a concern Thomas also had.

Abby opened the classroom door and three dozen eyes looked up. The professor was an older German man who had a handlebar mustache and always wore tweed. Standing at the chalkboard, he glanced over for a moment, but long enough to make her blush. With a sweater over her shoulder, books in her arm, and a pencil in her mouth, she hurried to the back and found a seat.

Taking out her notebook, she copied the sentences on the board as the professor recited them. German was so strange, she thought, the long words and harsh pronunciations. She didn't know why she chose it, other than that she had seen Marlene Dietrich in *The Flame of New Orleans* and loved her accent. George had joked that it might come in handy if they got invaded, a remark their mother scolded him for. With the threat of war so real and so near, there was nothing funny about it. Abby probably should have taken Italian, a language she was more familiar with, but it was too late in the semester to change.

When the class ended, the professor read out names one by one, and students went up to get their exams from the week before. Abby was called last, unusual considering they were in alphabetical order, and she didn't think it was a coincidence. She approached with a timid smile, and Professor Bauermeister held out her test. As she took it, she saw the score at the top and cringed—51% with a red circle around it.

"Ms. Nolan," he said, peering up from his glasses.

"Yes, professor?"

"Please, have a seat."

She put her book bag down and took the chair next to his desk.

"You're having difficulty with my class."

She wasn't sure if it was a question or a statement, but it was the third test she had failed.

"I've never taken German before."

"You've been late a lot."

"Sometimes the trains are delayed."

He squinted, and his expression changed.

"You're a day student?" he asked, a phrase she had never heard.

"I live at home."

"I was a day student. University of Bonn. We lived outside Cologne. I got up every morning before dawn. The trains were sometimes late too…"

Clutching her sweater, she listened closely, and the way he spoke reminded her of how her father used to reminisce about Ireland.

"Are you on scholarship?"

While she kept a straight face, inside she churned. Since starting college, she had been asked the question more times than she could count, and sometimes she felt like a charity case. She knew she wasn't the only one at B.U. on a scholarship, so she worried something about her clothes or accent gave it away.

"I am," she said, finally.

"As was I."

When he smiled, she smiled back, realizing he had asked out of sympathy, not criticism.

"We day students," he said, clearing his throat, "have more burdens than other students. Do you work?"

"I just started. A bakery. A few days a week."

Again, he seemed touched like it brought back memories of his youth. He thought for a moment, rubbing his chin, his thick fingers stained with tobacco.

"Abigail," he began. "You're going to take my exam over."

"Sir?"

"Next week. It won't be the same test, of course. Do you have any favorite subjects?"

She hesitated, not sure what he meant.

"Like academic?"

"I mean in life."

She shrugged her shoulders.

"I like going to the beach."

It sounded cliché, but she was only being honest. The one place she felt at peace was by the ocean, and she did none of the interesting activities of the other girls she met: skiing, travel, dance, or art.

"Very well. All things coastal. I'll provide you a study guide. You can pick it up Wednesday after class."

He wrote something down and nodded with a smile.

"Thank you," she said.

She stood up, so relieved she got emotional. She held it in, walking out with her back arched and chin high, the dignified posture her mother always taught her to show. But by the time she reached the end of the corridor, she had tears in her eyes.

"Abigail?"

She looked ahead and saw Harold from her English class, dapper in his checkered jacket and tie. As he got closer, he looked at her and his mouth dropped.

"Oh, my dear. What's wrong?"

She shook her head, lips pressed together, afraid she might break down.

"Little overwhelmed," she blurted.

They came to a large atrium with portraits of former deans and professors where students rushed by in every direction. She was embarrassed to be crying in public, but everyone seemed too busy to notice.

"Is it school?"

"That's part of it," she said.

When he put his arm around her, she didn't feel uncomfortable. His affection was more like a brother's than anything romantic or seductive, and she trusted him. In class, he always made her laugh, his silly observations and dramatic expressions.

"You know what you need?" he asked.

She shook her head, peering up.

"A stiff drink. And I know just the place."

"I'm only nineteen."

"Darling, age is for debutantes. Any doorman worth his salt can be bribed. When's your last class?"

"Biology at four."

"Good," he said, holding his finger in the air. "Let's meet in front of Marsh Chapel."

Abby hesitated, more out of nervousness than because she had other obligations. They didn't have volleyball practice on Fridays, and Arthur was at his grandfather's birthday party in Salem. Harold had been asking her to go out since they met, and she always had a reason to say no. She was feeling lonely enough at school that she had considered quitting, something that would have broken her mother's heart, and her father's. Socializing was always a good remedy for despair, and there was nothing like the company of a friend.

"Sounds terrific," she said.

"Delightful. See you then!"

......

AFTER SCHOOL, Abby and Harold stopped to freshen up at his place, a second-floor apartment outside of Kenmore Square. It was large enough for a half dozen students, yet he lived alone. The décor was wild, the furniture a mix of elegant and gaudy. On the walls, he had everything from a leopard skin tapestry to a framed portrait of an aristocrat on a horse.

The first thing he did when they arrived was put on some jazz and make cocktails. Like most of her friends, she was no stranger to alcohol and had been drinking since high school. It was usually wine and on occasion hard liquor. The one time her mother caught her, she berated her not for drinking but because it was beer, which she said was unbefitting of a lady.

"Daiquiri?" Harold asked.

She took the glass with a pirouette.

"Why thank you," she said, and they both chuckled.

They sat by the bow front windows on a green velvet sofa that looked like it was from the twenties. Outside, a haze of dusk descended over the street, the foliage on the trees still vibrant but fading. Harold crossed one leg over the other, exposing his argyle socks. She sipped her drink with a smile, and something about his company put her at ease. He had always been nice, but the first time she met him, she was intimidated and maybe even a little suspicious, something she got from her mother. For all her middle-class pride, Mrs. Nolan was anxious about her family's status, and she could be as contemptuous of the wealthy as she could of the poor.

After getting to know Harold, Abby realized the rich had problems too. He was born in Paris, the son of a diplomat from California. When he was ten, his parents divorced, and he and his younger brother moved with their mother to Larchmont, New York. A year later, he was sent to boarding school in Vermont, where he was kicked out for something he didn't want to talk about. While away at another private school in Boston, his brother found their mother dead in the pool, drowned after drinking all day. Harold's life had been tragic by any measure and hearing about it made Abby less bitter about her own misfortunes.

"Was your daddy a lovely man?" he asked.

She couldn't help but grin. Her brothers always made fun of her for calling their father *daddy*, a word she hadn't used around Harold.

"He was."

"It's a tough go. Losing a parent so young…"

His sympathy felt more genuine now that she knew about his mother's early death.

"And your first year at college," he added, shaking his head.

"He never wanted me to go. It was my mother, really."

"Nevertheless, he would have been damn proud."

"Not with my grades."

"Why? Are you failing?"

The semester had been so hectic she couldn't say for sure. She had received some 50s and 60s on exams, but she also got some high marks.

"It's just so much work. I've been thinking of quitting volleyball."

"Has Ms. Stetson been putting the moves on you?"

"What?" she asked with a laugh.

"She spends more time in the girl's locker than her own classroom."

Abby tilted her head, confused.

"She's a regular dike," he said.

"A lesbian?"

When he nodded, she raised her eyes, a look of shocked disbelief. She had heard rumors of homosexuals but never actually met one.

"You really think so?"

"Oh, darling. Trust me, I know."

She put her hand to her mouth and giggled, already feeling tipsy. With her glass empty, Harold took it by the stem and got up.

"Shall we be off?" he asked.

He walked over to the record player, which was playing *Moonlight Serenade* by Glenn Miller, one of her father's favorites. As he went to shut it off, she was tempted to ask him not to, but instead asked, "Where to?"

"Cocoanut Grove. A lovely little place."

"It's hardly little."

"You know it?"

"We went there after my graduation."

Grabbing his jacket, he walked over to a tall mirror beside the bar and put it on, smoothing out the arms, fixing the cufflinks.

"So you're familiar with the Melody Lounge?"

"Am I ever."

When Abby stood, he extended his arm like a duke at a cotillion. With a cute smile, she took it, and together they walked out. For the first time ever, she felt like a lady, which meant so much more than just being an adult. Despite all her doubts about college and life, she knew she could get through both with a friend like Harold.

CHAPTER THIRTY-TWO

Thomas waited by the fence until finally, the factory door opened, and women started filing out. As tired as they looked, they were still chatty, laughing and breaking off into groups. He wondered what it was like inside, whether there was ventilation or like in the guardhouse, they were subject to the whims of the weather. Small manufacturing firms weren't known for the concern and treatment of their employees. They popped up everywhere around the city, usually in rundown neighborhoods, hiring immigrants who couldn't advocate for themselves, either out of ignorance or because they didn't have green cards. Many of the companies were shady, which explained the working conditions, and Thomas understood why his father had been so pro-union.

For once, Connie wasn't last, walking out with the crowd and stopping at the sidewalk. She lit a cigarette and then looked around. When Thomas waved, she smiled and ran over. Leaning forward, she kissed him on the lips. Some older ladies smiled, and a few made sweet remarks. But by now they were used to it because Thomas met her almost every day.

"I thought I'd have to wait forever," he joked.

She looked at him, a hint of sarcasm in her eyes.

"And would you?"

He grinned and looked down, never one for romantic innuendo or double meanings. As he did, he saw a bandage on her finger.

"What happened?" he asked, and they started to walk.

"I put a needle in my finger."

The way she said it sounded funny, but he knew what she meant.

"What do you make?"

"It was stockings and girdles," she said. "Now uniforms."

"Uniforms?"

"Uniforms for the American Army."

When their eyes met, she smiled sadly. She never said much about her husband, other than that they were from the same town and that he had died in Greece near the border of Yugoslavia. But Thomas realized why she was upset and sewing military outfits must have been a painful reminder of the loss. He put his arm around her, and they headed to Maverick Station.

They caught a streetcar and sat alone in the back, snuggling close. By now it was dark, and the temperature had dropped. Thomas stared out the window as they went up Bennington Street. With the shops still open, the road was a long stretch of streetlamps and neon with cars darting in and out of traffic. Some corners had gangs, mostly teenagers, but it was starting to get too cold to linger, and there was always less trouble in the fall and winter because of it.

With only a few weeks until he started police training, he wondered where he would be stationed. He hoped it wasn't East Boston, where he would see people he knew and probably have to arrest a few. But he had no choice, and rookies always got the worst assignments.

When they approached their stop, neither one moved because they weren't going home. They continued another few blocks and got off at Orient Heights, catching the bus to Point Shirley.

Thomas felt mischievous, sneaking off with his girlfriend to the family cottage. He hadn't been back since August, and the ride across the strand was bittersweet. His father's death had shocked him in ways he was only starting to understand. He always considered himself tough, and even as a child, he would never cry. In high school, Coach Fidler had taught him to never show any emotion in the ring, whether it was the thrill of triumph or the agony of defeat. Thomas had carried that lesson into his life, where he was always polite but never said too much.

Now, whenever he thought of his father, he experienced a wave of grief that sometimes left him gasping for air. He always heard that pain lessens with time, but it only seemed to get worse. The week before, he was buying eggs and saw a picture of Heinie Manush behind the counter, his father's all-time favorite player. Mr. Nolan never got over the fact that he left for the Dodgers, and when he was listening to a game, he would blurt out, "Heinie would have hit that!" Thomas must have looked shaken because as he went to pay, the owner, a short German with Windsor glasses, gave him a concerned smile.

As he sat daydreaming, Connie took his hand, and he was startled. The bus pulled over at the last stop, and they were the only ones left. With the wind off the shore, Point Shirley was even colder, but he had her for warmth. He put his arm around her, and they started to walk.

With most homes shuttered for winter, the road was dark and quiet. They turned the corner, and the lights were on at the Loughrans, one of the only families on the block that lived there year-round. Thomas put his finger to his lips, and they crept around to the back. As he reached for his keys, he could hear Mr. Loughlin on his ham radio, his voice muffled by the windows.

Opening the door, he reached for the wall switch, and they walked into the small kitchen. The painted cabinets and cracked countertops looked shabbier in the off-season, or maybe he just never noticed before. Under the icebox, he saw a yellow stain from the ice they had forgotten to throw out. They used to close up the cottage, but last summer was different. With everyone so distraught, they had struggled just to turn the water off and take any food that would go bad.

"So lovely," Connie said.

"It's old, but it's solid."

He waved and she followed. As they walked, the floor creaked, and he could feel a draft. When they reached the front parlor, he smelled mildew and even the faint scent of his father's pipe, although it could have been his imagination. The cottage always reeked, odors trapped from decades of use, and on humid summer nights, it was the worst.

The room had a lamp, but the light from the kitchen was enough, so he didn't turn it on. People on Point Shirley were nosey, and he didn't want to draw any attention. He took her bag, and she sat on the sofa, crossing her legs and running her arm along the back.

"I'll put these in the bedroom," he said, and she gave him a sexy smile.

He went up the stairs, ducking at the top, and down the narrow hallway. As he walked, he could feel the cottage sway and remembered how, as a boy, it seemed so sturdy. At the end, he opened the door to the bedroom. Something didn't seem right, but it was too dark to see. Groping for the lamp, his foot hit something, and he almost fell. The moment he turned the light on, he froze.

Scattered across the room were dozens of boxes, powdered eggs and canned milk, chocolate bars and cooking oil, sacks of sugar and dried beans. Most of it was food, but in the corner, he also saw some Army first aid kits and bottles of cleaning solution. He stood stunned, a quiet rage growing inside him. He didn't have to wonder because he knew. Everything was from the depot at the shipyard; Lend-Lease supplies headed overseas. Not only was George stealing from the War Department, but he was also depriving their allies of aid they needed, a crime that made his activities with the *Christian Front* seem like jaywalking.

"Are you coming?" he heard.

"Be right there."

He turned off the light and shut the door. Opening the closet, he got two blankets and went back downstairs.

"We'll sleep here," he said.

"Why not the bedroom?"

"Um...it's filthy."

"Are you okay?"

He hesitated, distracted, and he still couldn't believe what he found. But nothing about George surprised him anymore, and he wouldn't let it spoil their night. Forcing a smile, he looked across at her.

"How could I not be?"

He made pancakes from a box of Pillsbury mix he found in the cupboard and cut up some apples he had brought from work. They had dinner in the parlor under candlelight, and it felt good to finally be alone with her.

When he asked if she was done, she took a slice of apple, put it in his mouth, and he ate it. They both laughed, and he got the plates and took them into the kitchen. With the plumbing off, he had to wash everything with water from a jug they kept beside the sink.

Thomas had been secretly going to the cottage for years after they closed it up, and he wasn't the only one. Once, he arrived to find George and his friends drunk off whiskey they had stolen from a truck. Whether their parents were ever aware, he didn't know, but he always cleaned up and never made any noise. No one was supposed to be there after August, and they got an abatement on their taxes because it was a summer house.

He walked back into the parlor where Connie was now laying across the sofa, her hands under her head. She moved aside, and when he sat down, she started to rub his leg. It didn't take much to get him aroused, and he immediately crawled beside her. With the shadows of the candles flickering on the walls, he found her lips, and they kissed. Too chilly to get naked, he just undid his pants, and she pulled up her skirt. Once he was inside her, they wriggled and squirmed, their movements restricted by the narrowness of the couch. It was over in minutes, and they lay sweaty and embraced.

After they both finally caught their breaths, she brought her face to his and looked him in the eye.

"I love you," she said.

His mouth twitched as he tried to form a smile. Stumped by her words, he said nothing and pulled her closer. Maybe he was scared, he thought, because he had been crazy about her since the day they met. But he was only nineteen and starting a career in two weeks. With his mother struggling at home and war on the horizon, it seemed an awful time to fall in love.

Still, he couldn't imagine life without her, their rendezvous after work, weekends at the movies, or an occasional show in town. Even on days they didn't go out, he enjoyed just taking the streetcar home together, walking her to her house. As he held her, he experienced a feeling of peace and contentment like never before.

Sometime later, he woke up alone on the couch. For a second, he panicked until he noticed her shoes on the floor. He got up and looked around, listening to hear if she was in the bathroom. Smelling cigarette smoke, he opened the front door and saw her on the porch steps.

"Connie?" he asked, whispering.

When she glanced back, he walked out and sat down beside her. The air was brisk, but it didn't feel uncomfortable.

"You snore," she said, and he chuckled.

"My father snored."

"Are such things inherited?"

"Habits are, maybe."

"Which explains my love for cigarettes."

"Your parents smoked?"

"Just my mother. My father was a boxer. He said it was bad for the lungs."

Thomas' face brightened.

"I used to box," he said.

"I know."

"How?"

"Chickie told me."

He smiled, thinking about the strange little girl next door. In high school, he used to train in the yard on weekends, doing calisthenics and shadowboxing around the old elm tree. Chickie would often stand by the fence and watch, laughing every time he punched the air. Sometimes she would say something, but he could never understand her.

"What's wrong with her?" he asked.

Connie narrowed her eyes, smiling dreamily. He hoped the question wasn't too harsh.

"Nothing," she said, tapping the ash off her cigarette. "She is just a different kind of child."

He accepted the answer with a warm smile. All his life, he had met people who didn't fit in, cripples and crackpots, drunkards and the demented. When he was a boy, there was an old lady who would walk around in a nightgown and talk to herself. Behind the horse stables on Bennington Street, a homeless veteran missing one eye and one arm used to growl at kids. In the hardscrabble streets of the city, no one escaped the afflictions and savagery of life, and Thomas sometimes wondered what his curse was.

"A light," Connie said, pointing.

When he looked up, he saw a tiny flicker in the harbor. It would flash for a second, stop, and then start again.

"Morse code."

She turned to him, her dark hair tousled from the breeze.

"What is Morse code?" she asked, sounding more like *Morz*.

"Signals. For the Navy."

"To prepare for the war?"

Thomas chuckled, but it was mainly from nerves. With a bright future ahead, he didn't want to think about the war, and losing his father seemed like enough tragedy for one year. But everyone knew it was coming, and the only question was when. For Connie, the prospect must have been particularly horrifying. Her husband had been killed, and she got out of Italy just in time. Thomas didn't know if she had expected salvation or safety in America, but he could sense the panic in her voice, and some part of him felt it too.

"Come," he said, avoiding the question. "Let's go get some rest."

CHAPTER THIRTY-THREE

Three days a week Abby got up before dawn and went into the bakery. She only worked until 8:30, catching the trolley to class right after, but at forty cents an hour, it gave her spending money. And on weekends, she could usually pick up a longer shift. She had been working so long at Betty Ann Bakery that she had known the original owner, an old Italian woman who died when Abby was in eighth grade.

As the sheet came out of the oven, she would sprinkle powdered sugar or drizzle icing, depending on the item. Normally, it was donuts, tarts, and pies, but tomorrow was Armistice Day, and the baker had made shortbread cookies in the shape of lilies. While the girls worked the front, Abby finished the pastries in the kitchen and took them out to the display cases. But she didn't always get that far because Tuesday mornings were busy.

"Abby...?"

She glanced back to see Eve.

"Two dozen Danishes, quick!"

Abby worked fast, but she was still dragging from the weekend. Friday she had gone to the Cocoanut Grove with Harold where he got so drunk he knocked over a palm, shattering its terracotta vase. At first, he was horrified until the staff came over and one of them was Mrs. Ciarlone's son. Sal was the head waiter, which explained why he worked late and Abby never saw him. Either way, he had been incredibly kind, cleaning up the mess and even giving them free drinks.

Aside from the mishap, it was the most fun she had had in months. Harold made her feel better about college, and life was easier when you had an ally. After several Martinis, they danced the rumba, and she didn't feel guilty, knowing Arthur wouldn't have minded.

"Abby?" someone called.

She looked back, and this time it was Loretta.

"Almost ready."

"Someone's here for you," she said, leaning in the doorway, her face beaming. "A man."

As surprised as Abby was, she had to smile. The counter girls were always so giddy around men. She put down her piping bag and wiped the frosting from her fingers. Shaking the flour off her apron, she walked out to the front where she saw Arthur standing by the wall in his service uniform. Just his presence seemed to change the mood of the place, housewives staring over, and Abby got a twinge of jealousy.

"Arthur?" she said.

"What time are you off?"

She glanced over at the clock.

"Ten minutes."

"I'll wait."

She nodded nervously, wondering why he had come.

"Okay," she said.

She hurried back into the kitchen and finished the last three pans of pastries. As she washed up, Eve walked over with a wide grin. Short and mousy, she was the gossip of the staff, and Abby had worked with her for years. She graduated from East Boston High when Abby was a sophomore, going from part-time to full-time at the bakery while continuing to live at home with her parents.

"Is that him?" she asked.

"How'd you guess?"

"What a dreamboat."

THE LAST HAPPY SUMMER

Abby rolled her eyes and rushed to get her coat and bag, Eve following close behind.

"Is he Italian?"

Abby stopped and turned. She used to believe shallow qualities like religion and ethnicity weren't important. But the more time she spent with Arthur, the more she worried about what people would think. In East Boston, like everywhere, ancient prejudices always simmered below the surface of polite society.

"Actually, he's Jewish."

Eve's expression changed, but her reaction was unclear.

"Even better!" she said, finally.

Abby smiled, some small relief in days of uncertainty. When she walked out to the front, the crowd had thinned, and Arthur was gone. One of the girls pointed, and Abby could see him through the glass. She buttoned up her coat and went outside.

"What a surprise," she said.

Usually they would kiss when they met, but the sidewalk was too public, and she felt dirty after working all morning.

"Abigail," he said.

He smiled but seemed distracted.

"What is it?"

"I'm leaving…"

She looked up at him, frowning in confusion.

"This evening," he added.

"Tonight?"

He nodded.

"I fly to Camp Pendleton then to Hawaii."

Her mouth started to water as she felt herself getting upset.

"Hawaii?"

"Gonna learn to fly planes," he said with an anxious grin.

"I thought you're in the Army?"

"Army *Air Corp*," he said with emphasis. "Now we're called the *United States Army Air Forces*."

"When will you be back?"

"Our training is eight weeks. Possibly for a weekend in January. I don't know."

When he first returned, he told her his orders could arrive any day. But he had already been home three weeks, and she had hoped it would continue. She'd even bought them tickets to see Eddie Cantor in *Banjo Eyes* on Saturday, a surprise for his birthday which, coincidentally, was the day after George's. She wanted to give him something to remember her by, some sort of insurance, and if it had to be her virginity, she would have done it.

They faced each other, their eyes locked, and although she wanted to be angry, she couldn't.

"I've gotta go," he said.

She dropped her bag, jumped forward, and wrapped her arms around him.

"I'm gonna miss you."

"Me too."

After they finally let go, she pushed her hair from her face, secretly checking for tears. Arthur backed away, not breaking his stare.

"Write me," she said, standing on her tiptoes and waving.

"I will."

"Soon."

"The first chance I get."

He opened the door of his father's Buick and gave her one last smile, a tender smile that was tragic too. Then he got in. As he pulled into traffic, Abby watched the car until it crested the hill and was out of sight. Standing on the sidewalk, she had never felt more alone, and the gray sky now seemed gloomy. She had never expected Arthur to be around forever—she didn't know what she expected. But after her father's death, she couldn't take much more heartache, and it was hard to lose two men.

Hearing the bell of a streetcar, she reached down for her bag. Her first class started at nine-thirty, and she couldn't be late. As she turned to go, her eyes swept the windows of the bakery, and the entire staff was looking out.

......

THE LAST HAPPY SUMMER

ABBY GOT to class on time, but the professor was late. The room was filled with quiet chatter. Looking around, she smiled at some of her classmates, but she really didn't know anyone, and college was much more impersonal than high school. Harold was out until Wednesday, having gone to see an aunt in upstate New York whose husband recently died. With his brother attending nearby Cornell, he said he was going to try to visit him too. Abby wondered why he didn't wait for a long weekend or Christmas break. He didn't seem to worry about school like she did, which was one of the reasons she liked him. While she took things too seriously, he didn't take them seriously enough. Either way, she was sure that without his calming influence, she would have cracked up by now.

Of all the times she could have used Harold's company, it was now. Arthur's sudden departure left her stunned, and she couldn't think straight. They had only just started to get to know each other, and he had been whisked out of her life. It was the same hollow feeling she had two summers before when Jack Ellsworth left Point Shirley, and she never saw him again. She didn't know much about love, but if this was what it was like, she thought, then she'd rather be a spinster.

Ms. Stetson entered, and the room went quiet.

"My apologies," she said.

Clearing her throat, she opened the textbook and called out the poem: *Sonnet Written in the Church Yard at Middleton* by Charlotte Smith. She got her pointer, something she always held even when she wasn't pointing. She was sterner in the classroom than she was at practice, where she sometimes smiled and even got excited. They had played three games so far, all with local female colleges, and she once threw a fit after the referee made a bad call. Abby couldn't say she liked Ms. Stetson, but she respected her, knowing it was hard for any woman to be a professor, never mind a coach.

"The assignment is to write a poem in the spirit of the English Romantics…"

There was a collective sigh. It was their first creative writing assignment—everything else had been reading and analysis.

"About someone important in your life," she added. "Due the Tuesday before Thanksgiving break."

With class over, students started to get up. Abby put her things away and was almost at the door when Ms. Stetson called for her.

"Yes, Miss?"

The teacher peered up, her small mouth pursed. She was the only woman Abby ever met who could stare without blinking.

"You seemed distracted this morning."

"I'm sorry."

"Are you unwell?"

"A little tired. I had to work this morning."

Their eyes remained locked, and Abby got uneasy. So far she had gotten a B- and two C's, her lowest grades ever, and she didn't know if she was in trouble.

"I understand," the professor said, finally.

With a quick nod, she returned to her work, and Abby walked away.

"One more thing," she said, and Abby turned. "Good play last week."

Abby smiled. If she couldn't get praise for her grades, she would take it for athletics. In the game against Emmanuel College, she had closed the gap with a spike. Although they lost in the final set, she was so thrilled she told her mother, who knew nothing about volleyball but said *at least it was a Catholic college.*

"Thank you."

CHAPTER THIRTY-FOUR

Thomas walked down the dock past the *HMS Newcastle*, a British Navy cruiser whose six 4-inch guns were pointed at the city. It was the first foreign warship to arrive at the facility and made a mockery of American neutrality. At six hundred feet, it took up two berths, larger than the merchant ships usually in port.

He waved to some soldiers on the top deck, who stood smiling and smoking cigarettes in the crisp autumn sun. Unlike the crews of other allied countries, the British weren't required to quarantine. Or if they were, they ignored the rule, and the MP's who now guarded all military ships didn't seem to care. Two nights before, a dozen sailors showed up blind drunk at the main gate, having walked all the way back from downtown.

As Thomas passed the security building, someone whistled. He turned and saw Barrett standing at the door, calling for him. The shipyard was busy enough that he went days without seeing him, but after the meeting with the police and FBI, he dreaded this moment.

"Sir?"

"In my office…please."

Before Mr. Nolan died, Barret would never have said *please*, and Thomas appreciated the courtesy. He followed his boss down the hallway into his office. Barrett removed his hat, something he always did, a remnant of military or old-world etiquette. Then he walked behind his desk, took the chair, and looked across to Thomas, his hands clasped.

"You know I could terminate you right now?"

The question caught him off guard, but then Barrett was never subtle.

"Sir?"

"For not disclosing future employment intentions."

"I start police training next week."

Barrett frowned.

"So you're submitting your resignation?" he asked.

"I already did…at the business office."

"And when were you going to inform me?"

"I thought they would."

Barrett made a sour grin like he had been outsmarted. But Thomas had only followed company procedure, taken from his employment handbook.

"Any more on all this Christian Front business?"

Thomas stayed calm, but he was starting to sweat, and it was over his brother's crimes, not his political affiliations. Stealing from a shipyard was a federal offense, and the fact that it was military property made it worse. Although he had agonized over the situation, it was mostly disappointment because he had never once considered snitching on George.

"I've seen the newspapers in his bedroom," he said. "That's about it."

"You two live together?"

"At home…with our mother."

"Has he been associating with anyone new? Has he said anything unusual?"

"To be honest, we don't talk much."

"Since the accident?"

"Long before that."

"A bit of a hooligan, is he?"

Thomas smiled. The question reminded him of how his father used to talk.

"He's always been a handful."

Barrett nodded, a hint of compassion in his expression.

"I had a brother like that. Alan, was his name—"

"Was, sir?"

His boss looked up, and their eyes locked.

"He died at seventeen, trying to steal a mare. A farmer shot him."

"I'm sorry."

In their five months working together, it was the most Barrett had said about his personal life. While he was strict, Thomas always respected him, maybe even liked him. When he was called into his office the week before, Barrett had put on a good show for the police and FBI. But it was obvious he didn't care, and the politics of the workers weren't the responsibility of the guards.

"Nolan," he said, standing up. "You've been a good watchman."

"Thank you, sir."

With the meeting over, Thomas felt relieved. He had expected his boss to be angrier.

"I don't know much about this priest nonsense. But they're watching your brother, and close. You might want to tell him to mind who he fraternizes with."

Thomas nodded but didn't respond, knowing that George would never take the advice. Barrett extended his hand, and they shook for the first time.

"Come see me when the shift ends Friday. We'll grab a few of the lads and go have drinks at Sonny's."

"I will."

......

THOMAS WALKED with Connie up the hill, and they stopped in front of her house. It was strange living side by side, like a modern-day Romeo and Juliet, and sometimes they even waved between the windows. He liked that she was so close, but it could also be difficult. Whenever he got the urge to see her, he couldn't just walk over, and she said she felt a similar frustration. Her aunt still wasn't aware they were together, and Thomas hadn't told his mother. Considering they always parted with a kiss, he was sure some of the neighbors knew, especially with Mrs. McNulty always looking out the window.

"See you tomorrow," he said.

He tried to pull away, but she held onto his hands, staring with a playful grin. Then she let go and dashed away, glancing back every few steps, teasing him with a smile. Thomas stood watching, as amused as he was captivated. She was the only girl who could make him blush.

When she got to the porch, Chickie opened the door, and she went in. Thomas walked over to his house, hanging up his coat and loosening his boots, his feet sore from work. Abby was in the dining room, her books spread across the table. With its mahogany China cabinet, credenza, and silk wallpaper, it was like a European salon, and as kids, they only ate there on special occasions. But Abby said she couldn't use her bedroom, which was too small and didn't have a desk, and Thomas was surprised their mother let her study there. Whether Mrs. Nolan had lightened up or given up, one thing was certain; somewhere between George's delinquency and her husband's death, she had let her standards go.

"Where's Ma?" Thomas asked.

"Church."

"Church?"

"She joined some ladies' group."

Although he smirked, he was glad to know she was getting out. He drifted into the kitchen, where he saw something on the stove under tinfoil.

"She left you some meatloaf," Abby said.

"Thanks."

Reaching for a fork, he had a few bites, but he wasn't too hungry because he had had a late lunch. When his coworkers found out he was leaving, one of them brought in pizzas from his parents' diner. Thomas had never had it before, his mother calling it *peasant food*, and he was amazed at how good it was. They had a small going away party in the cafeteria, and even some of the longshoremen joined in. Thomas had always known the job was temporary, but he realized he was going to miss some of the guys. And with his father's death, the shipyard now had sentimental significance.

He washed down the meatloaf with some milk and went upstairs. At the end of the hallway, the light was on in George's room. While the house had four bedrooms, he and his brother used to share one because their mother wanted to keep a place for guests. Back when their uncle and aunt would visit from Maine, it made sense. But once they passed away, Thomas took the room, and his parents couldn't object. For all Mrs. Nolan's pride about her family's history and legacy, they had no one left in East Boston, and their nearest relatives were some second cousins in Belmont.

He nudged open the door and saw George lying on the bed in his work clothes, a can of beer on the table and his ear against the radio. The window was up, and a cigarette was smoldering in an ashtray on the sill.

Before Thomas could speak, his brother said, "The Brits just invaded Libya. 750,000 of them."

Thomas smiled. Any news about an offensive against the Germans was good. But he hadn't come to talk about the war.

"Can you turn that down?"

Taking a drag, George reached for the dial.

"What's up?" he asked.

Thomas walked in and shut the door.

"I was at the cottage last weekend," he said.

"That's good for you."

Thomas ignored the sarcasm.

"What the hell was all that in the bedroom?"

"Just some stuff I bought."

"You mean you stole?"

George's expression sharpened, and he sat up.

"I didn't steal nothin'. Some guys at work were selling it."

Thomas hesitated. It was an excuse he hadn't anticipated and one that could be true. Petty theft had always been a problem at the shipyard, so common the owners even factored it into their business costs. But with the Military Police onsite and security at an all-time high, he found it hard to believe that any workers would be so bold.

"You bought all that?"

"Cold cash."

"For what? What're you gonna do with powdered eggs and powdered milk?"

"Maybe I'll make a powdered omelet."

Thomas smirked. As he turned to go, he saw some copies of *Social Justice* on the nightstand.

"You still reading that shit?" he asked, nodding.

"If the truth is shit then I'm drowning in it."

When their eyes locked, Thomas wanted to bring up the *Christian Front* to see what he would say. He had also considered telling him about the meeting with the police and FBI. But Thomas had learned long ago that trying to protect his brother from his own mischief would only get him caught up in it. George always had to learn the hard way. Thomas didn't owe it to him to reveal that he and his cohorts were being watched. If his brother was foolish enough to spread racist propaganda at work, he would have to pay the price. Since their father's death, they had reached a place that, although not quite a truce, was a fragile peace. And Thomas didn't want to upset it.

As he walked out, George called to him, and he stopped.

"What?"

"Mind shutting the door?"

CHAPTER THIRTY-FIVE

As Abby walked down the hallway, it was much quieter than on other floors. They were all offices for professors and other staff, nameplates on the doors, file baskets filled with mail on the walls. She had never come to see a teacher before.

The makeup exam from her German professor had been hard, but the topic she picked gave her confidence. Somehow it was easier to remember things when you could visualize them, and the seaside vocabulary was etched into her mind: badeanzug, springflut, liegestuhl. Even the grammar part was eerily relevant to her life: *The girl met her boyfriend at the beach.* (*Das Mädchen traf ihren Freund am Strand.*) or *The tide comes in at 9 a.m.* (*Die Flut kommt um 9 Uhr.*) Because she had difficulty saying his name, he even included a surprise question on its pronunciation, although she didn't think it would count towards her score.

She was touched by the professor's kindness. Her first semester had been one of the loneliest times in her life. Unlike her mother, she was proud but not stubborn, and she was willing to take all the help and support she could get. Abby knew it wasn't just college; her father's death was still as fresh and painful as the day it happened. Combined with the whirl of school, work, and volleyball, at some points, she thought she was losing her mind. The only thing that kept her going were those glimpses of encouragement, just in time and always unexpected. Without Harold and Frances, she would have surely dropped out, and they taught her more about friendship than all her years in high school.

Turning the corner, she read off the numbers until she got to Dr. Bauermeister's office, the last one on the right. As she approached the door, she fixed her sweater and smoothed out her dress, nervous but eager. She went to knock but stopped. Scraped into the wood were some words, faint but unmistakable:

NAZI GO HOME

SHE GASPED, horrified beyond belief. While some part of her was angry, another part felt afraid. Since Hitler's rise to power in the 30s, people had been quietly scorning the Germans, and in a city of immigrants, it didn't take much to arouse prejudice. But aside from the professor, the only German she knew was the old man who owned the grocery store on Bennington Street. George had grumbled a few times about *Krauts*, but the German community in Boston was too small to be a threat.

As Abby stood frozen, the door swung open. Standing there was Dr. Bauermeister, dressed in his tweed coat and not wearing a tie.

"Miss Nolan," he said, greeting her with a polite smile.

She was so stunned she couldn't speak. He looked at the door and then at her, frowning subtly.

"Come in, please."

She nodded and followed him into the office, where he invited her to sit and flipped through some files on his desk.

"I see you noticed the eloquent message inscribed on my door?"

"It's awful. I'm sorry."

With his back to her, he lifted his arm.

THE LAST HAPPY SUMMER

"Very kind, but don't be. I could've had it removed weeks ago."

"And you didn't?"

He turned around, a paper in his hand.

"No," he said, bluntly. "The only way to fight bigotry is to expose it..."

When he handed her the test, she took it but didn't look.

"I expect it to get worse before it gets better, as they say."

"What could be worse?"

Folding his hands, he glanced down thinking.

"The sentiment is not altogether ignoble," he said, and she had to unravel the words in her head before she understood them. "Mr. Hitler is a devil of a man. But the anger is misdirected. Not all Germans are Nazis."

She hesitated, not sure how to reply. The world was complicated, and sometimes she was ashamed of what she didn't know.

"Of course."

"So," Bauermeister said, becoming suddenly cheery. "How are your studies?"

"Better. It's been a difficult adjustment."

"To university or to adulthood?"

"Both."

He let out a quiet laugh. In the confines of the small office, she smelled cigar smoke on his breath, and it reminded her of her father.

"You're working, is it?" he asked.

"Parttime, at a bakery."

"And have you any siblings?"

"Two brothers."

"Oh, dear," he said, raising his eyes. "Are they in school?"

"One is starting with the police next week. The other works at the shipyard."

"Fine occupations, both. And quite necessary considering the state of the world at present."

Like most professors, he came off as formal, which was sometimes intimidating. But aside from Harold and Frances, he was the first person at B.U. to ask about her life, and the more they talked, the more she liked him.

"And your parents? They must be quite proud."

"Yes..." she said, stumbling. "Actually, my father passed away in August."

When his face dropped, she cringed, wishing she hadn't mentioned it. Her father's death was starting to feel more like a mark than a misfortune, and she was tired of the sympathy.

"Miss Nolan, I am so very sorry."

Although no different from the dozens, maybe hundreds of other condolences, it somehow sounded more sincere, and she responded with a warm smile.

"Thank you."

He cleared his throat and sat up.

"Now, you keep it up. Nose to the grindstone. I've been in this business a long time. You've the brains. All you need is perseverance."

Holding back tears, she reached for her bag and got up to leave.

"Thank you, Professor."

As she walked out, she didn't look at the door, knowing it would only ruin the pleasant meeting. They parted with a smile, and she continued down the hall, composed but also anxious. The moment she turned the corner, she glanced down at her test. Written on the top, in black marker with a circle around it, was her grade: 92%.

......

ABBY GOT to the gymnasium right before seven and would have been earlier except she had to turn in a project for World History. She had finished it on Monday, but after someone spilled batter on her bag at the bakery, it had to be retyped. The assignment was on Pompeii, a place she found so fascinating that its destruction by a volcano was just a sidenote. The city was as vibrant and cosmopolitan as any, with restaurants, theaters, public baths, and even brothels. Reading that the street signs were in five different languages, she couldn't help but think of East Boston.

When she walked in, she was surprised to see people in the stands. But she knew most were family and friends because no one came out to watch girls' volleyball. Tonight was a home game, the first in two weeks, and they were playing Mount Ida College, a small private school in Newton.

Over in the corner, the team was standing around Ms. Stetson. In her elegant gray suit and oxfords, she looked out of place in the dingy gym, but she always dressed up for games.

"Miss Nolan," she said, looking up from her clipboard.

"Sorry I'm late."

"Get changed, please."

Abby ran toward the locker room, Frances waving to her as she passed. She found a bench, quickly undressed, and took out her uniform. Although their shirts had numbers, the university budget for girls' sports was so low they couldn't afford names or decals.

"Abigail?"

Startled, she turned around to see Ms. Stetson. Sitting in her bra and panties, Abby was uncomfortable enough that she blushed.

"Miss?"

"You'll be setter tonight. Miss Davison is out sick."

"Yes, Miss."

Abby stayed calm, but inside she got anxious, knowing it was a hard position. As someone new to the game, she usually played libero, and once, middle blocker.

Pulling on her shorts, she felt a curious chill, and when she looked back, Ms. Stetson was still there.

"Miss?" she said.

The professor blinked like she had been daydreaming. Then she collected herself and gave Abby a curt smile.

"Match starts in five."

The game went for almost two hours and by the fifth set, Abby was exhausted. She had made a couple of good saves, and at one point, even set Frances up for a spike. But in the end, they lost, and no one was surprised. One of their best players was out, and Mount Ida, although much smaller, was an all-girls college so had more talent to choose from.

Abby came off the court, sweating and gasping for breath.

"Good show," Frances said.

Abby smiled, but she never took praise well, whether it was deserved or not.

"Wish it had been better."

"C'mon, Abby. Mount Ida is 5-0. They're top in the league."

As they headed to the lockers, Abby heard someone call her name, and they both stopped. Looking over, she saw Harold coming down the bleachers, a wide smile on his face. Dressed in a blue chalk stripe suit and silk tie, he made Ms. Stetson's outfit look like hand-me-downs, and even some of the female spectators turned.

"Now who's that?" Frances whispered, gripping Abby's arm.

Abby chuckled but mostly from excitement. Considering Frances and Harold were her two best friends at college, she had been excited for them to meet.

"How was New York?" she asked as he approached.

"My auntie was gloomy, poor thing. It's not easy."

"And your brother?"

"I left him passed out blotto on a statue of Ezra Cornell, if that's any indication."

"Harold, this is Frances…Fran," she said.

Taking a bow, he motioned as if removing a hat, which was ironic because he never wore one.

"A pleasure, *Frances Fran*," he said.

They all laughed, and he looked at Abby.

"Say, Abigail, why don't you spiffy up and we go grab a quick bite?"

After a long day, she was tired, and nothing with Harold was quick. She had to get up early for work and had an algebra exam in her first class. Her mother had been struggling at home, drinking every night, and even with her brothers around, Abby worried about her. In high school, she used to feel careless going out, and now she felt guilty.

As Harold stood waiting, he looked at Frances.

"How 'bout you, dear? Won't you join us?"

"I'd love to!"

They both turned to Abby who, much like the game against Mount Ida, felt outmatched. With her grades suffering, she had a thousand reasons to say no, but she knew friendship was as much about being spontaneous as it was about socializing. All her life she had been cautious, and if going out on a weeknight with friends set her back, she was willing to take the risk.

"Sure, let's eat."

CHAPTER THIRTY-SIX

Thomas sat at the table in Sonny's, a rundown barroom across from Maverick Station. Situated between a fleabag motel and a liquor store, it had a brick façade and neon sign. The bulb of the "S" had been blown for so many years that everyone called it *Onny's*.

Inside there were four pool tables in the back, and a jukebox in the corner, which played a steady stream of Duke Ellington and Cab Calloway. A few laborers lingered at the bar, men from the shipyards and plants along the waterfront. But it was long past happy hour, and the place was filling up with people from the neighborhood, guys in flashy suits, girls in tight dresses.

When Barrett ordered more drinks, a chunky waitress nodded and went to get them. Two dozen coworkers had shown up to say goodbye, but most just stayed for one beer. Although barely in their twenties, a lot of them were already married with kids, which gave Thomas a feeling of romantic urgency. Many were familiar, men he had started with back in July, but with almost eighty guards now on staff, it was hard to know them all. And although flattered by the turnout, he knew they would have been heading to the bar anyway.

"To our dear, departed colleague," Barrett said

"He ain't dead," someone joked.

"Then…to our dear *departing* colleague."

Everyone laughed, and they clinked their glasses. Taking a slug, Thomas winced and wiped his lips. Although he hardly ever drank, he was experienced enough to know the beer was cheap. But quality had no bearing on effect. It was their seventh round, and while Barrett still looked as sober as a judge, Thomas was close to blotto.

By ten o'clock, there were only six of them left. When Barrett announced he had to go, it seemed to signal an end to the night. With the after-work crowd gone, it was all locals, and although no one said it, they were starting to feel unwelcome. The waitress had stopped coming by, and some rough-looking guys took two of the empty chairs without asking.

"Thomas," Barrett said as he stood up. "You've been a fine employee. I wish you well."

"Thanks, sir."

Then to his surprise, his boss stepped forward and gave him a big hug. Thomas smiled, and he couldn't tell if Barrett's glassy eyes were from sentiment or Schlitz. He shook all their hands, and they headed for the door, people staring over as they passed. It was hard to think his father used to go there, even though he didn't drink, and Thomas wondered if any of the barmen remembered him.

On the sidewalk, they all shook hands again, his colleagues congratulating him, making jokes about getting them out of trouble. Thomas appreciated the camaraderie, knowing he would think fondly back to his days at the shipyard. It was the place where he started his adult life and the place where his father ended his.

"Don't be a stranger," Barrett said.

"Never."

The group dispersed, men going off in different directions. Thomas knew that a couple of them lived in East Boston; he had gone to high school with one of their brothers. But they were from all over the city, from Brighton to Hyde Park, and one guy even took the train down from Gloucester.

As he lingered a few minutes alone, the streetlamps looked hazy, and the ground seemed to wobble. He threw his bag over his shoulder, now empty because he had turned in his uniform, belt, and billy club. The only thing he kept was his whistle, some small token of his time spent there.

Crossing the street to Maverick Station, he noticed some guys on the corner but thought nothing of it until they started walking toward him. Despite his condition, he could always sense danger, an instinct he had either gotten from boxing or that boxing had helped him to sharpen.

"Hey tough man," he heard.

Thomas stopped. Looking down the sidewalk, he watched three men emerge from the darkness.

"I heard you quit?"

Realizing it was Angela's brother, he cringed. They had tussled during the strike and fought at the beach. He had hoped the tension died down, but it was hard to know at the shipyard, where starting trouble with a guard would have been a serious infraction. Now that he was no longer employed there, any problem between them was a private matter.

Still, Thomas refused to be intimidated.

"Maybe I did," he said.

As the man got closer, he smirked.

"I just wanted to give you a going-away gift—"

Ugh! He punched Thomas straight in the jaw, sending him to the pavement.

"Son of a bitch!" Thomas growled.

His adrenaline surged; his temper flared. In an instant, he jumped back up. He had been knocked down plenty before. As he swung back, he felt a sharp pain from behind and was stunned. He couldn't tell if it was a fist or a weapon, but they were all around him and swinging. If he wasn't so drunk, he knew he could have fended them off, and now all he could do was cover up.

Suddenly, a whistle.

Two policemen burst from the station doors, and the men scattered.

"You alright?"

Putting his hand on the wall, Thomas leaned over, his head throbbing and dizzy.

"Yeah, yeah," he said.

"They take anything?"

He glanced over, their faces blurry.

"Not a robbery," he said, gasping for air. "I think they thought I was someone else."

Considering his first day of training was Monday, lying to two cops seemed like a bad start. But he wasn't a snitch, and he didn't want to make things worse.

"You need an ambulance?"

Thomas shook his head, too exasperated to speak. With a reassuring smile, he backed away from the officers. Then he turned around and walked off.

······

By the time he reached his street, he knew it was late. In the distance, he could hear the rumble of the freight trains, which always left after midnight. He had walked the whole way back, stopping at the fountain at Putnam Square Park to wash off the blood and have some water.

The time had helped him calm down, but he wasn't really upset. His nose was sore, and he had a bump on the back of his head, nothing he wouldn't have gotten after a few rounds in the ring. If anything, his pride was hurt, but he didn't want revenge, and he never held grudges like his brother. He even had a strange exhilaration, and it wasn't from the booze. With a new career and a woman he loved, he finally felt like his life was on track.

As he came up the hill, he got suddenly mischievous. He turned into the Ciarlones' yard and snuck between the houses. In the darkness, he reached for some pebbles and tossed them at the second-floor window.

Hearing it open, he looked up.

"Thomas?" Connie whispered.

"Come out."

"What are you doing?"

"I wanna see you."

"It's late."

"I won't leave until I see you," he said, chuckling.

She stepped away and moments later, the back door opened. There she stood in her nightgown, her hair bushy and wild. When he walked up, her face dropped.

"My dear, what happened?!"

She touched his face, and he winced.

"Ouch, please. It's okay."

"Who did this to you?"

"I got robbed," he said, the second time he lied.

"Who?"

"I don't know."

"Where?"

They sat on the steps, and he put his arm around her.

"Maverick Square. They didn't get anything."

Before she could ask more, he leaned forward, and they started to kiss.

"No..."

"Everyone's asleep."

When she hesitated and looked around, he knew she was considering it. Connie had dignity, but she was also daring, and things like modesty meant little to a woman who had lost a husband and lived through war.

"Okay," she said, nodding with an eager smile. "Quick—"

Thomas grabbed her before she could finish, licking her lips, squeezing her breasts. While he undid his trousers, she lifted her gown, and she wasn't wearing any underwear. In seconds, she was on top of him, her hips rocking, muffled groans. It was over before he wanted it to be, and even she looked a little surprised, if not disappointed.

They sat embraced, their chests heaving, and she rested her head on his shoulder. Although the air was cool, they had worked themselves into a sweat. Under the bliss of passion, Thomas always got the urge to ask her to marry him. But he never trusted decisions made under passion, whether it was rage, joy, or bitterness, and he knew he would have to wait. Still, he didn't want to let her go. Holding her close, he noticed a shadow in the dining room window, just inches above them. As his eyes adjusted, he saw Chickie staring out.

CHAPTER THIRTY-SEVEN

*A*bby stood waiting as the baker took another sheet pan out of the oven. Carlo was a middle-aged Italian with big ears, his mustache always dusted with flour and yeast. He had been working at Betty Ann Bakery for decades, but all she knew about him was that he had one grown daughter and that he had fought in the Great War, which could have explained his limp. He never said much, rushing around the small kitchen, usually doing several tasks at once. Although they looked nothing alike, he reminded her somehow of her father, his quiet humility and devotion to his work.

With a smile, he put the hot tray down in front of her. She reached for the powdered sugar and went up and down the rows, tapping the shaker to spread it.

"No, Ab!"

When she glanced back, Eve came over. Using a towel, she began to wipe off the sugar.

"Croissants get egg wash," she said.

"Croissants?"

"Croissants. They're French. They're savory."

Abby had never heard of them, but she wasn't surprised. With the war, business owners everywhere were trying to honor America's allies. Just the week before, they had made a batch of British crumpets, although they didn't sell well.

"Sorry, I didn't know."

"I guess they didn't teach you that at B.U.?"

Abby frowned—the remark stung.

"What would you know about it?"

Eve stepped back, and their eyes locked.

"C'mon Ab," she said. "Just a joke."

Abby nodded with a halfhearted smile. She knew her reaction was harsh, but it wasn't the first time she had been teased. As working-class girls, none of her coworkers would go on to college, and the only one pursuing a profession was Loretta, who had applied to nursing school.

Abby watched as Eve tried to get the sugar off, but by now it was melted on.

"Don't worry about it," she said. "We'll sell these as sweet ones."

She walked away, and Abby finished.

By the time she had glazed the fifth tray, it was almost eight-thirty, and she had to go. After washing up, she grabbed her coat and bag.

Like most mornings, the timing was exact, and the moment she walked out, a streetcar was coming down Bennington Street. She hopped on and sat squished between two heavy men, one with too much cologne and the other with not enough. It was crowded for a Tuesday morning and not just with commuters. With Thanksgiving only two days away, people were heading into town to shop.

When she got off at Scollay Square to change trains, she heard chanting. Over by the station entrance, there was a dozen women, some holding signs that said CHARITY STARTS AT HOME and STAY OUT OF EUROPE'S WAR. They were mostly older, dressed in traditional hats and wool coats, one even wearing a corsage.

Anti-war protests had been popping up around the city for months, usually small and never much of a nuisance. If people were conflicted, they didn't show it, and pacifism was a hard thing to justify with a man like Adolph Hitler in the world. In one of the family's few conversations about the possibility of going to war, their mother said,

"Mr. Roosevelt knows what's best for the country," and everyone else agreed.

Walking by the women, Abby saw a pin on one of their lapels, an American flag shield. They were with the *America First Committee*, a national organization whose spokesman was Charles Lindberg. When the lady tried to hand her a leaflet, Abby declined with a smile.

She got to class ten minutes before it started, and by now, she was used to being early. Her grades were still terrible, but she was determined to pass all her classes. She took a seat at the back, but Harold still hadn't arrived. She never could understand how he did it, showing up late, taking off days to travel, and still getting A's.

Abby was glad they met, but she also had doubts. The Thursday before, they had gone out after her volleyball game to a diner in the Back Bay. While she and Frances had club sandwiches, Harold drank four Martinis, maybe more. They did most of the talking, subjects as foreign to Abby as sailing in Chatham or the best places to eat in New York City. They had even gone skiing at the same resort, Mont-Tremblant in Quebec.

At points, their conversation bordered on flirting, and when Frances burst out laughing, Abby felt the sting of jealousy. She always thought of Harold only as a friend, too suave for her tastes, and now she wondered if she was having second thoughts.

Ms. Stetson cleared her throat, and the room went silent. As she started to speak, Harold dashed in like he was making a stage entrance. He had on a striped jacket and silk tie, his face smooth after a fresh shave. When he tried to charm the professor with a smile, she nodded coldly, and he ran to sit down.

"Now, class," Ms. Stetson began. "As you know, your poems are due today…"

Abby reached into her bag, taking out the single sheet of paper, neatly typed, the title capitalized. She had worked on it for weeks, mostly at night and hiding it so her brothers wouldn't see it.

"I've decided to have each student read aloud his or her work…"

Abby froze. If she had known they would have to recite them, she would have made it far less personal.

"You'll be judged on both the content and delivery."

She glanced over at Harold, who rolled his eyes, mouthed something she couldn't understand.

"Any questions, Mr. Merrill?"

Harold looked up.

"None at the moment, Madam."

"We'll go in alphabetical order."

Considering the size of the class, Abby knew they couldn't get through everyone, but *Nolan* was in the middle.

Ms. Stetson called out a name, and a young man walked up to the front, taking a bow before starting. The readings went quicker than Abby expected, with students laughing, sighing, and even groaning at points. While some poems were funny, others were tender, and one girl had written an ode to President Roosevelt. When Harold's turn came, Abby heard something about the moon and a birdcage, but knowing she was up soon, she couldn't focus.

"Miss Nolan?"

She took her poem and stood up. Walking down the row, she felt dozens of eyes watching and got self-conscious.

"Title?" the professor asked.

Abby looked over with a nervous smile.

"Point Shirley Beach."

"Very well. Proceed."

Arching her back, she held out the paper and faced the class. Then she started to read:

> At three years old, he held my hand,
> We walked the beach along the sand,
> The waves were big, the ocean wide,
> But I was safe with him beside.

> At six, I found a robin dead,

JONATHAN CULLEN

Beneath the tree, behind the shed,
He told me she was still asleep,
To let her be and not to weep.

At nine, when I slipped on the rocks,
And cut my foot and tore my socks,
He carried me five blocks away,
To our small cottage by the bay.

At twelve, he taught me how to fish,
To cast a line and make a wish,
And not complain of what you caught,
Be grateful for the things you got.

By fifteen, I thought I was grown,
and left him to be on my own,
With friends, I'd go out every chance,
Days in the sun, nights for romance.

At eighteen, I was too mature,
For idling 'round the sea and shore,
A summer spot with childish themes,
Was no place for a girl with dreams.

Now that he's gone, a sudden end,
I yearn to have those years again,
To share another sunset view,

Or sit and hear the seagull's mew.

Point Shirley Beach will always be,
A sacred place, the lock and key,
To simpler times, the life we had,
The memories of me and my dad.

THE ROOM WAS QUIET; no one moved. Abby stood staring at the words long after she finished, too terrified to look up. With the whirl of emotion she felt inside, she was amazed she had not cried, and all she could think was that love was stronger than sorrow.

When someone clapped, everyone else joined in, a roaring applause that seemed to rattle the walls, shake the floors. At that moment, she felt incredible joy, or was it relief? Since her father's death, they rarely talked about him at home. If he was mentioned, it was always offhanded, usually about something else. She had spent more time on the poem than on any assignment before, including high school, and she finally felt like she was able to honor him.

Outside in the hallway, students were leaving classrooms—the period was over.

"We'll continue tomorrow," Ms. Stetson announced.

As everyone started to get up, Abby handed her poem to the professor, who was collecting them to proofread and grade. She returned to her desk, her eyes downcast, her heart still racing. At the back, Harold stood waiting with his arms crossed, a warm smile on his face.

"My dear," he said. "That was indescribably beautiful."

His reaction gave her a chill. As someone who had lost a parent too, his opinion meant a lot.

"Thanks."

She reached for her bag, and they started to walk.

"How about we celebrate with some light refreshments? My place?"

She waited until they got out to the corridor and stopped.

"I can't. I've got biology…then German—"

"Not now, silly girl. After classes."

Abby smiled. Volleyball practice was canceled that week, and she didn't have work again until Friday. Students had already started leaving for Thanksgiving break, the hallways noticeably quieter. As much as she always worried about going out and having fun, she really had no excuse.

"I'd love to."

CHAPTER THIRTY-EIGHT

Thomas sat on the bench with his head down. But with a hundred other recruits, he knew it was going to be hard to hide a black eye. The police class was larger than he expected, and as he looked around, he saw a few familiar faces. Beside him was his duffel bag filled with three t-shirts, two pairs of sweatpants, socks, a water thermos, and a box of crackers—everything the hiring packet told him to bring. He had a jacket too, although the officer at the front said they didn't go outside much in cold weather.

Thomas was anxious but not nervous, a distinction he had learned from boxing. Anxiousness was the body's natural response to the unknown; nervousness was born of doubt. He wasn't afraid; he had been waiting for this moment all his life. He knew he wanted to be a cop since, at eight years old, he saw one tackle a thief who had robbed an old lady at knifepoint in Day Square.

Finally, two police officers walked in, a tall man in his mid-forties with beady eyes, and another who looked ten years younger.

"Gentlemen, I'm Captain Llewellyn. This is Sergeant Flynn." He paused, scanning the room. "Today begins your journey in law enforcement, one of the oldest professions in civilized society. And the timing is auspicious…"

He was the most well-spoken policeman Thomas had ever heard, with only the trace of a Boston accent.

"With our brethren across the Atlantic engaged in a war against the most unimaginable evil, we expect our country to join them before long…"

A few men nodded, but no one acted surprised. People had been talking about America entering the war for so long that any anticipation was gone.

"When that happens, your duties will take on a crucial significance. Policing in war is different than in peacetime. Not only will you be enforcing civilian laws, but you may also be required to assist in military matters."

He stopped again, creating a dramatic silence.

"Any questions?"

When someone raised his hand in the back, the sergeant pointed.

"Sir, by assist, do you mean fight?"

"It's possible. What Hitler is doing is unprecedented. Even in the Great War, the battle was largely confined to Europe. Who knows if the Germans will try to come across the pond? In the least, you'll receive some special training on medical triage in case of an air raid or, God forbid, a land invasion."

"Sir?" another man asked, standing slightly. "What if we don't…go to war?"

"Then it'll come in handy when your wife goes into labor."

Everyone chuckled and looked around. The humor helped break the tension, especially with such a grim topic. Like a lot of men his age, Thomas didn't talk much about the war, too distracted by the excitement of youth. He followed events, of course, but with the vague interest of a sport whose rules he didn't understand. When his father was alive, they would discuss the news, the Battle of North Africa or the German advance into Russia. But even with the world crumbling, it was hard to worry when you were young and in love.

"Very well, men. Sergeant Flynn will now take you to your lockers," Captain Llewelyn said, then glanced at his watch. "You'll meet in the gymnasium at 0800 hours."

The whole class filed out and went down a narrow stairwell that smelled of coal and mildew. They came to the basement, a long room that ran the length of the building. Along the walls were rows of lockers with water pipes above. Metal lamps hung from the ceiling at regular intervals, casting a harsh light over the cracked cement floors.

It wasn't an elegant start to a career, but Thomas didn't complain. Training was new for the department. Men from previous generations had received nothing more than a nightstick and instruction on how to use the alarm boxes. Back then rookies went to work immediately, sent out with seasoned officers to learn on the job.

Once everyone had changed, they marched back up the stairs. They were directed to the gymnasium, which was nothing more than an old storage room with leather floor mats and some punching bags. The captain was gone, but Sergeant Flynn walked in carrying a clipboard and stopwatch, another officer with him. Thomas didn't see who it was until they got closer, and when he did, they were both surprised.

"Tom Nolan?! I didn't know you got called up."

Thomas smiled, and they shook hands.

"I've been waiting a while. I applied in June."

Nick DiMarco had been two grades ahead of him at East Boston High, and they met on the boxing team. Short and bowlegged, he made up for it with good looks with straight black hair, blue eyes, and a large nose that was somehow flattering. Everyone said he looked like Rudolph Valentino, and all the girls in school had crushes on him.

"I see you're still sparring?" DiMarco said.

Thomas cringed. The swelling on his face had gone down, but it was still obvious he had been in a fight.

"I guess you could say that."

"It's good to have someone here from Eastie. There should be more of us."

Thomas smiled, well aware of the implication. As a heavily Italian neighborhood in a city run by the Irish, East Boston had less influence, which meant fewer jobs.

As they talked, Sergeant Flynn stood with an impatient smirk.

"Welcome to the force," DiMarco said.

"I look forward to keeping the peace."

"Not much of that these days. But we'll keep our side of the world safe. Good to see you, Thomas."

"Good to see you, Anthony."

The two men walked to the front, and the room went quiet.

"Gentlemen, I'm Lieutenant DiMarco. Along with Sergeant Flynn, I'll be supervising your training for the next two weeks..."

He was young for a lieutenant, Thomas thought, but it wasn't unusual. With so many men leaving for the military, cops were moving up the ranks fast. Either way, Thomas was glad a friend from high school was in charge. It always helped to know someone.

"Now, I need you to get into lines," Flynn said, clapping his hands. "Quick, quick!"

In an instant, his expression stiffened. With his paunch and slumped shoulders, he didn't look like a drill sergeant, but he tried to talk like one. Everyone started to move, clumsily forming rows, not sure how many to make. The welcome and induction part was over; training to become a Boston Police officer had begun.

......

Thomas was on the train by 3 pm., the earliest he had been out of work in months. They only got half pay for training, but once it was over, he would make seventy cents an hour, twenty more than at the shipyard and over twice what he made at the movie theater.

The first day was easier than he had expected. Flynn only made them do an hour of calisthenics, one of the benefits of having an out-of-shape instructor. Thomas kept up, but he got more winded than he used to, which he blamed on inactivity. In high school, he played two sports and boxed, and even on days he didn't have practice, he was always out and about.

Next, they broke into groups and practiced restraining suspects with handcuffs. They had a quick lunch and then listened to a department attorney talk about the American legal system, the difference between civilian and criminal law. After another hour of exercise, they met in the room where they started and were dismissed.

Thomas got off at Maverick Square and changed to the streetcar, knowing that in a few hours Connie would be passing through there too. He couldn't go more than five minutes without thinking about her. At the shipyard, he understood why because he had so much free time. But now it felt like an obsession, and although he knew he loved her, it made him feel weak.

By the time he got home, the temperature had fallen, and for the first time, it felt like winter. As he went up the front steps, he heard a noise and looked over to see Chickie waving from the porch, dressed in a wool coat and gloves. He waved back with an awkward smile, still embarrassed by what happened a few nights before. He wondered what she saw or if she had seen anything, and a girl who spoke like a five-year-old couldn't have known much about sex. Still, he knew she was lonely, and there was nothing more tantalizing than seeing two people embraced.

When he walked inside, the house was quiet. He peered into the dining room, and Abby was hunched over her books, her head in her hand and writing.

"Where's Ma?"

She turned, almost like she was startled. With glasses on, she looked much older, and there was no question they were both adults now.

"She went down to the shop."

"Where's George?"

"Where do you think?"

As she said it, they heard feet moving above. He glanced up with a frown, and she giggled, the silent humor they shared as twins.

"How was the first day?" she asked.

"Guess who I saw."

"Cary Grant."

"Close. Nick DiMarco."

Abby rolled her eyes.

"Hardly close."

"All your friends were crazy on him."

"Maybe they were. I'm not interested in a man who's prettier than me—"

The front door opened. Thomas went out to the parlor, and his mother was walking in with a grocery bag. He quickly took it from her and looked inside to see some potatoes, turnips, canned peas, and butter.

"I could have gotten all this for you," he said.

Taking off her scarf, she looked over with a sour smile.

"I'm still capable of doing things myself," she said, then ironically, turned so he could help her take off her coat.

"Yes, Ma."

Her cheeks were red, but it wasn't just from the cold because her eyes were glassy too. Since her husband's death, her mental state had been getting worse, and Thomas didn't know if her drinking was the cause or a symptom.

He took the bag into the kitchen, and they started to put everything away.

"They were clean out of spices. No sage, no thyme. They didn't even have marjoram."

"What's marjoram?" Abby asked from the dining room.

"It's for the squash."

As they talked, George walked in wearing the green wool cardigan their aunt had knitted years before. Thomas had also gotten one but lost it at the frozen marsh behind Saratoga Street where they played hockey.

"They didn't even have parsley," Mrs. Nolan added.

"You need parsley, Ma?"

"Who doesn't?"

Although the war seemed far away, everyone knew it was only time before they were impacted. Supply problems with chemicals had increased prices on everything from ladies' pantyhose to radios, and there were rumors of an oil shortage. Retail stores were packed, and it wasn't just for the holiday season. People were hoarding goods out of fear that they would soon be scarce.

"I can get it," George said, coming out of the pantry with a beer. "Anything else, too. Just tell me what you need."

Thomas stared at him, but he wouldn't look back.

"Thomas?"

He turned to his mother, who was waiting for him to hand her a can of peas. She gave him a confused look and then glanced over at George. Thomas forced a smile and said nothing, not wanting to upset her.

George popped the cap off his beer, flicked it in the trash, and walked away. Something about his attitude sent Thomas into a quiet rage. After their talk the week before, it was arrogant to be bragging.

Once everything was put away, he tried to help make dinner, but she wouldn't let him. Instead, she asked him to put on some music. It only took a few seconds to go into the living room and turn on the radio, and by the time he came back, she had made a highball.

"How was your training?"

Thomas watched in pity as she diced the potatoes, her hands jittery, a dirty apron around her waist. In the past, it would have been her first question, and now it sounded more like an afterthought.

"Good," was all he said.

Abby walked in, rubbing her shoulders.

"I'm freezing."

"Then put on a sweater," Mrs. Nolan said.

"What's for dinner?"

"Ham hash."

"No onions on mine," Abby said, and when their mother gave her a sharp look, she added, "Please."

As Thomas turned to go, his mother called him.

"Mind putting some more coal on?" she asked.

"Yeah, would you mind?"

He looked at his sister, and she stuck out her tongue.

"Sure, Ma."

He opened the basement door and reached for the light, descending the narrow staircase. The air was cold and dank, and when he reached the bottom, he had to duck under the low ceiling. All his life, it had been dingy, the floor made of dirt, cobwebs between the rafters. As children, they were so afraid to go down there that their father used it as a threat for bad behavior.

He made his way to the back, reaching for the spade against the wall. Opening the furnace hatch, he started to shovel coal from the bin beside it, sparks flying and the smoke making him wince. With prices rising, four scoops were enough, and it would keep them warm at least until bedtime.

As he turned to go, he noticed some boxes under the old workbench his father had built. Crouching down, he opened one, and the hair on the back of his neck stood up. Inside were dozens of women's blouses, dresses, gloves, and hosiery, brand new and still in their packaging. He looked in another box and saw more of the same, enough department store merchandise to outfit a society luncheon at Fairmont Copley Plaza. If he didn't have a reason to be mad at George before, he did now.

He tossed the spade and went back upstairs. As he walked through the kitchen, his mother said something, but he didn't respond. He went straight up to George's room and stormed in without knocking.

"What the hell?" George shouted, lying on the bed with his head against the radio.

Thomas tapped the door shut.

"Maybe you should tell me?"

George sat up.

"What's this all about?"

"Are we gonna keep playing this game?"

George reached for his beer and took a sip.

"I don't know what you're talking about."

"All that loot in the basement."

"Loot?" he snickered. "Brother, you been watching too many Chandler films—"

"Get it out of the house!"

George wiped his mouth and stood up.

"It's mine. I bought it fair and square."

"It's stolen and you know it!" Thomas said, his temper rising.

"I don't know nothing! Guys at work sell stuff. Everyone buys it. Maybe it's extras from factories?"

Thomas stepped closer until they were only inches apart. With his teeth gritted, he looked his brother dead in the eye.

"I want it gone by tomorrow," he said.

For a moment, he thought George might try something, and he hoped he didn't because he was beyond furious. They both knew the items were stolen and bringing them into the house was an insult to the memory of their father.

George shook his head.

"Fucking cop."

Thomas grabbed him by the collar, and his brother's eyes bulged.

"Thomas!"

Startled, he looked back and saw Abby. He let go, and George fell back.

"What?"

"Dinner's ready."

Thomas nodded, but she wouldn't leave, lingering in the doorway with a worried look.

"We'll be right down."

After a short hesitation, she slipped back into the hallway, and Thomas waited until he could hear her walking down the stairs. Then he pointed at George so fast he flinched.

"By tomorrow. All of it!"

His brother stared back with a defiant scowl, but he wasn't foolish enough to argue. Thomas turned to go and saw some copies of *Social Justice* on the dresser. He didn't know much about the magazine or the organization, other than that its followers were nutjobs. As he walked out, he swiped them off with all the fury he would have vented on his brother.

"And stop reading that trash!"

CHAPTER THIRTY-NINE

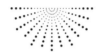

Abby walked out of her history class with a grin. She had gotten an A- on her project about Pompeii, which made up for the sixty on her midterm exam. The professor, an older man from England, praised her for writing about the people and culture, not focusing on the disaster. When he mentioned her optimism, she was surprised because she never thought of herself that way, especially in recent months. The semester had been a frenzy of work and school, and for much of it, she had been miserable. Harold and Frances had helped her get through it, but all the friends in the world couldn't save someone who felt defeated by life. Now she was finally passing all her classes, and with Thanksgiving only a day away, there was no better time to be grateful.

As she walked out of the building, Dr. Bauermeister was coming up the steps, his jacket open, his shirt untucked in places.

"Good afternoon, professor," she said.

He stopped and gave her a confused look.

"Abigail," he said, lifting his hat. "How are you?"

Squinting in the sun, his face was tense, his eyes bloodshot. She wanted to ask if everything was alright, but it didn't seem appropriate.

"I hope you have a nice Thanksgiving."

He responded with a wide grin that seemed to mask some deeper despair.

"Thank you, dear. You too."

With that, he walked away, lumbering up the stairs. She watched him until he went inside, curious but also concerned. Of all her teachers, he had been the most supportive, always asking about school, her job, and her life.

She headed down the sidewalk, uncomfortable in her winter coat. There had been a heat wave since Sunday, temperatures reaching the mid-seventies, the warmest she ever remembered for fall. She had already put away her summer clothes, stored in her trunk in the attic, the accumulation of things she had owned for years.

When she turned into Marsh Chapel, the courtyard was quiet, many students having already gone home for the long weekend. Someone whistled, and she looked over to see Harold leaning against an archway, one hand in his pocket and the other holding a cigarette. He flicked the butt and came towards her.

"Don't you look lovely?" he said.

Abby turned her head, running her fingers through the pin curls she had set that morning.

"You like it?"

"Darling, you look like Betty Grable."

She smiled, appreciating the flattery. Her mother always told her she was *competently pretty*, a phrase that sounded like a compliment and an insult at the same time.

"I just saw one of my professors. He looked unwell."

"The German?"

"Dr. Bauermeister. How'd you know?"

"A friend of mine has him too."

"He's been so kind to me."

"The world hasn't been kind to him, unfortunately," he said, and she tilted her head. "His daughter and son-in-law live in Cologne. They've been trying to get to America for months. Their visas were denied."

"Cologne?"

"It was hit terribly by the Brits a couple weeks back."

She took a deep breath, as shocked as she was saddened. After the harassment Dr. Bauermeister had experienced, it was an outrage that he had to worry about his family too.

"Yoo-hoo!"

They turned, and Frances was walking toward them. In her petticoat and hat, she looked dressed for a banquet. While most girls with fair skin didn't look good in white, she did, her blue eyes glistening.

"It's hot as blazes," she said, fanning her face.

"Welcome to June in November."

Frances looked at Abby, and it was obvious she noticed her hairstyle.

"I love it," she said.

"You don't think it's too—?"

"Not in the slightest. You look like Veronica Lake."

"Harold said Betty Grable."

"What do men know, anyway?"

"Trust me, darling, more than you think," he said, and they all laughed.

"So," Frances asked. "Where to?"

"I know a little juke joint on Beacon Hill. Quarter Martinis before nine."

Abby shrugged her shoulders.

"I'm game."

Frances turned to Harold.

"Lead the way."

They walked out to Commonwealth Avenue and caught the first trolley downtown, laughing and joking the entire ride. At Arlington Street, they got off and went through the Public Gardens, the flower beds dry and lifeless, the trees all bare. Still, it was elegant, the winding paths and marble statues. By a small footbridge, an elderly woman was taking donations for the Salvation Army, ringing her bell. Harold reached for his wallet and stuffed a ten-dollar bill into the box, more money than Abby made in a week at the bakery.

They came out the other side of the park and crossed over to

Charles Street, a bustling thoroughfare of brick storefronts and restaurants at the foot of Beacon Hill. Up ahead, Abby saw a hanging wood sign, *Churchills,* and the figure of a man in a top hat. Harold got the door and waved them in with a theatrical sweep.

Inside was dim, the air warm and smoky. It was busy for late afternoon, but the day before Thanksgiving was always a popular time to go out. They found a table in the corner and took off their coats.

"What's your pleasure?" Harold asked.

"I'll take a Manhattan," Frances said.

He pointed at Abby.

"I don't know. Maybe just a glass of wine?"

"Wine? My dear, this isn't a cotillion."

She chuckled.

"You choose."

He walked over to the bar, where a dozen sailors stood drinking. With the Navy Yard just over the bridge in Charlestown, they were everywhere, wandering the streets and alleyways in their uniforms, crisp and white.

Moments later, Harold came back, somehow carrying all three glasses without a tray. He put them down and loosened his tie while he sat.

"I should've worn linen," he said, wiping his forehead with a napkin.

"It's supposed to cool down this weekend," Frances said.

"Whatever the weather," he said, raising his glass with a sentimental smile. "We're all together, and first semester is almost done."

"I'll drink to that."

They toasted, and Abby took a sip, wincing from the sting of the liquor. She wasn't familiar with cocktails, but she guessed it was a Manhattan because Martinis had olives.

Over the next two hours, they drank and talked as the bar filled with patrons. By the third round, it was probably close to dinnertime, but Abby couldn't tell because the place had no windows. Either way, the conversation was so absorbing she lost track of time, an intimate exchange of stories, observations, and even a few confessions. Harold admitted he had stolen a paper on the American Revolution from his brother; Frances said she had lied in her application essay about being the setter on her high school volleyball team. At some points, Abby laughed so hard she had to cover her mouth; at others, she got teary-eyed.

They were interrupted only when music came on, the thumping rhythms of Artie Shaw's *Back Bay Shuffle.*

"What do you say we cut the rug?" Harold asked.

He hopped off his chair and extended his hand to Abby.

"I just need to use the ladies' room first."

"I'll dance," Frances said.

She took his hand, and they made their way over to the jukebox where some of the sailors had already started moving to the beat. Standing up, Abby got dizzy, and she didn't know if it was the alcohol or from sitting for too long. She headed towards the back, swerving around tables, men smiling at her as she passed. At the end of a dark hallway, she found the lavatory, which was nothing more than a closet with a seatless toilet and broken mirror.

When she came out, she heard shouting and the sound of breaking glass. She hurried back to the bar and was shocked to see Harold kneeling on the floor. While Frances helped him up, a young sailor stood over them, his fists clenched.

"What the hell happened?!" Abby shouted.

"Stay out of this, toots!"

Finally, Harold stood, a look of stunned humiliation on his face.

"Why'd you hit him?"

The sailor turned to Abby.

"I said *stay out of it!*"

All at once, her rage flared. She lunged and punched him straight in the teeth. Instantly, every man in the bar ran over and got between them.

"Crazy bitch," the sailor said, wiping blood off his mouth.

She tried to swing again, but people were holding her back.

"Let's go!" Frances said, taking her by the arm. "He's getting our pocketbooks."

Abby looked over and saw Harold at their table, fixing his jacket and leaving money for the bill. She snarled once at the sailor and then turned to leave.

They burst outside into the evening air, which had cooled since they arrived. For the first few minutes, no one said anything, and it seemed an awful way to end a fine day. Abby didn't know what the incident was about, but she wasn't surprised. Sailors were always causing trouble in Boston with their rowdiness and drunken antics. Just a week before, a group of them had brawled with the entire Tufts football team at a nightclub in Scollay Square.

By the time they reached the corner, Harold looked calm enough to talk.

"Are you okay?" Abby asked.

When she scanned his face and saw no bruising, she assumed he had been shoved, not hit.

"I've been knocked about before."

Frances stood with her arms crossed, lips pressed together.

"They were so obnoxious," she said.

"And you," Harold said, looking at Abby. "You've proved yourself a city girl after all."

She smiled, but only to hide her shame. She had come to college to improve her mind and her manners. Even if the sailor deserved it, there was nothing more unladylike than fighting.

"What exactly happened?" she asked, changing the subject.

As Frances went to speak, Harold held up his hand.

"A little jostling in tight quarters," he said, and he seemed to enjoy the irony. "I bumped into him, that's all. It's over."

He lit a cigarette, and they lingered in silence as people walked by. With the mild breeze, it almost felt like a summer night, and Abby could smell the ocean.

"Well," Harold said. "Let's get you to the station."

"I can walk."

"My dear—"

"It's only a few blocks."

"Abby, are you sure?" Frances asked.

They all locked eyes, and Abby nodded.

"There you have it," Harold said, a reluctant acceptance in his voice. "A modern, independent woman."

"Get used to it," Frances joked.

She stepped towards Abby, and they kissed on the cheeks. Then Abby turned to Harold, and they hugged, the smell of his cologne faint after a long day.

"Happy Thanksgiving!"

"See you at practice Tuesday night," Frances said.

They all said goodbye, and Abby crossed the street. When she got to the other side, she glanced back, and they were still waving. She smiled to herself and went up Chestnut Street, cutting through Beacon Hill because it was quieter than the main roads.

The narrow lane was lined with elegant brownstones, lamps shining through lace curtains. Now that she was alone, Abby felt drunker, or maybe it was her mood. She was still angry about what happened, and the only reason she didn't show it was so Harold wouldn't feel bad. She never liked barrooms for that reason, having seen her brother George come home with fat lips and black eyes. But she couldn't blame it entirely on the place or even the soldiers. There was a strange feeling in the air, a nervous energy that had been building for months. With the holiday season, it was more obvious, if only because people couldn't hide their fear.

As she went up the sidewalk, she saw a woman coming toward her with a poodle. With a smile, she moved aside, and the moment she passed, Abby looked ahead and froze. Hanging from a pole in front of a brick townhouse was the Nazi flag, the swastika shining eerily in the dull haze of the streetlamp. She thought it was a dream or a nightmare until she got closer and saw a bronze plaque beside the door: German Consulate.

CHAPTER FORTY

Thomas stepped quietly out the front door and down the steps, dressed only in his shirtsleeves. Although the sky was overcast, the air was warm, and it had been mild all week, almost like spring. In past years, he wouldn't have minded, but it made his police training harder, and all week the stuffy gymnasium felt like a sauna. Never in his life had he wished more for the cold weather.

He went up the Ciarlones' steps, anxious and even feeling a little mischievous. In his hands was an apple pie, bought the day before at Betty Ann Bakery. Realizing they would sell out fast, he had asked Abby to set one aside, and she did. Connie didn't know he was coming by, and he worried how she would react. For weeks, they had discussed telling her aunt about their relationship, but she still wanted to wait.

Beyond that, he wasn't even sure the Ciarlones were having Thanksgiving and not because they were Italian. Two years earlier, President Roosevelt had changed the date to extend the holiday shopping season. With many states protesting, it created confusion across the country, and Vermont and New Hampshire were celebrating the next week.

As he approached the door, he could smell fish and garlic. He knocked once and moments later, it opened. Standing there was Salvatore, dressed in a white t-shirt and pleated pants. His dark hair was matted like he had either just woken up or just got home from work.

"Hey," he said, scratching his head.

"This is for your mother."

Thomas held out the pie, and Sal took it.

"Thanks a lot," he said.

"Happy Thanks—"

Chickie appeared suddenly at the door.

"Thom-ah," she said.

"Hi, Chickie."

She looked up with a wide grin, her eyes almost closed.

"Thom-ah," she said again.

Thomas smiled, and it was hard not to feel some tender affection for the girl. Sal thanked him again and turned to go. As he did, Connie came to the door in a long-sleeve dress, a string of pearls around her neck.

"I thought I heard your voice."

"I brought your aunt a pie."

She gently nudged Chickie inside and came out onto the porch.

"You're a rascal."

"You look beautiful."

When she paused, he knew it wasn't from embarrassment because she could always take a compliment.

"And you're thin."

"It's the training. You don't like thin guys?"

"I didn't say that."

As he stared down into her eyes, she had a soft and sensual gaze. He knew the look, that expression of restrained desire, something he felt too. If they had been anywhere else except the front porch, he would have taken her there and then.

"I wanna see you later—"

"*Concetta?!*"

Thomas cringed and not just because they were interrupted. Mrs. Ciarlone's voice always sounded like a mule in distress.

"We have to go to my uncle's grave," Connie said, glancing back.

"How about after?"

"Maybe."

"Concetta?!"

"In the shed," Thomas said.

With a quick nod, she smiled and then rushed inside.

He walked back to his house, as aroused as he was elated. When he came in the door, he was met by the rich smell of roasting turkey, vegetables, and gravy, those reminiscent odors of childhood. There were spices too—nutmeg, rosemary, and bay leaves—and he knew George had gotten them because all the shops were out. Even with America still neutral, everyone had been expecting shortages. It seemed strange, if not poignant, that some of the first to go were the things that added zest to life.

"Where were you?"

Thomas looked up, and Abby was coming down the stairs. With her hair primped, she was ready for dinner, but she also seemed tired, her face pale.

"Next door," he said. "Are you okay?"

She made a grim expression.

"I am. She's not."

"Whaddya mean?"

When she nodded, Thomas looked towards the kitchen. He walked in and found his mother hunched over a pot, her sleeves rolled up, stirring potatoes with a wooden spoon. On top of the oven was the turkey, steam rising from the tin foil.

"Can I do anything?"

With her back to him, she shook her head. On the counter beside her was a drink, and he could tell by the way she moved that she was tipsy, if not drunk.

"Ma—?"

She put up her hand, and he stopped. All morning she had been irritable, running around, yelling out orders, sighing, and groaning. Thomas knew Thanksgiving was hard without her husband, which was why he and his brother had swept the whole first floor and set the table. Abby had wiped down the good silverware and dusted the furniture in the dining room. Still, nothing was enough, and even with everyone ready and available, she at one point cried, "I never get any help!"

As Thomas went to go, she turned around.

"Get your brother. Dinner is in twenty minutes."

Their eyes met, but only for a second before she looked away. Her back was hunched, her expression almost vacant. She had never looked so fragile.

He went upstairs and got changed, putting on clean slacks and the two-pocket cotton shirt Connie had given him. She got it from work, one of a huge batch of military dress shirts her company had produced for the Army. Using a little Brylcreem, he slicked his hair back and then dabbed on some cologne.

When he came back down, George was already at the table, and Thomas was surprised to see him wearing a tie. Abby was bringing out dishes of vegetables—glazed carrots and squash—but Thomas didn't dare offer to help. While Mrs. Nolan was liberal enough to send her only daughter to college, she always believed men shouldn't do women's work and vice versa. And now wasn't the time to test whether those opinions had changed.

Finally, everyone sat down, their mother still clinging to the rag she had been using all morning. Abby took it, and as she went to put it in the kitchen, Mrs. Nolan asked, "Could you get my drink?"

Abby returned, and they said a quick prayer and started passing around the food. Other than a few small remarks, their mother was quiet, eating with her head down. When Thomas looked across at Abby, her eyes were teary, and she chewed in slow, solemn bites. George didn't seem to notice the tension, or if he did, he ignored it, instead talking about the news. Fifty-three thousand Jews were reported killed by the Nazis in the Ukraine; the Russians were driving back the Germans outside Leningrad. Closer to home, a bomber had crashed in Bangor, Maine, killing four Army airmen.

Hearing about the war only made things worse, and when Thomas looked over at his mother, she had put down her utensils and stopped eating.

"Enough," he said, and George looked up.

"What?"

"I said *enough!*"

His brother paused, looking around the table like he suddenly realized he had been the only one speaking. With a subtle frown, he reached for his beer, but he didn't argue.

The meal was over fast, and Thomas missed the endless conversation and silly chatter of previous Thanksgivings. He remembered when his aunt and uncle used to come down from Maine and stay in the guestroom. In the morning, the women would cook while the men played horseshoes in the yard. After they ate, neighbors would come by for dessert, sometimes staying late for drinks and card games by the fire.

This year was different, more like the afterparty of a wake, which was no small irony considering the tone hadn't been so grim since their father's death. Mrs. Nolan was sullen the whole time, and the liquor seemed to have done nothing to lift her mood. Seeing her so down made Thomas angry, which was always a poor substitute for sadness. He wanted to blame George, but for the first time, it wasn't his brother's fault.

Abby and her mother cleared the table in silence while George snuck out to the porch for a cigarette. Thomas brought the turkey into the kitchen, the one task his mother would allow because it was heavy. There was enough remaining for a small banquet and plenty of vegetables too. She always made use of leftovers, and with the price of meat and poultry so high, nothing would go to waste.

When she went into the pantry to get something, Thomas waved Abby into the hallway.

"What's wrong with her?" he whispered.

"I don't know."

"Should we get her to see a doctor?"

"Who's available Thanksgiving?"

"I have ears, you know?" his mother said as she came back out, but Thomas knew she couldn't hear them.

"Keep an eye on her."

Abby shook her head, looking uneasily towards the kitchen.

"Okay."

......

THOMAS STOOD in the darkness in the shed behind his house. His father had built it years before and always called it *the garage*, even though they never owned a car. He used it as a workshop, with saws, chisels, mallets, and drills hanging from the walls and rafters. Anything he made was more the result of amateur enthusiasm than skill, however, because he had never been taught carpentry.

Aside from the tools, there was a rusted reel mower and a handmade bench that was smooth enough to be a piece of furniture. But Thomas couldn't sit and had to keep moving. The temperature had dropped, and after an hour of waiting with no jacket, he was starting to shiver.

He was just about to leave when the door creaked open, and in stepped Connie.

"You made it."

"Not yet," she said with a smile.

He loved her innuendoes, those seductive flirtations. When she walked over, he sat on the bench, and she sat beside him. She had changed since dinner, putting on a simple dress and sweater, and he knew why. With no place for them to be alone, they had to improvise. The month before, he had finally convinced her to get a hotel room, but most weeks it was easier and cheaper just to meet in the shed. At first, she had been horrified, but now she seemed to like it, even remarking once that it felt mysterious and exciting.

"How was the cemetery?"

She turned to him with a sour smile.

"I never met Salvatore."

"Salvatore? Like his son."

"Boys don't take their father's names in this country?"

"Sometimes…" Thomas said, getting distracted.

She reached under her dress to undo her bra and take off her panties, if she was even wearing any. It felt so mechanical, having sex on a cold bench in the dark. But they wouldn't have privacy until they had their own apartment, and they wouldn't be able to get an apartment until they got married.

Still clothed, she turned to him, and they started to kiss. She reached down and rubbed his thigh, sending a chill through his body. While she stayed seated, he knelt in front of her, and she pulled up her dress. The position was awkward, if not painful, but by now he was used to it. As he moved closer, she put her hands on his cheeks, moaning softly as he entered her.

Suddenly, a scream.

"What was that?!"

Thomas quickly stood and pulled up his pants.

"I don't know," he said, listening.

When he heard it again, he knew it was Abby.

"Wait here!"

He flew out, tying his belt and fixing his shirt, and went down the side yard and up the front steps. Bursting in the door, he saw Abby leaning over their mother in the kitchen.

"Ma?!"

His sister looked over, her face wracked and sobbing hysterically.

"Thomas!"

He ran in and his mother was lying still, her eyes drooping and mouth slightly open. Thomas gasped when he saw a large gash above her wrist, blood pulsating from it, pouring down her arm.

"She cut herself! Do something!" Abby cried.

Just then, his brother came out of the basement door with something in his hands. As he did, Thomas went over to the wall phone and picked up the receiver.

"I already called," George said.

"Do something! Do something! Do something!" Abby shrieked.

George knelt down, and Thomas saw that he had a first aid kit, U.S. Army Medical Department stamped across the top. Opening it, he took out a canvas strap that looked like a belt. As he got it ready, Thomas raised his mother's arm; he had just learned about tourniquets in training a few days before.

Blood was pooling on the floor, and he knew that if they didn't stop the hemorrhaging, his mother could die.

"Quick!" Thomas said.

George glanced at him once and pulled the strap. They both watched as the flow slowed to a trickle, then a drip. Finally, it stopped.

Thomas sighed and slid back against the wall, running his hand through his hair. George picked up a knife off the floor and tossed it on the counter. Thomas wanted to ask if it had been an accident, but he knew the answer. He looked across to Abby, who was crouched beside their mother, rubbing her head with tears rolling down her cheeks. His sister's anguish was almost as heartbreaking as the act that had caused it. Of everyone in the family, Thomas always worried most about her.

Soon sirens came up the street, lights flashing through the windows. Thomas pulled himself up off the floor, careful not to slip on the blood. After everything they had been through, what happened was more than a misfortune, it was a tragedy. Somehow he knew that by opening the door, none of their lives would ever be the same again.

CHAPTER FORTY-ONE

When Abby walked into the cafeteria, Harold and Frances were at a table in the corner. In the milder weather, they would all meet outside, either in the courtyard at Marsh Chapel or the small park beside the science building. But now it was cold, and with the wind coming off the Charles River, it felt like winter. The days were shorter too, the sky a sheet of gray, which only added to her gloom. After finally bringing up her grades, they were starting to slip again, and there were only two weeks left in the semester.

"Abigail," Frances called, fluttering her fingers.

Seeing them together often made Abby jealous, especially because she had introduced them. She didn't know if Frances was prettier than her—she was always a bad judge of such things—but her style got the attention of men and women alike, her pleated skirts and berets.

Harold was no less striking, always impeccably dressed, and some days Abby felt like a pauper around them. While she liked, maybe even loved him, she could never tell if the feeling was friendship or something more. She had come to college under a haze of grief, and romance had been the last thing on her mind.

JONATHAN CULLEN

"We're thinking of going to see *I Wake Up Screaming* tonight at the Paramount," Frances said.

"Sounds fun—"

"Betty Grable."

"Your twin," Harold joked.

"Thank you. I...I...can't," Abby said, stumbling for an excuse. "I have to work."

Frances looked confused.

"The bakery is open nights now?"

"Extended hours...for the holidays."

Even as she said it, she felt guilty, and somehow half-truths always seemed worse than lies. The bakery was in fact open later, but she wasn't working.

"Ah, right," Harold said, raising his eyes and tapping his cigarette on the ashtray. "Mr. Roosevelt and his economic brilliance."

He slid one of the chairs out with his foot.

"Won't you sit?"

"I have biology."

"You weren't at practice Tuesday," Frances said.

"I wasn't feeling well."

It felt like an interrogation, but Abby knew they were only concerned. She glanced over at the clock, and it was almost one.

"I've gotta get to class."

"Well, snap to it!" Harold said.

Although he sounded cheery, she could tell he was disappointed. Forcing a smile, she waved and walked away. She was almost at the doors when she heard Frances' voice and turned around.

"Is everything okay?"

"Yes. Why?"

"You seem out of sorts."

"Just a little tired."

Frances stepped closer and took her gently by the wrist.

"I'm having a little shindig before finals. My parents' place. I want you to come."

"Duxbury?"

It was more a murmur than a question. She knew the town only by reputation, and even the name was intimidating.

"Father will drive us. You'll stay over. Be my guest."

"How will—"

"Father will drive you home too. Easy as pie."

Abby stood thinking, and for once she had no reason to say no. Aside from the occasional night out for drinks, she never had much time for fun. It wasn't just her schoolwork and family problems that were wearing her down. The slog to and from East Boston every day was exhausting, and she knew she needed a break.

Finally, she looked up.

"I'd like that."

......

ABBY GOT off the trolley in Mattapan, a dense neighborhood of three-decker homes and apartment buildings on the southern end of the city. It was all Jewish, the shops along Blue Hill Avenue a mix of kosher delicatessens, bakeries, and butchers. In some ways, it reminded her of East Boston, and even the people looked the same. She saw elderly men with gnarled faces, women in florid dresses, the weary looks of immigrants and their descendants. Everyone smiled, but she felt like an outsider. With many of the signs in Hebrew, it might as well have been an Eastern European village because the area was completely foreign to her.

She had her pocketbook over her shoulder, but the paper bag in her arms was starting to feel heavy. Turning at the corner, she continued down Morton Street. She crossed at the next intersection where the blocks of houses gave way to an expanse of woods and scattered fields like the city had come to an abrupt end. In the distance, she saw a large sign: *Boston State Hospital*.

She went towards it and through the gate, embarrassed and yet sure that no one she knew would see her. As she passed the guardhouse, a black security guard tipped his hat, and she smiled. The entrance road was lined with old elms and dead leaves fluttering across the open grounds. She came to a brick building and walked up the steps, hesitating a moment before going in. She had been there over a dozen times, and it never got any easier.

Inside was a large but empty lobby. The walls were bare, and the air had the stale smell of a government institution. She walked over to the front desk, and an overweight woman with glasses looked up.

"May I help you?"

"I'm here to see Katherine Nolan."

She opened a binder and began flipping through the pages. As Abby waited, she glanced around and saw a barefoot man in a robe talking to himself. Over by the stairs, two orderlies were trying to get an older lady into her wheelchair. Each time they touched her, she would shriek, sending a chill up Abby's spine.

"Name?"

Startled, Abby turned back to the attendant.

"Abigail Nolan."

"Relationship?"

"Daughter."

The woman picked up the phone.

"You can wait over there," she said.

She pointed to a waiting area with a row of shabby chairs and some pedestal ashtrays. Abby stepped over, but she was too anxious to sit, and she was relieved when, moments later, a nurse called to her from a doorway.

Abby smiled and followed her down a corridor. Patients looked up as they passed, all in various states of psychological distress. While some looked simply troubled, others seemed downright crazy. The hospital was originally the *Boston Lunatic Asylum* until State authorities tried to soften its image. But calling something by a different name did nothing to change it.

They turned down another hallway and came to a room. When Abby looked in, her mother was in a chair facing the window.

"Miss," the woman said, glancing at the paper bag. "If you please."

"Oh, of course."

Abby handed it to her, and she checked it before giving it back.

"Thank you."

The nurse left, and Abby went in.

"Ma?"

Mrs. Nolan moved, but she didn't look back. Abby put her pocketbook on the table and opened up the bag.

"I brought you some ham sandwiches," she said.

Of all the inconveniences of being in a public facility, her mother complained most about the food.

"Thank you, my dear."

"And something else," Abby said, taking out some Huntley & Palmers biscuits.

With metals scarce, they now came in a box instead of a tin.

"Any gin to go with it?"

Abby gave her a sour smile.

"Ma, you know I can't—"

Mrs. Nolan waved her hand and looked away. If she craved a drink, it was probably more out of habit because Abby could tell she was already medicated by her dazed look and tiny pupils. When her mother first arrived, they had her on something strong, worried she would try to take her own life again. Now the doctors assured Abby it was just a light sedative to stabilize her moods.

Mrs. Nolan had denied it was suicide, claiming the knife slipped while she was washing it. But she wasn't anywhere near the sink, and the gash was too straight, too deliberate to have been an accident. If anything, Abby believed it was a flash decision, motivated by despair and encouraged by drunkenness. Alcohol always made the worst things possible.

After opening one of the sandwiches, Abby folded the tin foil to save it, knowing it would soon be hard to find. As she did, her mother mumbled something.

"Pardon?" Abby asked.

"School. How is school?"

Abby stopped and looked over, her mother gazing outside. In the yard patients in white outfits hobbled down pathways past dried flower beds and barren trees.

"School?" Abby asked, her eyes welling up. "It's fabulous."

It was the first time her mother had mentioned it, which seemed some small sign that she was improving.

"You were always the brightest in the family."

Abby smiled and put the sandwich on a napkin.

"Here. Eat."

"Is there horseradish?"

"Plenty."

As Abby stood watching, her mother chewed in long, thoughtful bites. Her expression was still distant, but her skin color was better than before.

"It's good," Mrs. Nolan said, peering up.

Abby smiled, struggling to hold back tears. While her father had always been reliable, her mother was the strongest in the family, and it hurt to see her so frail. In some ways, Abby felt responsible, although she knew it was foolish.

Someone knocked, and she spun around. Standing at the door was a nurse. And there beside her, holding a bouquet of flowers, was Abby's older brother.

"George?" she said.

"Hi, Ab."

"George?" their mother said, craning her neck.

He nodded to the woman and walked in. Kneeling down, he held out the flowers, and their mother's face beamed. Abby was as touched as she was surprised, not sure how often he, or her brother Thomas, had been coming by. She could have blamed it on their schedules— they were all busy. But the truth was, as siblings, they never talked much about serious things. With their father dead and their mother mentally unwell, they were as lost and confused as orphans.

For the next few minutes, George chatted alone with their mother, and Abby didn't mind. She had been visiting her every day, their conversations limited to either gardening or the war. In the past, the two topics would have been entirely incompatible, and now they seemed normal.

Soon an orderly came to get Mrs. Nolan for dinner. After Abby kissed her mother, George did the same, rubbing her back and whispering goodbye. Seeing his tenderness was shocking, and if it didn't make up for all his years of trouble, it was a strong step in the right direction.

After escorting their mother to the dining hall, they walked back to the lobby in silence. They left through the front doors, and Abby saw a black car, parked and idling. When George went towards it, she stopped.

"Aren't you coming?" he asked.

"I took the streetcar."

"I'll take you home."

She crept over and peered in to see three young men. In their leather jackets and neck chains, they all looked shady, but after such an emotional visit, now wasn't the time to criticize George's friends. She was about to get in the back when he opened the passenger door and barked, "Out! My sister gets the front seat."

The guy jumped out, arms flailing, and Abby just stood with a hesitant grin. With his quick temper and wild ways, George had always been a handful, but she realized then that sometimes it helped to have a hoodlum for a brother.

CHAPTER FORTY-TWO

The class filed into the gymnasium, and everyone collapsed to the floor, sweaty and out of breath. After two weeks of exercising inside, Sergeant Flynn had decided to take them out. They had run five miles through the city, down the narrow streets of the financial district and around the Boston Common. People looked over, and some even cheered, but with the men dressed in sweats and the unit not bearing a flag, it probably wasn't clear who they were. At points, they went along the harbor where the cold air whipped off the water and made them shiver. By now there were so many military ships, from Coast Guard cutters to light cruisers to Army dredgers, that it looked like a port on the eve of battle.

As Thomas sat stretching his legs, Lieutenant DiMarco walked in holding a stack of envelopes.

"Gentlemen," he announced, and they all got up. "I wanna congratulate you on your last day. Tomorrow you'll be fitted for uniforms and issued firearms. Monday we'll have a small ceremony at City Hall. Captain Llewellyn will be present. Mayor Tobin, too. Friends and loved ones are invited."

Thomas exhaled and looked around, seeing a similar relief on the faces of his colleagues. The training had been hard, but he never worried he wouldn't make it. Out of a hundred and six recruits, they had only lost two, one who broke his arm falling from a rope ladder and another who left for personal reasons.

"Now," DiMarco went on, "I have your paychecks. When I call you, come up."

Thomas listened as he read off the names, which were a cross-section of Boston's ethnic landscape. The majority were Irish followed by Italian, and then smaller groups, Polish, Jewish, Greek, and Lebanese. There were three Nolans in the class, but they were all from other parts of town, and Thomas didn't know any of them.

The checks were nowhere near in alphabetical order, and by the time he got called, the stack was almost gone.

"Thomas," DiMarco said, handing him the envelope.

"Thanks, Lieutenant."

As he turned to go, DiMarco stopped him.

"We need to talk," he said, leaning in.

"Talk?"

"Upstairs. Room 274."

Their eyes locked, and Thomas nodded. He walked back to his spot, and the lieutenant ended with some words about duty, integrity, and honor that sounded like practice for their graduation service. Then everyone dispersed and headed back to the lockers in the basement.

After Thomas got his things, he walked up to the second floor and found the office at the end of a long hallway. He knocked once, and DiMarco called him in.

"Thomas."

"Hi, Lieutenant."

"It's Nick," he said with a tight grin. "…when no one's around."

"That's not too often."

DiMarco chuckled and pointed to the chair, and Thomas sat down.

"You still sparring?"

"Not since graduation."

"You always had a great left hook."

"And you had a good right one."

"It could've been better. I'm really a lefty, but I broke my shoulder when I was a kid. Had to compensate."

"You sure did."

Thomas had always liked DiMarco. He was tough without being a bully, which was a rare combination in Boston. But Thomas knew he hadn't been asked to his office to talk about boxing or high school.

"You wanted to see me?"

"I heard your father passed away."

"In August, a crane accident."

"I'm sorry."

"Thanks."

"I'm on a task force. It's us and the State Police. We've got a big investigation going on, involves stealing from some of the shipyards…"

All at once, Thomas felt his blood pressure rise.

"There's gonna be a dragnet this weekend. Two hundred suspects on the list." He looked up suddenly. "Your brother George is one of them."

Thomas tried to act surprised, but he wasn't.

"He's been working at East Boston Works," he said, like it was some kind of excuse.

"I know he's a little nuts."

It was such an understatement Thomas had to chuckle. But DiMarco knew his brother since they were both in the same year at East Boston High until George dropped out.

"He's a pain in the ass."

"You two don't get along?"

"Never have. But to be honest, he's been better lately."

"Really?"

"Yeah. Since my father died."

DiMarco paused, tapping his pen on the desk.

"Listen, if you want, I can make his name go away."

"Go away?"

"Take it off the list."

Thomas shifted uneasily in the chair. The conversation had all the undertones of a backroom deal.

"What do I have to do?"

"Nothing. If you want, I'll remove it."

Thomas raised his eyes, as surprised as he was grateful for the offer. Part of him wanted George to get arrested to teach him a lesson. But he knew he would probably go to jail because he had a record. With their mother recuperating, Thomas didn't want to put her through the heartbreak and humiliation.

"If it's no trouble," he said.

"None at all."

"I'll keep an eye on him."

"You should."

Thomas gave a nervous smile, and they both stood up.

"I appreciate this," he said, and they shook.

"Welcome to the force."

......

THOMAS GOT off the trolley in Day Square, a busy junction of shops and restaurants a mile from his house. He walked down the sidewalk with a new exhilaration. The training was over, and by Monday he would be a cop. Aside from the thrill and prestige, he would also be making more money, which was why he didn't hesitate to go into Agri Jewelers.

The bell above the door rang, and the owner came out from the back, an old Italian in suspenders. Although small, the shop had cases of fine jewelry, from diamond necklaces to ruby brooches. And while it looked like an easy target for crooks, at least two of the family's four sons were always there, and Thomas had no doubt they were armed.

"Mr. Nolan," the man said. "Come to make a payment?"

"More than that."

The owner smiled, and walked over to a case, unlocking it with a key. He took out a small purple box and brought it to the counter. When he opened it, Thomas saw the ring, its gold band smooth and diamond glistening.

"Beautiful," he said.

He reached in his bag and got his wallet, filled with bills after cashing his check. It wasn't enough to cover the whole price, but he had been making payments since September. As the man watched, Thomas counted out two hundred dollars, and once he was done, he felt a tremendous relief and joy.

"Thank you."

He held out his hand, and the owner gave him an amused look before shaking it.

"Good luck, boy."

Thomas walked out and went towards the streetcar before deciding just to walk. While there were always pickpockets, he worried more about himself, so excited he feared leaving his bag on the train.

He was home in ten minutes, and the first thing he did was run upstairs and put the ring in his dresser. When he came down, Abby was studying in the dining room, and George was frying a steak with mushrooms on the stove. Thomas had never seen him cook; his brother relied on their mother more than anyone for his meals. But beyond that it was obnoxious, making something only for himself.

Thomas went over and looked in the icebox, where he saw five steaks in wax paper. As he took two out, George glanced over, a spatula in hand.

"Those are mine," he said.

Thomas' mood changed in an instant. He shut the icebox and walked over.

"Yours?"

"I bought them."

"What? From a friend?"

"Prime rib ain't easy to get these days."

Thomas stared at him, shaking his head, and it was tense enough that Abby got up and came over.

"More stolen stuff," he muttered.

"It didn't bother you when it saved Ma's life—"

He slapped George across the face, and he stumbled back into the stove. Whether he raised the spatula as a reflex or to strike, Thomas didn't know, but he swiped it out of his hand.

"Stop!" Abby shrieked, getting between them.

"Bastard!" George said.

Thomas had only hit him with an open hand, knowing a punch would have knocked him out. But when he looked, George's nose was bleeding.

"For chrissakes," Abby said, tears rolling down her cheeks. "We have to stick together…"

Thomas stood fuming, his eyes focused on his brother.

"If Ma doesn't come home, we're all we've got!"

The angst in her voice softened his rage, and he even got emotional, something he had never experienced before in an argument or fight. When he finally stepped back, it wasn't just for her sake but for the family's. He nodded once to his brother which under the circumstances, was the closest he could get to a reconciliation.

Then he stormed out of the kitchen.

CHAPTER FORTY-THREE

*M*s. Stetson's office was in the basement of the Charles Hayden Memorial Building, which had only opened two years before. While the walls were new, there were no windows, so the air was stale, the light harsh. As Abby walked, she could smell oil from the giant furnaces, yet the hallway was colder than the main floors. She wondered if, as a younger professor, Ms. Stetson didn't have enough seniority to be upstairs, or if it was because she was a woman. Aside from her, all of Abby's teachers were men, and most of the females she saw were either secretaries or librarians.

She found the room, *Janet Stetson, English Literature* embossed on a plaque. She knocked once, and the professor opened the door.

"Ms. Nolan," she said with a curt smile. "Please, come in."

She had on a skirt and a cardigan sweater, her hair in a neat bun. The office was small, with a dropped ceiling and bookshelves on the walls. Hearing a hum, Abby looked down and saw a small electric heater in the corner.

"I used to have more tolerance for the cold," Ms. Stetson said. "One of the advantages of being from New Brunswick."

Abby smiled.

"Canada," she said.

"Saint John. I went to college in Montreal."

As she said it, Abby noticed a framed diploma behind her, *McGill University* written across the top in fancy script.

"Have you been to Canada?"

Abby had never been outside of New England, something she was always ashamed to admit.

"No. But I hope to visit someday."

Their eyes locked, and Abby got the urge to look away. She was never comfortable around Ms. Stetson, whether in the classroom or at practice.

"Now," the professor said. "Have a seat."

There were two chairs in the room, but she pointed to the one next to the desk. They both sat down, and she grabbed a stack of papers.

"I was very impressed by your work..."

Abby got a nervous excitement.

"There are some punctuation problems, however, which I'll need you to change..."

Crouched over the desk, their arms were almost touching. When Abby tried to move back, the professor waved her closer and pointed.

"In the first stanza, every line ends in a comma, regardless of whether it's a complete sentence or not. Poetry is a flexible narrative form. But once you choose a convention, you must stick to it."

Abby nodded, and the professor gave her the pen. She took it and made the changes, her hand tense as she wrote.

"Good," Ms. Stetson said. "Now, *seagull's mew*? I assume you mean the general sound of seagulls by the shore?"

"Yes."

"Plural possessive, not singular."

Abby fixed the apostrophe, the professor now so close she could feel her warmth, smell her breath. Her fingers started to tremble, her body tingling from nerves. Then suddenly, she felt Ms. Stetson's hand on hers. She froze. Swallowing once, she glanced over, and the professor was staring back with a hazy smile.

"All done," Abby said.

Ms. Stetson hesitated for what felt like an hour, and Abby began to quietly seethe. Whether the professor sensed it or not, she finally took her hand off.

"Good," she said, as if nothing had happened.

She reached for the pen, and Abby handed it to her. Taking the paper, she reviewed the changes and with a quick flick of the wrist, wrote A+ at the top. Abby gasped, her face beaming. The relief she felt almost made up for the awkward interaction.

"Thank you," she said.

"You've earned it. And he'd be very proud."

Abby smiled, the mere mention of her father enough to make her teary. She reached for her bag, and they both got up. As the professor walked her to the door, Abby felt a creeping dread, but she stayed composed.

"Keep up the good work," Ms. Stetson said.

"I will."

"See you at the game tonight."

......

ABBY STOOD HUNCHED OVER, hands on her knees and trying to catch her breath between sets. Looking over at the clock, she saw it was almost eight o'clock. Except for a few students, the stands were empty, and the audience had been dwindling since Thanksgiving. The game against Pine Manor College was the last of the year, and with finals coming up and Christmas only three weeks away, even their diehard fans had lost interest. But it wasn't unusual, or even unexpected, and girls' sports were seen more like a cute pastime than a serious collegiate pursuit.

"Stay alert!" Ms. Stetson shouted.

When Abby stood up, the serve came at her, and she knocked it back just in time. For the past hour and a half, she had tried to stay focused, but she was exhausted. With the holiday season in full swing, she had worked every morning that week.

The ball came over the net, sailing high in the air. She and Frances ran to get it at the same time and almost collided before another girl spiked it. The whistle blew, and the game was over. They lost 3/2, which wasn't a surprise because two of their best players were out, one with a strained wrist and the other with the flu.

Walking off the court, some of her teammates groaned. Abby sympathized with their disappointment, but she was too happy to be upset. With classes over, she had one A-, two B's, and a C in biology. Even if she only did average on her finals, she was certain to pass the semester.

"You win some, you lose some," Frances said.

As Abby waited for her to catch up, she heard someone call. They looked over, and Harold was coming toward them. He had on a double-breasted suit, a pink tie, and a wool overcoat. In one hand, he held a suitcase and in the other, a *Gilchrist's* department store bag.

"Don't you look dashing," Abby said.

"Thank you, darling."

"What did you think of my save?" Frances asked.

"I'm afraid I only just arrived. I fly out in two hours."

"Fly out?"

"I'm going to see my father in Bermuda for Christmas. I couldn't leave without saying goodbye to my favorite girls."

"I thought he lived in London," Abby said.

He made a deep, sarcastic frown.

"As did I."

"What about finals?" Frances asked.

"I've made arrangements with all my professors. It helps to be the son of a diplomat, you know?"

They all laughed.

"Oh," he said. "I bring gifts."

He reached into the bag and took out two boxes, wrapped in striped paper, topped with a bow. He handed one to each of them. Not thinking, Abby started to undo the ribbon before he stopped her.

"Not here. Put it under your tree."

She smiled, but the remark stung. With her mother in an institution, Christmas was the last thing on their minds, and they hadn't gotten a tree.

"I will."

"Good girl," he said, then he looked at his watch.

"I must be off, unfortunately."

He leaned towards Frances, and they kissed on the cheek. Turning to Abby, he took her in his arms, squeezing her so hard her feet left the ground.

"I'm gonna miss you, lady," he said.

When he let go, any envy or suspicion she had about him and Frances went away.

"Me too."

In the intimacy of the moment, she felt guilty not telling them about her mother. It was more out of consideration than shame, not wanting to drag them into her troubled home life. She always saw going to Boston University as a chance to start over and to become a new person, far from the prejudices and limitations of her neighborhood. But sometimes she felt like she was living in two different worlds.

"Let's get dressed," Frances said. "Father will be waiting out front."

Harold put his hands to his mouth and blew them kisses. Picking up his things, he said, "Au revoir."

He backed away with a theatrical flair, bowing and spinning around. As they stood laughing, something caught Abby's eye, and she got suddenly uneasy. She looked over and saw Ms. Stetson by the locker room door, her arms crossed and watching.

······

Abby sat in the sleek leather seat of the Cadillac sedan. It was not only the nicest but also one of the few automobiles she had ever been in. As a girl, her uncle Walter, who had lived on their street, owned a car, but he died when they were young. Her family had always traveled by trolley or bus, and all her life she had watched people zoom past her with a mysterious curiosity. George was the only one with a license, but it was mainly for work because he couldn't afford a car. In East Boston, the world was so compact, everything within such a short walking distance, that none of them ever needed to drive. Still, Abby couldn't deny she felt important going thirty-five MPH through the city streets.

When she looked over, Frances smiled back from the darkness, her coat buttoned up, her eyes tired. Her father had insisted they sit together, and with the passenger seat in the front empty, it was like they were being chauffeured. They drove through places more crowded than East Boston with endless blocks of apartment buildings and brick rowhouses, and the hazy glow of cheap diners and barrooms. She could always tell rough areas because the basement windows had bars, something that, so far, her neighborhood didn't need.

Finally, they pulled out onto a wide boulevard where she saw a sign for Blue Hill Avenue. It was the first familiar street since leaving the B.U. gymnasium, and not for good reasons. As they continued south towards the suburbs, she got a sinking feeling,

"Everything alright?" Frances asked.

Abby nodded, forcing a smile. She was surprised her friend noticed, but then she could never hide her emotions. They came to an intersection that Abby recognized, having been there only the day before. As they drove through it, she looked down Morton Street where, in the darkness, she could almost see the entrance to Boston State Hospital. In that instant, all her excitement about going to stay with Frances went away, replaced by simmering guilt and worry in knowing her mother was in there alone.

.

CHAPTER FORTY-FOUR

Thomas got home after dark, his uniform, badge, and belt in his duffel bag. Under everything was his pistol, stored in a shiny metal box. They wouldn't get bullets until Monday. With so much war materiel being sent overseas, there was a shortage of everything from copper to gunpowder. Even their billy clubs, produced by a company that also made stocks for Army rifles, wouldn't be available for another few weeks.

After such a long day, he had taken a taxi home, something he never would have done in the past. But with a new job, he wasn't worried as much about money, and he didn't want to be carrying a weapon on the trolley anyway.

The first thing he did when he walked in was put his things away. There was no lock on his bedroom door, but he knew they would be safe. The captain warned them to take care of their equipment, that if anything was lost or damaged, they would have to pay for themselves. If their weapons were stolen and used in a crime, they could even be held criminally liable, although DiMarco said it never happened.

Thomas went downstairs and into the kitchen to find his brother at the stove. With some pots boiling and a drink on the counter, it was almost as if he had taken the place of their mother.

"Abby home yet?" he asked.

"She's staying with a friend for the weekend."

"Where?"

George glanced over and shrugged his shoulders.

"Some rich town. South Shore, I think."

Thomas just nodded. Their conversations were always like that, cold and matter of fact, like the best they could do was tolerate each other. But with their father dead and their mother in the hospital, the hostility seemed unnecessary, if not unfortunate.

"I made dinner," George said.

He took the potatoes off the stove and dumped them into a colander, the steam rising around him.

"There's a ham in the oven," he added.

Thomas didn't respond, watching with slight amusement as his brother took the carrots, drained them, and tossed them in a bowl. Not only had he never seen George make a full meal, but he had never seen him so enthusiastic.

Thomas glanced over at the clock.

"I gotta go," he said.

George looked up, a faint disappointment on his face. For a second, Thomas thought he saw that boyish innocence he remembered from their youth, long before his brother got bitter and reckless. As he turned to go, George said, "I talked to the doctor today."

"Yeah?"

"He thinks Ma could be out next month."

When their eyes met, Thomas smiled, but what he felt was more a mix of relief and regret. He had been so busy with police training and with Connie that he hadn't been able to visit her as much as he wanted.

"That's good news."

"I can borrow a car to take her to church and such."

Thomas nodded and walked away without a word. He had only gotten as far as the foyer when he stopped. Putting aside his pride, he went back to the kitchen and saw George knelt by the icebox.

"Hey," he said.

His brother stood up and faced him, a stick of butter in his hand. "What?" he asked, but his tone wasn't cold.

"Thanks."

......

When Thomas and Connie stepped off the bus, Point Shirley was dark, and if it wasn't for the streetlamps, they would have needed flashlights. Pulsifer's Market, which was open the last time they came out there, was now shuttered for winter.

Carrying both their bags, he took Connie's hand, and her fingers were tense. They walked down the road, and with no wind, there was a majestic silence. When they came around the bend, the cottage shone under the moonlight, the water still across the bay. In the distance, the city sparkled against a starlit sky, and somewhere out in the harbor, a light was flashing. Although the air was frigid, the scene was as tranquil as a summer night in August.

While Connie waited on the porch, Thomas went around back and opened the door. They walked inside, and he put their things down next to the table. Upstairs was too drafty, so they would sleep on the couch.

He told her to wait and then went up to the bedroom. When he peered in, all the contraband from before was gone. Whether George had sold it, moved it, or thrown it out, he didn't know, but he was glad it was gone. DiMarco's help had spared his brother an arrest, but Thomas knew he couldn't keep him out of trouble forever, nor did he want to.

When he came down, Connie was standing at the fireplace like she was imagining its warmth. Beside her was a small stack of logs from the tree his father had cut down two years before, the wood now dry and cracked. As he watched her, he crept over and went in his bag. He had wanted to wait for a tender moment, a poignant situation. But if he had learned anything in the past few months, it was that life changed fast and there was no perfect time for anything.

Walking back over, he opened the flue and crouched down to put a log on the rusted andiron his great-grandfather had made by hand. He reached into a box of sticks and twigs and spread them around it. When he pointed to the matches on the table, Connie went to get them, giving him just enough time to go into his pocket. He lit one on the first try and the kindling caught, casting a soft glow in the room.

Still kneeling, he held out the ring and peered up, but she was so captivated by the flames she didn't notice.

"Concetta?" he said.

She blinked once and looked down at him, her expression dreamy.

"Will you marry me?"

She stood frozen with her lips pressed together, shadows from the fire flickering across her face. For a moment, he worried she would say no, something he had never considered, the blind determination of love. Then slowly her head began to move up and down, and he got goosebumps. When she finally spoke, they were the most beautiful words he had ever heard.

"Yes, Thomas," she said, her eyes filling with tears. "I will. I will marry you."

CHAPTER FORTY-FIVE

𝒜bby sat alone on the couch, heat coming off the hearth like the hottest summer day on Point Shirley. Around her were two dozen of Frances' friends, some from childhood and others from the Academy of the Assumption where she had gone to boarding school. Everyone talked and laughed while music played from a console radio. Over at the bar, a man in a tuxedo made cocktails, and although everyone wasn't old enough to drink, Frances' father allowed it as long as guests either got a ride home or slept over.

The house was stunning, a ten-bedroom mansion on the shores of Duxbury Bay, the finest home Abby had ever been in. The living room was the size of her whole first floor, with mahogany furniture and bookshelves that went up to the ceiling. The walls were covered in oil paintings of street scenes of Paris and Rome, and behind a grand piano was a framed poster from some important yacht race.

The party was mostly women but there were also a few young men, including two guys in Army uniforms who had a group of girls around them. At one point, Abby got the urge to ask if they knew Arthur before realizing it was absurd. Over in the corner, Frances' teenage brother was dancing by himself, his plaid jacket open and his

THE LAST HAPPY SUMMER

hair slicked back. While her father stayed upstairs, her mother came down a couple of times to check on things.

"You okay?"

Abby turned, and Frances was sitting on the back of the couch, one leg over the other.

"Yes," she said with a smile.

"Whaddya say we blow this joint? Go out on the porch?"

Abby chuckled—the slang didn't sound right coming from her.

"The porch?"

"The stars should be lovely."

"Sure."

She looked at Abby's hands, which had been clutched to her purse all night.

"Lady, you need a drink!"

When Abby got up, Frances went over to the bar, cutting in front of a small line before returning with a Martini.

"Here," she said, handing it to her. "This will take away your worries and your woes."

Abby laughed at the corny remark, but in some ways she understood it. All night, she hadn't had a drink, afraid of saying or doing something foolish around so many strangers. But with her mother in the hospital, she couldn't relax, and there was nothing like the temporary comfort of alcohol.

"Come," Frances said, taking Abby's hand.

They walked into the next room, past a table filled with elegant appetizers, Frances waving and smiling at people. Along the back wall was a set of glass doors, and when she opened them, Abby flinched from the cold.

They stepped out onto a large terrace that overlooked the bay, the shapes of sailboats rocking in the harbor. Frances took out a pack of Chesterfield cigarettes and gave Abby one. They sat down on two Adirondack chairs facing the water.

"Are you chilly?" Frances asked, giving her a light.

"I'm glad I wore a sweater."

"Drink up. It'll warm you."

Abby took a sip and then leaned back and stared at the sky. The stars seemed brighter than in the city, or maybe she just never noticed them back home with all the buildings.

"Are you having fun?" Frances asked.

"Yes. A wonderful crowd."

"I'm sorry there aren't more boys."

"I saw you talking to one of the soldiers."

"Byron Merritt? He's just someone I grew up with. Truth is, I really miss Harold."

Abby got a chill, and it wasn't from the cold. For weeks she had wondered about Frances and Harold, and now seemed a good time to ask.

"Do you fancy him?"

"Of course. He's a gas. Don't you?"

"I mean, do you *fancy him*?" Abby emphasized.

Frances looked over, but in the darkness, Abby couldn't see her face.

"He wouldn't fancy me, that's for sure…"

When Abby hesitated, Frances sat up in the chair.

"Oh dear, you can't be serious?" she asked.

"I'm curious, that's all."

Frances giggled so hard she burped.

"Darling, Harold's as queer as a quaker."

All of a sudden it made sense, and Abby was ashamed for being naïve. Her feelings for Harold had always been so intimate she mistook them for attraction, and it was a relief to know they could just be close friends.

"I…wasn't quite certain," she said.

"And I thought you city girls were so savvy."

Abby grinned and drank some more, and already she was feeling tipsy. Talk of men combined with booze always made her giddy, and she even got a little mischievous.

"Ms. Stetson touched my hand," she said, almost like it was a confession.

"That's no surprise. She spends more time in the girls' locker than on the court."

"Should I tell her?"

"Tell her what?"

"That I'm not that way."

"Oh, hardly," Frances said, waving her cigarette. "Let her wonder. You got an A, didn't you?"

Abby laughed, but inside she was torn, not sure if her grade was earned or some kind of bribe. Either way, she was less anxious than before, and talking with Frances always made her feel better.

By now, they were both starting to get cold. When Frances stamped out her cigarette, Abby took a few last puffs and did the same. She hadn't smoked as much since going off to college, worried people would think she was low class, and she missed the sensation.

As they stood up, Abby noticed something on the horizon.

"A flashing light," she said, pointing.

"Probably just Morse code. The Navy patrols at night."

"I see the same thing from East Boston."

Frances smiled, and they walked towards the doors.

"You see," she said. "Our worlds aren't so different after all."

......

ABBY OPENED HER EYES. For a moment, she didn't know where she was. Leaning up, she looked around the small room and everything was white: the walls, the dresser, the writing desk, and even the doorknobs. Except for summers on Point Shirley, she hadn't slept away from home in years, and waking up somewhere strange gave her a fright.

She got out of bed, her head pounding and throat dry. Running to the bathroom, she turned on the faucet and guzzled for a minute straight. Slowly, memories from the previous night came back. She had gotten drunk—that much she knew. But she also had a good time, dancing until after midnight, wandering with some girls down to the shoreline in the dark to soak their feet. After her chat with Frances, she had a new confidence, even smoking cigarettes with the two soldiers on the veranda. They were both from Duxbury, and while one was stationed nearby at Fort Devens, she was surprised to learn the other was in Texas. When she asked if he knew Arthur, he said no but didn't scoff. There were thousands of troops at Randolph Field—even she realized that. She did it mainly for attention, knowing how men were jealous of other guys, but a part of her still missed him.

Hearing voices, she cracked open the door, and Frances was coming down the hallway. There were two girls with her, all dressed in short skirts and carrying tennis rackets. One she didn't recognize, but the night before the other had been trying to get her to join the *Massachusetts Women's Defense Corps*, an organization Abby had never heard of.

"Morning, sunshine!"

Abby squinted in the light, still groggy.

"What time is it?" she asked.

One of the girls looked at her watch.

"Just after eleven."

"Why don't you go get something to eat downstairs? Meet us for tennis after."

"Tennis? Where?"

"On the courts, of course. Just behind the pool."

Abby smiled, and they all skipped off. They seemed too cheery for such a late night, which made her wonder if rich girls didn't get hungover or if they just hid it better.

She washed her face and changed into a clean dress, putting on her saddle shoes because her feet were sore from wearing heels. With her pin curls flat, she pulled her hair back in a bow. Once she was ready, she went downstairs where the man who had been bartending was now serving brunch from chafing dishes. The room was empty, the tables cluttered with plates of melon rinds and half-eaten omelets. Through the glass doors, she saw a couple of girls smoking on the patio. Otherwise, it seemed that most guests had left, and she was embarrassed she had slept so late.

After having a croissant and some coffee, she found the front doors and walked out. The air was warm, filled with the sweet smell of lavender and rose bushes. In the distance, she could hear the thwack of a tennis ball, the squeak of shoes. She crossed the circular driveway and went down a path, passing a large pool with a tile deck and diving board. When she got to the courts, Frances was playing against the soldier from Fort Devens, who looked even more handsome in shorts and a polo shirt than he did in a suit.

"Abigail, this is Richard."

"Hello," Abby said, even though they had already met.

"Wanna see how to put the Army on the run?"

Without warning, she tossed the ball in the air and fired it across the net. The young man lunged, but he was too late, and by the time he swung, it was gone.

"Not fair!" he said.

"Did I catch you *off guard?*"

Abby laughed, and it might have been the first time she watched a couple flirt without feeling envious.

As the game continued, she leaned against the fence and looked around at the beautiful property, the sprawling house with its peaks and weathered shingles, the lush gardens and manicured lawns. She never fretted over social status like her mother did, but she couldn't deny that being there made her feel important. Despite all that had happened, she'd managed to get through the semester and made some good friends. Whether what she felt was joy, gratitude, or just relief, she couldn't tell. But she knew she had the will to go on living, without which none of those other sentiments would have been possible.

"Care for a match?"

Abby looked over and Richard was holding out his racket.

"I'm heading out anyway," he said.

She hesitated for a moment before a smile broke across her face.

"As a matter of fact, I would."

For the next two hours, she and Frances played in the hot sun.

While Frances was good, Abby held her own. In her neighborhood, tennis was considered snobby, but she had learned it at the local YWCA from a woman who said the sport was good for a girl's posture and confidence.

It was the best of three and in the end, Frances won. When they finally left the court, Abby's dress was soaked. But her headache was gone, and she always felt better after exercise.

"This calls for a drink," Frances said.

"I hope you mean lemonade."

"Is a Tom Collins close enough?—"

Suddenly, a car sped into the driveway and skidded to a stop.

"Frances!" a voice shouted.

They both turned, and her father was looking down from the hedges, dressed in a summer suit and hat. Even from a distance, Abby could tell something was wrong.

"Father?"

"Everyone must leave at once."

Frances glanced over at Abby, her face a mix of worry and confusion.

"But Abigail will need a ride home," she said.

"I'll drive her. Quick! Let's go!"

CHAPTER FORTY-SIX

It was the first weekend Thomas had had off in months, and it had all the magic of a fairytale. The night before, Connie had cooked dinner, polenta with mushrooms, something he had never heard of, let alone tried. She said it went well with red wine, but he hadn't brought any. Remembering what it did to his father, he'd always been wary of alcohol, and seeing how it now affected his mother, he had grown to despise it. But Connie didn't mind, and she was never hard to please, something he loved but also made him wonder. He still didn't know much about her, and considering he had his own secrets, he had no right to complain. He had lied to her about his mother, saying she had broken her hip and was recovering in the hospital.

On Sunday morning, he woke up naked under the blanket, his arms wrapped around her like he was clinging to a rock in a storm. The fire was out, but the room smelled of ash, the air so cold he could see his breath. He got up quietly and as he started to dress, she turned over.

"Your head," she said.

When she pointed, the ring on her finger glistened in the shadowy light. He went over to the mirror and saw that his hair was standing straight up.

"You make me aroused," he joked, licking his hand to smooth it down.

He walked into the kitchen and lit the stove, which worked year-round because it ran on propane. After a breakfast of coffee and stale biscuits, they bundled up and went out. In the December cold, everything was gray, but there was something poignant in the bleakness. They walked the rocky shoreline, their hands clasped, the only sound the seagulls and the waves. He hadn't checked the clock, but they had slept late, and he could tell by the tide it was early afternoon.

With so few full-time residents, Point Shirley was desolate, and they circled the whole peninsula without seeing another person. After an hour, they were both tired, and Connie's cheeks were red from the wind. They came around the bend, and Thomas heard someone knocking. As they approached the cottage, he saw the neighbor standing on the porch in a robe and slippers, a cigar in his mouth.

"Mr. Loughran?"

"Thomas. We've been attacked."

"Attacked?"

"The Japs. In Pearl Harbor, Hawaii. I just heard it…on the ham radio."

Thomas glanced over at Connie, who looked as shocked as he felt.

"Will the Germans attack too?"

Mr. Loughran shook his head.

"I don't know, son," he said, somberly.

It was something people had been worrying about for months. At the shipyard, Thomas had seen the damage from U-boats and heard stories about entire crews lost at sea. Living on the east coast, they were more vulnerable to an invasion than anyone.

Thomas stood frozen, his mind racing.

"What do we do?"

"Nothing. It probably won't be announced for a couple more hours. But don't say anything. You don't wanna get people panicked. Go home. Tell your mother you love her."

The advice was kind but bittersweet. With a tense smile, the man nodded and walked away.

"How'd you know we were here?" Thomas asked.

Mr. Loughran turned around.

"I was young once too, you know…"

······

THERE WERE no busses on Sundays, something that, with the excitement of proposing to Connie, Thomas had forgotten to consider. So they walked back to East Boston, across the neck of the peninsula and through the town of Winthrop. They went fast but didn't run, Thomas carrying their bags through the eerily quiet streets.

All his life, he had been fascinated by the ham radio next door, and when he and George were young, Mr. Loughran used to teach them about frequencies and call signs. Never could he have imagined that someday he would learn about such a horrific disaster over it. And with a five-hour time difference between Hawaii and Boston, he was sure they had heard before anyone else.

When they reached the bridge over Saratoga Street, he had to stop.

"Are you alright?" Connie asked.

"Yeah," he said, leaning over and gasping for breath. "Let's go."

They continued for another mile, slowing down only when they got to their street. They had been in such a hurry to get home that they hadn't talked about what to do when they got there.

"Are you gonna tell your aunt?"

She peered up.

"I think I ought to," she said, her voice shaking.

"And the ring?"

She nodded with a sad smile, and he understood why. With America now at war, it seemed an awful time to get married. They parted with a quick kiss, and he went up the front steps. When he walked in, Abby and George were in the parlor.

"Thomas," she said, running over. "We've been attacked."

"It's true? Have they announced it?"

"Not yet," George said, crouched by the radio and turning the dial. "We're waiting."

Thomas put down his bag and looked at Abby.

"Mr. Loughran said he heard it on the ham radio. I was hoping it was a mistake."

"Shhh," George said, and they rushed over.

As they listened, the familiar voice of CBS announcer John Charles Daly came on.

WE INTERRUPT this broadcast to bring you a special news bulletin. The Japanese have attacked Pearl Harbor, Hawaii, by air, President Roosevelt has just announced...

ABBY BURST into tears and threw her arms around Thomas, who hadn't hugged her in years. Shaking his head, George got up, and Thomas was surprised when he started to console their sister. They stood in a tight circle, the closest the three of them had been since they were kids. When Thomas looked over, George just stared back, but his expression had all the sincerity of a promise or a pledge. With their father gone and their mother in a psychiatric institution, the three of them were all they had, and somehow Thomas knew his brother was offering a truce. Whether it would be for now or forever, he didn't know. But with the country at war, they had to look after their mother and sister more than ever before.

"I'll go make dinner."

"I can help," Abby said.

When she pulled away and followed George to the kitchen, Thomas was relieved because he had to wipe his eyes.

ALSO BY JONATHAN CULLEN

The Days of War Series

The Last Happy Summer

Midnight Passes, Morning Comes

Shadows of Our Time Collection

The Storm Beyond the Tides

Sunsets Never Wait

Bermuda Blue

The Jody Brae Mystery Series

Whiskey Point

City of Small Kingdoms

The Polish Triangle

Sign up for Jonathan's newsletter for updates on deals and new releases!

https://liquidmind.media/j-cullen-newsletter-sign-up-1/

ABOUT THE AUTHOR

Jonathan Cullen grew up in Boston and attended public schools. After a brief career as a bicycle messenger, he attended Boston College and graduated with a B.A. in English Literature (1995). During his twenties, he wrote two unpublished novels, taught high school in Ireland, lived in Mexico, worked as a prison librarian, and spent a month in Kenya, Africa before finally settling down three blocks from where he grew up.

He currently lives in Boston (West Roxbury) with his wife Heidi and daughter Maeve.

Made in the USA
Middletown, DE
12 March 2023